Praise for Ted Krever's books:

Mindbenders

"…a storyline that takes hold in the first few pages and doesn't let go…"

"…really fast paced…I found myself unable to put it back down."

"…dialog that left me breathless."

"…[a] global, international conspiracy of corporate and governmental politics, mind control, murder and intrigue."

"OMG!...finally crawled into bed early hours of the next day."

"This is that rare piece of fiction based on fact in such a way as to make the two seem to blur."

"Mindbenders…will make you wonder if your mind really does belong to you."

Mindbenders 2: The Fiery Sky

"…a more than worthy followup to the 1st book, fast paced, well written and exciting!"

"…takes me places that were only in my imagination - I feel like I have been to that island in the South Pacific living on the water, and I've been parched in the Aussie desert - it's all real."

"…A complete thrill ride from beginning to end…great style and substance."

"…intense, memorable scenes…"

"…seamlessly weaves multiple storylines together, delivering a powerful punch of an ending."

GREEN

"…not your typical romance…

"…a unique look into the mindset of men, rather than the typical romance, which is told from the woman's point of view."

"… a smart, witty and wise look at love later in life…"

"I found myself laughing aloud more than once, only to shortly thereafter find myself deeply touched."

"The descriptions…of Ireland are alone worth the price of the book…"

"If you like reading about horses, Ireland, friendship, love in any form..."

"Part a love story, part a political thriller, and part a satiric commentary on life and politics…"

"Green is a charming book."

Howling at Wolves

"This book, simply put…is funny!"

"Keep your tissues handy as you won't stop laughing."

"Nothing is sacred…"

"…like Garp on steroids (or maybe Viagra?)

A Crafty and Devious God

"…a great read…"

"Weirdly excellent"

"[The] writing is very natural, loose and easy, yet deep and thoughtful."

"…an engaging character study… a tale of a man who's lost, looking for his way, and a girl who knows she is destined for great things and is determined to achieve it at all costs."

"I gave it a try. And kept reading, and reading, and reading. Just very well-written, scattered throughout with concepts that made me think (which I occasionally like to do)."

After

"…short stories of New Yorkers trying to make sense of their changed world in the immediate aftermath of 9/11."

"These stories are emotionally impactful but they are not grim. Each character finds some measure of hope or understanding or, at the very least, adaptation to their circumstances."

"…a masterful job of depicting the surreal dream-like state that trauma survivors inhabit…"

"Intricately woven stories of despair and ultimately hope…"

"…a tender tribute to the survivors of 9/11."

by
Ted Krever

Little David Publications
www.tedkrever.com

ISBN: 978-0615484761

Cover background photo:
(strada per clifden) by Leo Righetti,
with permission

Sections of this book appeared (in rewritten form) on
www.chronofhorse.com

Out of Ireland have we come
Great hatred, little room
Maimed us at the start.
I carry from my mother's womb
a fanatic heart.
WB Yeats

Beauty and madness to be praised
'Cause it is not easy to be brave
To walk around in so much need
Carrying the weight of all that greed
Joni Mitchell

History teaches us
that men and nations behave wisely
once they have exhausted all other alternatives.
Abba Eban

~~~~

Irish Glossary:
Punt: Old Irish currency, pre-Euros
Garda, Gardai: Irish police
Taoiseach: Irish Prime Minister
Guinness: Beer

~~~~

Songs:
The Blacksmith, Traditional
Molly Ban, Traditional
Arthur McBride, Traditional/mangled lyrics by Author

For Di

THURSDAY

MARCH 2003

The cab driver had been ranting all the way out from Manhattan about the Jews.

"Where do Jews come from? Iraq! Abraham the Patriarch come from Ur! Where is Ur? Iraq! Jews too smart to fight in Iraq— they send American virgins, innocents, to fight the Muslim! When this war start, it is fought for the Jews. The Jews are the terrorists!"

"I'm Jewish," I told him, just to be disagreeable.

"You? Not Jewish—you're Protestant."

"Excuse me? I'm Jewish. One grandfather from Lithuania, the other one from Poland."

"You don't wear the *kepah*?" he asked knowledgably. He was a wearing a brightly-colored djellaba—the hood held earpieces for at least two cellphones or maybe a music player and a cellphone.

"No."

"You eat pig?"

"Just in Chinese food."

"You eat Chinese food?"

"Sure—I'm Jewish."

"What about Jesus?"

"A great Jewish prophet," I said, trotting out the response that had fended off Jews for Jesus in the Grand Central mezzanine for years.

"Hmph! Unitarian!" he spat, like it was an insult.

"What's *that* mean?" Suddenly we'd swept past cab-driver-on-the-way-to-the-airport conversation. Now I was *involved*, Emily tugging at my shirt notwithstanding.

"Jew God don't take no shit," he said, turning off the Belt onto the JFK Expressway. "Jew God bury Sodom and Gomorrah, drop Aaron's sons into the chasm, tell Abraham 'Tie your son up and kill him for a sacrifice'—'Oh no, just kidding.' Jew God is tough son-of-a-bitch. No God of love and turning the other cheek, no God of 'Jesus, great Jewish prophet'. Jew God is God of Israel, ruthless killer God, you send twenty times the men, he still kicks the shit out of you."

He kept this soliloquy going all the way to the International Arrivals Terminal and I felt duty tugging at me the whole time. What's left to being a Jew anymore, if not a historical sense of outrage? Nobody told my generation we couldn't move into the neighborhood or marry their daughter. Our one chance to feel Jewish is to cry prejudice when they blame us for everything.

But then he smacked into the next cab at the terminal, trying to grab a prime curb spot and I gave up. I was planning to stiff him but once I saw the dented yellow nose of our cab and the dented yellow nose of the other, paint scraped and headlights shattered, tire deflated, rim bent out of shape, antifreeze leeching into the air like poison gas, what was the point? It would just leave him victimized again and superior. So I tossed the fare—and his tip—onto the seat. Let him learn his lesson from the next guy.

"You don't think this is an omen?" I moaned.

"Of what? We're not hurt," Emily said, bouncing out of her seat, an uncoiling spring, a jack-in-the-box, my smiling, breezy, bolt-of-light Emily. "We caught the cab two blocks before Penn Station so we're early even with the accident and we'll get the good seats in the lounge. One thing leads to the next leads to the next. That's how life works."

The drivers were really going at it now, flying elbows and accusations in English and Pakistani, clouds of visible breath in the late winter air.

"You pulled right in front of me!"

"This is New York—everybody is everyplace! You have to *watch*!"

I loomed over them until ours finally popped the trunk. I grabbed my suitcase and Emily's third and hoisted them onto the wide sidewalk. The road was rapidly jamming up behind the accident, honking and screaming at us to move but no one was moving.

"If we got the cab at Grand Central instead of two blocks away," Emily continued—you can pause twenty minutes and Emily will pick up a discussion right where she left off, "we arrive a second later and the other guy rams right through our door instead of the front fender. Fifty yards north of usual and everything changes. That's why travel's good for the soul. Sometimes it's where you're going—sometimes it's where you left. Sometimes it's just motion."

I was half-listening. *One thing leads to the next*, I heard. *Just motion*—God knows I heard that. The rest just washed away. When you really need help, everything sounds promising but nothing sticks. What I needed was *useful* advice. As far as I was concerned, we carry our connections—and our omens—with us as we go.

"What the hell is in this case?"

"Saddles."

"I'm hauling *saddles*? Plural?"

"Plural," Em nodded. "I'll take them if they're too much for you." She said this politely, as though she really might if I insisted.

She stepped out ahead, navigating the jampacked terminal like a general. A 44-year-old six-foot-tall blond runway-model-slim general in a crimson riding jacket and creased black denim, lugging an overstuffed backpack and two huge luggage cases on wheels. The crowd—teeming smooching Italians from the 4:43 Roma and 65 Sikhs in turbans, manicured beards and deep gravity filing off the 5:03 (arrived early) Islamabad—parted in front of her the way crowds always do with Emily, eyes panning as she passed. It's impossible not to stare at her. Actually, the Sikhs refused, which only proved the point. I caught the looks bringing up the rear, the same looks I've seen for twenty-five years, on and off. *Lucky son-of-a-bitch*, that's what they said.

"They don't have saddles in Ireland?"

"Not like these. If you want to ride, now I'll have a saddle for you."

"The last time I rode a horse, I was pretending to be Roy Rogers."

"Well, it's yours, so you haul it. Like every other onerous thing in your life, *there's a story in it*." We laughed an obligatory laugh. One of the privileges of knowing someone a long time is that a joke doesn't have to be all that funny if it keeps coming up—repetition itself becomes the punchline.

I followed her onto the escalator. She was ascending backwards, having marshaled her cases into an upright, organized phalanx.

"I haven't run out of stories," I protested. "I ran out of people who want to hear them."

"Well, Ireland's the place, you'll see. Nobody loves stories like the Irish. They don't care if they're making them up half the time. The pleasure's in the telling."

"So what do they need me for?"

"You need *them*," she said, tapping me on the chest. "You've been sleepwalking too long."

The escalator reached the top of its cycle. "C'mon," I said, stepping off the ramp, "let's parade a little."

Emily squared her shoulders, tossed her hair in one of those moves women commit to muscle memory before high school and slipped loose another button on her blouse. Not that anything *showed*, mind you. A sliver of skin on Em is more erotic than bare nipples and a g-string on a less dignified woman. We threaded through the crowd, past swiveling heads and furtive glances. Emily glowed at this little game and I swelled a bit, just being seen with her.

I've always believed that much of my value to Emily is that I draw attention—at least a little attention—away from her. I've always been big. My mother kept the charts for as long as she was around: 97th percentile at six months, 98th at a year. Later, my father scratched pencil marks on the bathroom lintel: Four feet tall at age six, five-foot-two at age ten. By junior high, I was accustomed to towering over everyone I met. It's hard not to see life as humorous when you spend all your time staring at people's bald spots. You'd be amazed how many *women* have them.

Even before I topped out at 6'7" and big boned, people took me for a formidable character accustomed to getting his way. Often they gave me my way before I knew what it was. I was elected ninth grade class president without campaigning or even wanting the job. I can't remember doing a thing in office but I remember being re-elected without opposition. Over the years, people have offered me all sorts of things—jobs, inside information, their virginity—that I would never have dared ask for on my own. People look up to me—not that they have much choice—and all too often confuse metaphor with reality.

Emily circled the stations of ascension at Aer Lingus, greeting everyone by name. "Omar, how are you?" "Mr. Robinson, did your daughter start school yet?" The woman behind the Emerald Club desk assayed our rolling armada and asked, "What is it this time?"

"Saddles," Emily smiled. She has a Julia Roberts smile, like the whole world is teeth. "One of my old ones is worn out. Are there any upgrades?" It wasn't much as conversation goes but just enough. The woman leapt to the terminal, fingers flying, to ensure that any available upgrades would go to Emily. When there were none, she seemed more disappointed than we were. She stepped out from behind the desk to lead us to the head of the bomb detector line.

The world's gone petty democratic in recent years; nobody likes serving *anybody* anymore. But people serve Emily and like it.

She flashes her laser smile and speaks politely and people act as though she's invited them to dinner at the Plaza.

Women try to resent her sometimes—you can see it in their eyes—but she's too nice for the feeling to linger. The baggage handlers and ticket takers and the guy with the humongo bomb detector that x-rayed our underwear all treated her like a beloved daughter returning from college. What's weirder than dirt is that she was older than some of the guys gazing at her paternally. In a few cases, paternally and carnally at the same time and *that's* the mother lode if you can strike it.

The receptionist at the Emerald Lounge asked for Emily's ID—she couldn't have worked there long. Em headed straight for the Internet terminals on the far wall. All the computers were taken but a man around my age leapt to his feet to offer his place before anyone else had the chance. A little runty, this fellow, maybe five-eleven, with that weak chin that screams British Upper Class and well-dressed in the taste of the day—black suit, black shirt, tie somehow a different shade of black (there are shades?).

"Market's closed," he announced in a dripping public school accent. "I suppose I'm entitled to a bit of leisure." *Leh-zhur.* He displayed the timepiece around his wrist for our admiration. I could quote the ad that sold the thing almost by heart: *Made of the same metals that sheathed the space shuttle, if not better.* That might not be an exact quote. Emily smiled and took his seat without a word. I grouped our carry-ons beside her and the fellow *glared* at me. I represent all kinds of things in people's heads—fathers, bosses, authority figures, the tall guy who gets the pretty girl. All I am is big but the connotations blanket the map.

Em proceeded to bang through her messages as though they had a ten-second half-life. A lot of people get clogged up in their past, gummed up by the preoccupations of half a lifetime. Not Em—she blasted on through as though she had no past at all, as though everything before today was a placemark.

I watched the carnage over her shoulder. "You want to check on anything?" she asked between furious fits of typing, not that anyone was getting up to offer *me* their seat.

"I'm fine," I said. It might even have been true.

In recent months I'd begun monitoring my psychic temperature several times a day but all I'd learned was that I had no baseline. Sometimes I was 97.6°, other times 102°. Fluctuation seemed to be my nature, at least for now, and it still beat hell out of being perpetually flattened like the French, Communists, Moors, Apaches, Cubs or Red Sox (maybe just the Cubs—the Red Sox are always convinced they got *robbed*). At least if you fluctuated, you could always come around.

"Have some food," Emily suggested, without taking her eyes from the screen. "It's free." She'd ripped through two bulletin boards—MBA's who still didn't know what to do with their degrees (a sizeable group), painters without a major exhibition (

smaller group but more desperate)—and had now moved on to horses, which was apparently thicker going.

Emily has a trust fund and land on two continents. Her family came over on the second ship to follow the Mayflower. Her great-grandfather developed the first detergent to come in packaged, easy-to-use form and *kept* his fortune, thank you very much. Which is a long lead-in to the reality that Emily is as cheap as they come.

Stereotypes piss me off. To be precise, it's people who *justify* a stereotype that eat at me. Being Jewish, cheap Jews annoy me a lot—I tip big even when I'm poor, in case the waiter decides I'm Jewish and is checking out the tip as a test. Of course, if he *is*, it's plain prejudice and he can go fuck himself. But at least I'm not giving the venal racist bastard any excuses. Cheap Jews, Italian mobsters, Pakistani cab drivers, lazy black people, Arab extremists—all these stereotype-enablers had to change, to become a little unpredictable, if only for the sake of dignity.

Emily was not a cheap Jew. She was a cheap Protestant trust fund Republican. She would drive all over Princeton looking for a parking space instead of pumping a couple quarters into a meter. She bought Christmas gifts for her friends from the duty-free catalog on the plane flying home.

Somehow none of it stuck. It felt like cruelty to hold her responsible for her own behavior—she just wasn't a self-made person like the rest of us. Social customs arose in her like genetic imprints, things she was no more likely to change than I was to become a (natural) redhead.

And she had her own brand of generosity—when I was unemployed for months after September 11th, she paid me a hundred bucks to drive her from the airport to her friend Bib's house in Jersey more than once and that was really crucial money for me at the time. Of course, it only made more inexplicable the meals I had to buy her because she never had currency (or only Euros) in her pockets. Cheap.

So I filled a dish with free food, the kind that gives 'free' a bad name—a dry cluster of red grapes, a little inedible chicory and some tuna wraps that had been left out too long. As long as the wine was plentiful, it wouldn't matter. I wandered the lounge, popping grapes and sipping wine.

The place was full of businesspeople making cell calls, checking their PDA's and watching the clock in several time zones at once. Many miles from the first pre-packaged home detergent.

"You're Paul Roget." All I have to do is stand still in a public place and some business hot shot will step up and pitch me his life story. I worked so many years to put myself in that position that it would be ungrateful to complain once it outlived its usefulness. Besides, you could never tell: any of these guys might be the vehicle back to a real life. This one had that impressive look: decent-sized, maybe six-two, haircut and suit costing as much as a

Hyundai. CEO or EVP maybe. Too young for Chairman but the hungry wolf's face of a contender.

"Guilty," I admitted.

"I like your stuff. I watch whenever I see you."

"That's what we work for," I said, bluffing the self-assurance of a year earlier, when I was still *on-air*.

He handed me his card, that thick matte-finish stock with the blue blobby logo all the designers love. Expecteron, Unimorph, whatever—all these companies sound like something out of a 50's sci-fi movie. CEO—bingo! Haven't entirely lost my touch.

"Haven't seen you in a while, though," he continued and my mood soured. Not that there should have been any confusion about it. No one shows business news *reruns*, so when I stopped interviewing CEO's and EVP's and Chairpeople after twenty years in TV and magazines, I disappeared, period. "Funny seeing you here—your name came up the other day. We're working something new. Extreme 'chairs—the ones paraplegics race, stripped-down, real maneuverable? We're rolling them out for advanced adults."

"Advanced adults?"

"Yeah, you know, getting past your 40's, body can't take the pounding from running anymore and swimming is boring. Maybe you've already had a knee replacement and don't want to go through that again. People *our* age. So this is extreme sports—very hip young image. You order your rig any way you want on the

Website—infinitely customizable—and we're underwriting theme parks all over the country to race them. Mountainous terrain, chutes that go up and down. You pay a subscription, practice every day if you want. Get the workout without the breakdowns. We'll have aerobatic chutes once the insurance company stops giving us hell about it."

"Sure," I nodded. When one of these guys gets up a head of steam, you just let them go until they finish. If you interrupt, they have to start over at the beginning.

"So we're talking infomercial to punch it out there, get the meme into the airspace. Figure an hour, Hollywood production values. And someone mentioned your name. You've still got some credibility from your news stuff. Interested?"

I was feeling a little whiplash; I think it was the segue from 'Never miss ya' to 'you still have some credibility'. And then my cell rang and I knew immediately who it was. I raised a finger for a moment's grace and answered.

"They think they've captured Bin Laden!" Ron said, feverish as ever. "Do you think that's bad for business?"

"*Who* thinks?"

"It's on the Web," he said and I could envision him sweating over the flatscreen on his spotless desk. "Some Pakistani politician says they caught him."

"Hang on, okay?" I urged. "Just one second." I shoved the phone in my pants pocket and turned back to the CEO. "Actually,

I might be *very* interested. I'm out of the country for a week. Can I call you when I get back?"

"No problem," he said. "You have my card." He returned to the bar to freshen his Scotch. I moved to the farthest corner of the lounge and retrieved the phone from my pocket.

"Who were you talking to?" Ron demanded.

"The bartender," I answered. "There's no reason to panic. The War on Terror won't be over even if they've bagged him. Have you reached anyone?"

"I have calls in to *everyone*! My Vision Advisor *and* my Process Consultant. But I'm not sure which this is—I mean, the End of the World is part of our Vision, but having a contingency plan if he goes away is part of our Process, right?"

"That's good thinking," I said. "Look, even if he's captured, whoever takes over will have to get even. That makes sense, right?"

"They're terrorists," Ron complained. "I'm not sure they worry about making sense."

"They're in *business* like the rest of us. The new guy's going to have to prove he's tougher than Bin Laden—and the other three guys who want the job. Competition is Nature. Maybe it'll only be a car bomb in Kansas City, but they'll do *something*. Besides, we've got thousands of troops on the Iraqi border—you've got to amortize that investment." The couple on the couch nearby were eyeing me; when I glanced their direction, they looked away. If I intended to board an airplane anytime soon, I had to cool it.

"That's a point," Ron admitted, his breathing returning to normal—Ron normal, but what more could you hope for? *"People are not predictable—"*

"—but the rules of their behavior are," I finished his sentence. Business aphorism #723.

"I don't know if this is a good time for you to leave," he repeated.

"If it makes you feel better, I'll be in the Western Capitol of Terrorism," I whispered. "If anyone's going to buy into the End of the World, it's the Irish."

I could hear him sigh. "Okay, that's right—you're right. *Business is The World.*"

"Business is The World," I chanted, knowing he'd make me if I didn't. "They're calling our flight—I have to go." I closed the phone before he offered any additional reminders of what I was escaping.

Emily was still working the boards. I sat over her shoulder, munching my tuna wraps and watching. You'd think that pleasure would have faded by now, but it seemed instead to have gained depth. As paint deepens, the bright bits become more incandescent against the dark backdrop and thus it's been with Emily and me.

"Remind me to take my pill or I won't sleep on the plane," she said. I hadn't even seen her look up—the woman must have phenomenal peripheral vision. "How's the food?"

"Best day-old tuna of my life. And grapes the size of grapes."

"Great," she chuckled. "With that attitude, you should actually start enjoying your vacation around the time you come home." Em really wanted me happy. I checked the look in her eyes twice to be sure. All my hopes were pinned on that look and there it was.

I'd had a year that knocked me flat. After effortlessly commanding the attention of strangers all my life, I'd gone translucent without warning. I was off the air for the first time in decades. The women I'd been dating stopped answering my calls. One even blocked me so I couldn't see her profile on the website anymore. But Em still wanted me.

From the moment she'd offered the tickets, I'd begun reaching for *good* omens. Desperation in its latter stages proffered an odd sort of lightheadedness.

Each preliminary step—renewing my passport, finding a cheap suitcase, buying up the art supply store with her before the cab to the airport—had been another gulp of hope. Four years after my divorce, thirty years after first making love to a woman, forty-nine years removed from the forceps, I was grasping after an odd brand of redemption. I'd taken a couple good punches and hit the mat hard. But here was a chance to get off the floor. This was no plane ticket—it was a get-out-of-jail-free card. Maybe the doubts and fears that had eaten me up in recent months could be swept away, the frictious blocks removed from my wheels; maybe I still had a small window of years left before I started feeling old *to make something happen.*

Something was going to happen. The thought alone was a revolution. Not just a revolution—a coup, a coup against myself, and a midnight coup, where you wake up in the morning and there's a new general on the television and everything on the street is the same and different all at once.

All I had to decide was what I was fighting for.

FRIDAY

It was so *quiet*. I'd been wavering in and out of sleep and wasn't sure, for long moments after waking, where I was. It was like stirring out of anesthesia—time out of time, dim light, soft breathing from far away and the sensation of floating in a really shallow basin. The continuous whooshing of air conditioning seemed to cast a liquid feel over everything. Awareness came with snatches of images or chunks of dialogue in my head but nothing useful to a wakeful mind.

And then light was coming through the cabin window, though I didn't remember raising the shade before falling asleep. The beginnings of sun, a rusty glint, seeping around the folds in the clouds. I could feel the plane dropping, our belly rushing into contact with the spiky woolen mass. *Attention passengers, we are beginning our descent...*

The cloudbank ran straight across the rim of sky; it took just a minute to penetrate. The layers were thickly woven, gaps of hundreds of feet between the folds and growing light shimmering through the fibers, each layer moving in a slightly different direction at a slightly different speed. It was like being *inside* the Dance of the Seven Veils. And then, without warning, it became a bumpy ride.

I'd thought she was asleep but at the second jolt, Emily gripped my arm. "I hate this," she murmured, working the cord of her headset like a rosary.

I looked out onto the shifting clouds, the wings shuddering, the plane wobbling in the heavy air. I worked through the checklist in my head: Flaps extended. Landing gear down, with that reassuring thunk of wheels locking into place. Bank for final approach, not that you could see anything but gray fuzz. Flaps whining out to their fullest outstretch—and then a glimpse through the veils of land beneath. Moss and mud, moody light and isolated patches of trees in vast fields.

Where were the houses? There was one, finally and another in the distance, across a long narrow channel of greenbrown slowmoving river. Each house isolate, fixed and stubborn against the landscape. A stillness slipped over me, a new mood settling in.

I really hadn't thought much about where we were going. Emily was taking me and that was enough. But the land peeping through the clouds presented an unyielding stubbornness that demanded recognition from 1500 feet.

New York was man's creation, trendy, self-regarding, nothing that couldn't be torn down and rebuilt at a whim. This land rolled to an impassive rhythm all its own. People built outposts here but they were as peripheral to this landscape as the dodo.

The turbulence increased as we descended, as if compressing the air beneath us. I waited for the inevitable mandala of shipping company hangars, wide highways and fast-food joints. It was, after all, an airport. Nothing. Sixty feet off the ground, we were still disturbing herds of cows and the flight path of flocks of geese. I rubbed Emily's shoulder—she was taut, barely breathing.

And then we were down. All at once we were over the runway and all that bucking momentum melted away and I swear all the wheels touched simultaneously. The whole cabin burst into spontaneous applause.

"That was fantastic," I said as we taxied to the terminal. "Great landing."

"They're always good," Emily said, dusting off her jacket as though she'd been through a sandstorm.

"The whole plane applauded!"

"They do that since September 11th," she whispered. "We're just glad to be on the ground."

Before we'd stopped moving, she was up and pulling her carry-on out of the overhead compartment. By the time I'd unfolded myself, stiff as cardboard, to follow, she was twelve ahead of me in the exit line. And then barely in sight up the corridor, heading for Customs.

The Customs people all knew her, of course, so she was through in three seconds. She stood a moment watching me, tapping her foot as though it was a competition. By the time they stamped my papers, she was pulling our suitcases off the luggage carousel and halfway to the exit.

I caught up, puffing, just before the doors. "Got a doctor's appointment?"

"It's just how I am in airports," she shrugged.

I was still pulling my coat on. I hate cold weather—I can never wear enough clothes to keep the chill out. But I couldn't get dressed and keep up with Em at the same time, at least not without a jetpack. Then the gates smacked open and I realized there was nothing to worry about—the air was delicious, damp, clean, with a temperature so neutral you didn't feel a thing.

Feel? Nothing. But *Hear*? Plenty. A bullhorn squawked nearby, words buried in metallic screeching but nothing you could make sense of. Cops in Kevlar jackets and plastic helmets clustered on the walkways directing foot traffic, passed on motorcycles, squatted on nearby rooftops with binoculars and tense expressions and massed at the far end of the terminal, holding a pack of demonstrators in a narrow end of the parking lot across the road.

The whole airport was smaller than the International Arrivals terminal at Kennedy. A couple of hundred yards away glistened the Shannon River—no wonder there'd been so little habitation visible on the descent.

The light changed and we crossed the curving service road into the parking lot—five rows back was Em's car. This was *long-term* parking at Shannon. I rejoice when I get an overnight spot that close to my apartment in Brooklyn.

Emily's car was a Suzuki, a little mini-SUV thing. It was probably silver. Or maybe bronze. Or copper or maybe even a paleish metallic green. Maybe. It needed a wash. Actually, it had needed a wash for a year, explaining the oleaginous colorscheme that changed hue every time you took a step around it.

Em opened the rear hatch and we lifted the big cases in, on top of rain slickers, motor oil, half-opened bags of carrots and a couple nasty-looking syringes. When I came around to the passenger door (on the wrong side of the car, of course, the Irish driving like Brits on the left side of the road), Em was sweeping debris off the front seat. I placed the syringes gingerly in the glove box.

"Wouldn't want you to have to explain these to the cops," I said.

"They would understand," she replied. "*Everyone* has horses over here, silly."

"Everyone *you* know," I said, folding myself into the seat. They were for the *horses*—I knew that.

Thank God the roof was high—I could sit without slouching. I got a good view of the patterned headliner, however.

"Everyone thinks it takes so much money," Em laughed. "I know lots of absolutely salt-of-the-earth people who own horses."

By your standards, maybe. She rolled out the exit road onto a two-lane that hugged the outer edge of the airport. The road was no bigger than Fourth Avenue in Brooklyn but marked like a superhighway. It started drizzling; Em flipped on the wipers just as we ground to a halt, watching the police herd a small group of protestors into a shrunken paddywagon. Up the hill behind them, you could see where they'd tried to clip the perimeter fence.

"Why break in right by the highway?" Em complained. "Why not just turn yourself in to be arrested?"

"Because that wouldn't get you on television," I answered, motioning to the camera crew coming around the back of the paddywagon. "What's the protest?"

"We're shuttling troops through Shannon to Iraq. So—" She shrugged.

"They're going to have to do more than cut a hole in the fence."

Emily shrugged again, removed an open bag of rice cakes from the instrument binnacle and threw them in the general direction of the back seat. "It's a fringe movement. There's not a country in the West that's more pro-American than Ireland. But this isn't Afghanistan—they didn't attack us."

"Let 'em get used to it. It's our newest growth industry: The War on Terror. You use up cruise missiles so you can buy new ones—creates employment. And by the way, there are still lots of angry people out there who really *do* want to kill us. You recall one victim, your husband."

"*Ex*-husband," she corrected. "And you can't really say that killed him."

"He died, didn't he? Like somebody said, he's the only husband you've ever had." Dyson had been in my dreams on the plane. Emily and I were traveling together; memories of Dyson were inevitable.

Dyson was a senior at Sarah Lawrence when I transferred in as a sophomore. There were few men there at the time and even fewer straight ones. More to the point, I'd told myself I wanted to be an artist but, confronted with a campus full of them, I *felt* like a straight man, in every sense of the word—I wasn't as passionate, flamboyant, entertaining or as sure of having anything to say as anyone around me.

Dyson became my safe haven and mentor, the physicist in the writer/sculptor/dancer/conceptual video performance horde. The couple science prodigies at Sarah Lawrence all wrote their own majors then—the school was working up to a pre-med program—so it was taken for granted he was a brainiac. His physical ailments seemed inevitable, as though he burnt so much energy cogitating that his limbs and organs couldn't be expected to function properly.

The first image you had of him was the heavy walking stick and his hips laboring to forward motion. Then the shadowed unhealthy eyes, all accusation. The rest of the world had the luxury of 'There but for the grace of God go I.' Dyson was one of God's examples and less than gracious about it. "At least legless beggars in Calcutta get charities," he'd growl. "I have to grade papers."

We were a complementary mismatch. As Dyson was precarious, I was robust. As I was cheerful and a bit childish, Dyson was a dark tragedy with attitude. He was fastidious and thorough; I was impulsive and scattered. We quickly discovered that we picked up girls more successfully together than apart, him with his tragic aura, me by making them laugh.

"It's all there," he would say in that guttergrowl voice of his, clearly audible in a bar shrieking the Clash or Ramones. "The Universe is being broken down into its component parts. Neutrinos, quarks, the stepping stones have been identified and their properties catalogued. It's possible we could know all the answers to all the questions within our lifetime. I just want to get out there before it's all done."

Emily arrived in my senior year, when Dyson had become a teaching assistant. They had grown up down the road from each other in Bucks County Pennsylvania, though it was simply proof that the setting didn't create the person. Emily, at first, was a bumptious tomboy, sunburnt even in winter, a ponytailed mess of wooly whiteblond hair and gangly limbs she'd just begun to grow into. Quiet and tense around people, she seemed wedded to the horses she'd left behind and that, at first, she drove home every weekend to ride. Dyson, by contrast, gave the impression he'd gotten through two decades on the planet without ever stepping outside.

There was something forcible and unpleasant about them from the beginning. "Em!" Dyson would bellow in the middle of a dorm or study hall, deaf to his surroundings, "let's get a drink!" or "I need meds. Take me to town." "We're not amongst the farmers anymore," he'd snap. "Don't you have jeans without shit stains?" But that situation didn't last long.

The weather hadn't turned cold yet—it was probably mid-October—and Emily showed up at the Pub one night in a bright blue and pink patterned sundress with her hair cut so it framed her face. The dress was a revelation—who knew she had boobs? And legs? She'd been Dyson's horsy friend. But even now I can summon the sight of her in that dress simply by encountering the smell of her perfume.

By the time she'd walked the thirty feet from the door to our table, the wind had changed, the flags had shifted direction and Emily was banging loudly on the sexual radar of every man and woman on our little campus.

And from that moment she was in control. She infuriated some of the more militant types on campus, who persisted in jeans and baggy sweatshirts while Em stalked the place looking like Lauren Bacall. She took to hanging out in a bar in Bronxville with a pool table and dance floor and Dyson started dragging me there, just by coincidence, the two of them pretending to ignore each other night after night.

After a week or two, I realized how entangled things were between them. Dyson had two women hanging onto his stoned deep-karma quantum physics rap (Einstein was not only wrong a lot; he was *superficial*) while Emily, who was supposed to be dancing with a boy she'd met on the floor, kept getting in the way. Whenever Dyson would begin to reel in one of his admirers, Em would appear for a sip of her drink or to drape her jacket over the back of Dyson's chair—and each time, she would take Dyson's concentration with her. With her, inevitably, back to the dance floor, where he, of the walking stick and the laundry list of infirmities, could never follow. He sat surrounded by other women, nursing his drink and popping his pills and watching Emily dance with other men.

My mother passed away when I was four. At least so the old man told me. I don't remember her being sick and I don't remember a funeral, though he swears I was there. The point is, I know longing when I see it, know it the way other men know lust or hunger or rage at the first sniff. Dyson was a hard man but that hollow space was visible in him and not in any healthy way. I've never seen any cruelty in Emily. If Dyson hadn't treated her well and she was now getting her own back, flexing her own wings, who could blame her? Or maybe it was just another proof of our ability to hide from our own worst behavior.

The Irish police now surrendered to reality and officially stopped traffic to let the paddywagon take the demonstrators away.

"This whole thing's a mess," Em continued. "Iraq's no threat to anyone except maybe someday shoulda coulda woulda. Did you hear Colin Powell at the UN? No evidence, just take our word for it."

"It works for them at home," I shrugged. "Look, what's the difference what we think? They're going one way or the other. It's all because Saddam tried to off Bush 41. "

"Oh please," she scoffed. "We go to war over personal neurosis?"

"Everything in life is personal neurosis! Jeb was the favored son—Dubya was a dead end, the alkie cokehead who failed at everything. Mom is prickly and distant, Dad is benign and distant. So you go in and knock off the guy who tried to assassinate Dad, the guy *he* couldn't knock off. Pay off family karma at the expense of the world. Shakespeare would love it."

"You know you're not as cynical as you sound."

"Who's cynical? I'm not even sure I'm against it. We're replacing an oil dictatorship with a democracy. If Clinton had suggested it, we'd be shocked at his idealism. I'm not knocking neurosis—sometimes it shows you the way." I know I should keep quiet more. I don't know if the motor's in my brain or down my throat but clearly the fucking thing just runs 24 hours a day.

"Well, I don't like the war and I don't like the demonstrations either," Em said. "Not once they start cutting fences and blocking the highway. You'd think the Irish would appreciate order."

"You just don't like the traffic jams," I nudged and she laughed as traffic finally started to move. But the paddywagon had conjured an ambulance in my head and there was Dyson again, bouncing around the walls of my skull.

He hadn't been feeling well and Dyson routinely felt so badly that not feeling well took some doing. Dyson lived ten blocks from the towers and had stood, transfixed, at the mouth of the subway station watching them come down. He was caught in the cloud of ash and hobbled out but it took time because he didn't move any better then than he had when I first met him.

His doctors wanted tests run. I picked him up a couple of days after, outside his girlfriend's apartment just north of Canal Street. "She doesn't want me to have visitors," he said when he came down, looking more sour than usual. "I might start feeling welcome." We rode the subway to a hospital in Chelsea, outside the emergency zone.

The halls were filled with gurneys and watch stations, armed guards and dispirited families, the chalky dust carried in with the EMT's and cops. The hospitals had girded for a major influx of injured and had to cope with receiving none.

"Hospitals should be my turf," Dyson griped. "They ask questions with quantifiable answers." We sat in green-and-white striped metal chairs as he filled out paperwork. "My address is unliveable, my conditions and known drug interactions take an hour to fill out and they don't care anyway." He looked up with those dark-circled eyes. "You can really get lost in a place like this. Just let go and sit quietly in the corner and everything drifts away. That's why *you're* here," he said. "To make sure I don't get lost."

"I'll get you one of those pendants with your name on it so you won't forget yourself."

Dyson smiled at that, in his way. His smile never changed— all in the eyes, more an indication that he was grateful for someone else's amusement than that he was ever able to share it.

"Remember when I told you we were going to know everything? Break it all down?" I nodded. I remembered. "You thought I was crazy, though you were too gracious—or too stoned—to say so. Well, we do. We know almost all the things we thought we would way back then. And we're farther from answers than we ever were," he laughed, a grunting hacking cough of a laugh. "Did you know observing electrons *changes their behavior?* Our consciousness affects the physical universe on a subatomic level. What say you of *that?*"

"I think it's the most encouraging thing I've ever heard."

"You would. To me, it's terrifying. There's a theory that's been gaining strength over the last twenty years or so—it fits the available data. It suggests one set of rules for matter at the subatomic level and a completely different set for collective activity above that."

"You mean the way a note is different as part of a chord than played alone?" I asked. I have this unreasonable desire to be *heard.* My marriage counselor said it was central to my psyche— and death to my marriage.

Dyson laughed again, a moment of genuine cheer. "No that's terrible," he said. "No, it's like rush hour. On one level, everyone's in their cars, driving nicely-marked highways heading for work at 9am. On another, they're cutting each other off, shaving and putting on makeup, talking on their cellphones, doing 75 and 40, having multi-car pileups and bumper-to-bumper traffic behind jackknifed tractor-trailers and getting to work at 8:30 and 10:45. Nothing is as expected and the rules are ignored as often as they're obeyed. Yet if you pull back a hundred miles and observe the process from outer space, you see an orderly procession of cars from the suburbs to the city and at night the whole process reversing itself."

He looked up—they were calling someone and for a moment it sounded like Dyson's name but wasn't. "So reality becomes a question of *perspective*. Reality is a goddamn liberal arts question. That is the shit I *hated*. I dug being the scientist among the wooly-headed artists. We had *facts*. Now I just want to go home and lock myself in but I can't even do that until the place is cleaned up." And then they called him for his tests.

We were approaching Limerick according to the roadsigns. The whole city looked like a Dickensian factory, low redbrick and granite buildings against the darkcloud horizon, punctuated by smokestacks and several impressive church steeples. All the cars on the road looked HO-scale, shrunken versions of familiar shapes, though the Europeans like hatchbacks a lot more than we do. A mournful sound filled the car and I realized Emily'd turned the radio on.

"What's that?"

"It's the Irish station," she said. "I thought you'd like it."

The song ended, followed by a short burst of commentary in Irish. The language was a surprise, ancient and guttural, almost Eastern European, a rough tongue that exposed English for the slick mongrel it was. Followed by laments and hymns, voices in the dark, desolate and mournful.

The sky was a roiling stew of red and orange and purple as Em worked around the edges of the town. The whole place felt haunted now, foreboding, because of the radio. A sprightly reel with fiddles and pipes a few minutes later felt like a consolation.

We turned North at a traffic circle ('Everything here is roundabouts,' Emily explained) and in minutes were deep in farmland. The landscape ran wide and high-waisted, soft rolling hills polluted with sheep and wide valleys sweeping shallow from horizon to horizon. Small houses stood behind stone and hedge walls set right along the road, across from neat forests of densely-packed trees. All this ten minutes from a major international airport. In the US, we'd have twenty-five more miles of strip malls and gas stations, cheap motels and topless clubs, all rutting shamelessly to put the other guy out of business.

"I love the way houses are added to the landscape here," I told her. "Man doesn't dominate. It's all so natural."

She giggled while turning onto a smaller road. "There's not a natural thing in sight," she answered. "The whole countryside was deforested hundreds of years ago to build ships for England. The government plants these stands of trees so the next generation will have some lumber. The old trees are on the estates of English Lords sent to keep the Irish in line. Nobody dared cut *those* down."

The roads kept getting narrower and more tunnel-like, though still marked like highways. We settled onto a paved path little wider than an American driveway—maybe a (narrow European) car-and-a-half wide—hurtling along at a startling clip.

When we first met, I visited Dyson and Emily at their adjoining properties in Bucks County. I had an old sports car and drove stupid fast. Emily jumped into her father's pickup truck and called out, "Follow me." I did—once and never again. She rocketed along the banks of the Delaware, bouncing from one shellhole to the next, cackling like a fiend, foot to the floor the whole distance. I told myself I was afraid of ripping the suspension from under the car but if I'd been at the wheel of a tank or Jeep or a rocket ship with air suspension I still couldn't have kept her in sight.

Now she was driving the same way on these teeny Irish roads. I played heroic as long as I could, then grabbed for the handle over the door and held tight, as though that would help.

A truck appeared at the top of the hill, rumbling straight for us. It was surely narrower than an American truck—we hog the world market in excess—but it still filled the road nearly from edge to edge. Emily inched closer to one hedgerow while the truck pulled slightly toward the other but it couldn't be nearly enough.

There was a sudden clawing noise and I jumped. The slit-open side window of the car was snagging bits of the hedge alongside. I grimaced, for just a second—and the truck was past us, heading away out of sight. I swear I didn't look away but I didn't see it pass either.

There were bits of hedge on my shirt and lap; I swept them off like they were radioactive. "Jesus! Cut those hedges down! Who cares about tradition—they're a goddamn hazard!"

"What tradition? Lots of them are new."

"*New*? How?"

"The government here doesn't have eminent domain. They can't just claim twenty or thirty feet of your lawn if they want to. If there are survey maps, they're several hundred years old so people put up hedges to settle the line. That way, if the government needs to expand the road, you get paid for the land."

"Sure—kill me for property rights," I grumbled.

"Wait till we're on a road with *stone* walls," she laughed— the woman always had a strain of pleasant-faced sadism. "I don't have a problem with people getting paid for their property."

"Damn Republican."

"And an MBA, don't forget."

"Okay, damn MBA's. What's the square root of a hypotenuse?"

"That's not an MBA," she insisted. "But if you can figure out the answer, I'll tell you the profit margin."

≠

"I've been looking at travel books," I said as we hurtled around another narrow turn. "There are a few places I'd like to go."

We'd been driving half an hour along the Shannon. The towns were smaller and more cheerful than Limerick—well-tended, squat houses and taller rowhouses in an array of neon colors, set into hillsides overhung with fast-moving clouds. Every few miles, you got a view that either made you smile or tear up. The whole place was desperately beautiful.

"Dingle Peninsula sounds good," I started.

"Where?" she asked, as though she'd never heard the name. That should have been a sign.

"Dingle Peninsula. It's in all the tourist guides. Pretty towns filled with Irish music...is it a tourist trap?" Em loved music—maybe these places weren't authentic enough for her.

"Don't know," she said, like it was a fly buzzing at her ear. She'd lived in Ireland for three years and this was news to her? "We can go to the Rock of Cashel. An Irish king lived there and it's pretty close by."

"Okay," I continued. "And south of Cork is supposed to be gorgeous and Dublin and if we could do Northern Ireland, that would be great." Her eyes were glazing over; clearly, it wasn't a good time. I was on vacation—she was coming home and probably hadn't slept much on the plane. I stuffed my notes back in my pocket. Sometimes I overestimate Emily, but it's easy to do. It just feels like she has the answer for everything.

They called Dyson three days after his tests and told him he was fine. No additions to the list of what was already wrong with him. We went for a drink to celebrate. He clinked glasses with me, took a sip and slumped over onto the floor before he'd finished swallowing. The drink had nothing to do with it, the doctors said. Neither did September 11th. His heart stopped. Just like that.

Dyson had been sick so much that I didn't imagine anything could kill him. Now, as I watched the bar owner administering CPR, there was no imagining. There was also no sense of infinity on Dyson's face, no consoling insight striking him in his last moments. Nothing was on his face like nothing was a thing, like nothing had a tangible aspect, like he was what nothing looked like.

I remained at the table until the EMS guys bagged him up in their disaffected way. Somebody asked if I needed help getting home but I just left. I walked until I ended up home and by the time I'd made it there, I'd decided to throw Dyson a shiva. He wasn't a Jew and I wasn't much of one, but I needed to respond somehow to…to the nothing, if nothing else. And Dyson was a determined, parochial outsider—the kind of man who could feel let down by the molecular structure of the universe. Was anything more Jewish? A shiva at least felt appropriate.

His apartment was in a penal-colony complex in Tribeca, fixed-income housing built back when there were still unfashionable neighborhoods in Manhattan. Three weeks after 9/11, it was once again a place no sensible person would choose to live. The fires were burning at the site and would for months. The smell in the air was awful. The chalkwhite dust clung stubbornly to every surface. Stores had gone out of business, the streets were cluttered with police and the posters of the lost flapped from a thousand lampposts whenever there was a breeze.

The newspapers were talking about a Federal cleanup but as soon as the EPA announced there was nothing to worry about — without ever explaining how they knew — residents were advised simply to mop up their apartments. I don't think anyone in their right minds really believed the air was safe but, for a little while there, it really felt like wartime — you buckled down and did your best.

I brushed the grit — of girders, telephones, windowpanes, computer monitors, bone and flesh — off Dyson's furniture. I pushed everything against the walls except his dining room table, which stood, leaves in place, waiting for friends to cover it with food. I mopped the floors and tossed the mop when I was finished. Dyson's sister Eileen called from Richmond with plans to show the

"My ex designed wedding dresses."

"Interesting we both picked people," she mused, "who spoke a language we couldn't understand." The sky was a sheet of artificial light. They were still moving girders and finding body parts on rooftops ten blocks away. I needed this connection with Emily. If I hadn't known it a moment earlier, I knew it now. I needed *something*.

"I like your hair," I said, idle flattery but also the truth. She'd achieved herself. Her hair was completely different, thinned out and straightened. Tamed.

"Oh, that was the chemo," she said nonchalantly. I was struck dumb. After a moment, she continued, "Dyson didn't tell you? I had a bout, just after we split up. Ovarian cancer. He acted as though it was my punishment for divorcing him. I yelled at him for two years about that. Probably did me good—gave me someone to focus my frustrations on," and she laughed again. Her face changed all at once. "Am I a widow?"

"You *divorced* him."

"He's the only husband I've ever had."

"Does it really matter? It's just a word."

"You're the writer," she said. "Don't words matter?"

"You just like wearing the expensive black dress," I needled and she went red with laughter.

And that's where we started. We met whenever I was in town and she was in the States for dinner. I started driving her to and from the airport. Then she sent me the date she was arriving and just assumed I'd be there.

There were unintended consequences of course, as with all else. Back in her orbit, I started writing fiction again. "You've got to do something with those tales in your head," she giggled. "They're *inventory*! You can't just waste them." It was the first time anyone had made writing sound practical—leave it to the MBA.

And then, all of a sudden, I had *time* to write, because I found myself suddenly out of work. The advertising market dried up after 9/11 and the network decided to 'reorient' their business coverage—more headlines and less feature stories like mine. Emily became my buffer, confessor and safety net, my contact when no one else returned my calls. I anticipated every visit, every email and phone call. She spent almost all her time in the States with me. She never mentioned any men on the other side of the Atlantic.

Finally, she suggested I come to Ireland. "You have to get away, take a break," she said. "Besides, you'd write a book over here. There's material around every corner in Ireland." I laughed—I had just started working for Ron, and at that point only part-time. I was financially wrecked. I dismissed the thought but she didn't stop bringing it up.

And then, one night, we went to some arthouse movie where the main character's wife ends up in an affair with his sister. When I got home, I found an email from Emily in my in-box:

```
I've thought sometimes I might be gay. I find
    I'm attracted to women but I can't bring
myself to do anything about it. It's strange
at this age to be so uncertain about myself.
You remember I wasn't always shy about what I
wanted. What do you think? How does someone
        know what they are? What they want?
```

I wrote back:

```
I'm sorry, sweetie but I'm a simpleton on
    these things. I've spent half my life in
    locker rooms with naked men without ever
getting a thrill. Meanwhile the waitress bends
too far over the table and I begin to salute.
So for me sex is the most obvious thing in the
world but I suspect that approach works better
    for men. We've sexualized women's bodies so
much I can't imagine anyone of either gender
    sitting around a locker room of naked women
and not getting excited. One of my girlfriends
told me she used to get turned on staring at
herself in the mirror in dance class. Forget
    penis envy—I want to be able to do that.
```

And then, I appended: You know I want you to be happy. It seemed gratuitous at the time. But it was, possibly, the start of something a bit underhanded between us. Actually, not between us—underhanded on my part.

That whole painful year, I couldn't understand why we hadn't dated, why we weren't a couple. At least I wondered when we weren't in the same room together. When we were, the void was hard to miss, at least on my end. No spark. I couldn't explain it—Emily was everything I wanted in a woman except that somehow I...didn't...want her.

All the same, I didn't believe she was gay. She wanted me, I knew it. And, spark or no spark, I needed her. My life was a shambles. Even if I was a misanthrope, I needed other people around to make me uncomfortable. So I added: You know I want you to be happy. I sent the message and waited.

The next day, she sent me the tickets.

In the distance, a wide valley sketched its outline through the haze. Water glimmered through trees to the North. The hillside below rippled like paper that had been crumpled and flattened out again in haste,

Emily lived on a dirt road off a small paved lane off the local main road. The pavement started up briefly just before her house and ran a few yards before disappearing as though it had faded away.

Five houses clustered in this narrow space where the land had temporarily flattened out. Each a different style, from the stucco boxes I'd seen along the highway to the steel-and-glass constructs from depressing Fifties English movies. What happened to the thatched huts from the John Wayne picture? Em caught me looking.

"Most houses here are concrete," she said. "The Irish expect a house to be cheap to make and to last two hundred years without maintenance."

"Wood houses don't last?"

"In this climate? It rains almost every day. Besides, the timber went to make English ships, remember?"

She pulled up a driveway alongside a yellow concrete blockhouse, L-shaped, one wing fronting the road and the other pointing away across the valley. An ancient black truck with vestigial fenders, vent windows and a rippling riveted skin sat comatose in the gravel square inside the L. A tarp had been thrown halfway across the hood; a watering can stood on the running board.

Walking to the back door, we passed drainage pans, old dead trees in pots, cinderblocks, old tires—and horse syringes, of course. I'd already become expert at spotting those.

Em pulled at the door and recoiled. "I've got to talk to the gardener—he always locks the place." She trudged to the black truck and pulled a key from under the floor mat.

"You leave it open?" I asked and she shrugged. But, unlocked, the door still refused to yield. "Hmm," she murmured, peering through the glass, "we'll have to move those boxes." Three huge cartons , several pair of knee-high rubber boots and bundles of blackish logs lay crammed in the foyer just behind the glass door.

"I'll break them up. Do you recycle?"

"No, I need them. They're for my computer and DVD player. If I return them, they have to go in the original cartons." She stared a moment longer. "I'll put them in the attic."

We managed to squeeze around the door. I broke down the containers while Em opened a hatch in the ceiling. She climbed a telescoping ladder and I handed up one box at a time. It took a long time to find space — there were evidently several generations of computer boxes up there already. I tried to figure how she'd gotten her suitcases out, leaving for the States two weeks earlier.

Finally the foyer was clear. Em got to the end and stopped dead, cursing. She grabbed a broom to sweep a path through a bed of newspapers, empty scrip bottles and indiscriminate dirt covering the floor. This had once apparently been the kitchen. Its counter lay under piles of dirty dishes, small opened (and strangely crunched) boxes of tea, old onions, turnips with roots growing out of them, prescription bottles, glasses filled with coffee grinds and unidentified hardened saps.

From there, the two wings diverged — the living room (and several others, unidentified) sat along the street, while the wing adjoining the drive jutting out beyond the foyer. Em tried to pull her big case into the living room and got nowhere. I came over to help and stopped dead.

Opened unfinished books and magazines lay several layers deep across the floor, along with riding jackets, horse blankets, boots, gift boxes filled with soft gauze wrap and assorted computer and television parts. Saddles, an unused semi-rolled-up fabric shoetree, a road atlas, a set of encyclopedias and four guitars lay in cases atop the piles. There were layers underneath, too, but I wasn't looking.

A love seat and chair covered in debris offered the possibility of seating, if you could reach them, but the point of the entire house appeared to be random storage. Random as in, everything to be found wherever it was first laid down. Em abandoned her case and trudged on into the streetside wing.

I was in a state of shock. My first thought was some angry neighbor or irresponsible cousin had trashed the place while she was gone. But she returned a moment later, chipper and energetic, totally oblivious to the level of carnage. This was, I realized, the first time I'd ever seen a house Emily owned herself. With Dyson, they'd had help (though I'd had no idea how much at the time). Since then, whenever she was in the States, she stayed with Bibs outside Princeton as a guest. It was surreal to see her in her immaculate hunting suit battling through the debris to throw on a standing lamp crammed into the far corner.

An ancient canister of butter cookies, open and crumbling, lay on the floor in front of me. I carried it into the kitchen, found a garbage bag, dropped in the cookies and Emily's floor sweepings as well. I ran the sink, washed the dishes and, pushing the pill bottles into a corner, wiped and scraped and scrubbed the counter. Once I'd finished, I was willing to consider eating there, but I was running hot water over any surface before letting it touch my tongue.

And then she was in the doorway, pointing down the back wing. "Your room is there, just beyond the bathroom. Let's get a couple hours sleep and we can think about dinner." She grabbed her suitcase and dragged it across the mosh pit, cursing as she went.

I lifted my suitcase across several pair of boots and what looked like a lavender parachute into my room. It was tiny, filled by two twin beds, one cradling a pile of pillows and hand-labeled CD's, the other, a video camera, about fifty tapes, two riding jackets and a magnificent boxed set of Proust in leatherbound hardcover. I stacked the pillows and CD's on the floor under the window and tried to ignore the feeling in my stomach.

I'd been a bachelor for four years. I came of age in an era of hippies and crash pads. This was the first house I'd ever been in that made my skin crawl.

I pulled the curtains open. A huge checkered cow stared back at me, two feet away, lazing over newly-chewed grass. Two or three others, one a mother sheltering a wobbly-legged calf, kept her company. A bowl of mountains stood across the valley under a wide sky. Swift-moving clouds drifted by like cotton balls, dragging their shadows across the landscape. A thicket of trees split the flickering glare of the lake below.

This was no good. I'd come over with plans for Emily—or at least hoping she had plans for me. People don't offer you transatlantic plane tickets without reason and Emily didn't offer to pay for them without a reason-and-a-half. Could she really be nuts? The evidence of the house left her looking real wobbly.

I pushed my suitcase and laptop bag into a neat grouping at the foot of the bed, joining several horsy prints and a heavy-duty professional tripod. I returned to the kitchen, dried the dishes and set them in the rack. Then I went back to my room and crawled under the covers without undressing.

When I woke, it was with a fully-formed thought in mind. I opened my laptop case and pulled out the guidebook with the fold-out map under the cover. I traced the route we'd taken that morning with my finger, parsing the scale and confirming that from Shannon Airport to Emily's house, we'd driven about 35 miles as the crow flies—but it had taken us almost two hours. And no wonder—any crow attempting our route would have spun to earth with a bad case of vertigo.

This country didn't know from straight lines. The cranky Irish landscape and roads built long after the farms they connected made every trip a stutterstep assemblage of local stages, instead of the grand processions Americans were used to. There was no driving from Dublin to Waterford, for example. You had to go from Dublin to Naas, take the left fork near Kilcullen in County Kildare, follow that south to Carlow, then the winding road west to Kilkenny, then south past Knocktopher and Ballyquin to Waterford. Okay—so at least I could understand why my travel plans seemed to overwhelm her. I sat slumped against the wall for a minute or two. For the moment, I would take my reassurances wherever I found them.

But there was more to it, just a murmur at that point, a pre-echo of something to come. I understood more than I knew. The sun was going down fast—lights were going on across the valley and in a cluster just down the hill. There was some kind of life down there—a town but not a big one, close but not too close. At that moment, all I had was the awareness of that space, of Emily's chosen solitude. There was more to come and I felt it but it was too soon to name it, to admit it. Most of the time, we have to learn what we know, even if it's inside us already.

When I came out, she was wandering the kitchen, straightening. She was straightening the dishes and glassware on the counter. She was straightening the prescription bottles. In the midst of Omaha Beach, she was straightening the things I had straightened before going to sleep.

"We should go into town," she said, "and get some things."

We drove over the unpaved road onto a slightly bigger paved road and then a slightly bigger road than that one. She was taking a different direction than the way we'd come and the terrain and even the vegetation seemed different, as though land here could be as moody as weather.

"Zinc mines," Em said as we passed a huge pit dug out of a hillside. "Used to be silver when silver was worth something." After two deserted churches, several shuttered farmhouses and endless stone walls, the town appeared through the trees below. "Lisheen-Ballynkill," Emily proclaimed. "Actually, we're coming into Ballynkill—Lisheen is down below, across the way. They built a bridge in 1720 so now it's one town hyphenated by a river."

"That's a good bit," I murmured, scribbling notes in my pad. "Thank you."

"It's not a story," she warned. "As far as the Irish are concerned, this is recent history. They can cite you chapter and verse on everything around here since the year 1000."

"Well, I'll probably make up the history anyway," I said. "Actually, I'll have you mangle it. You're the local American."

"I'm the local *Protestant*," she giggled. "That's why they leave me alone. I'm doomed to perdition anyway."

"Perdition...that sounds good—sounds lazy."

"No, no, that's not for *you*. You're Jewish—you're fair game. They can *convert* you."

"I'd have to become a better Jew first."

"You tell them that. They can go looking for some *serious* Jews to offer more of a challenge."

Ballynkill was a gem, brightly lit and polished, cute as a button. Cars crowded the narrow hilltop streets as couples meandered from one gleaming pub to the next, old-timey acoustic music poured out the doorways into the night. The narrow attached buildings were painted an array of brazen colors—bright yellow, several different purples, lavender, ochre, peach and forest green—they might sell blouses or even cars in those colors in the States but not houses. Complex, luminous colors—cheerful but not simple-minded.

We passed three town squares before Em found a parking spot next to a church, in a courtyard that was all odd angles. The shape surely descended from some open-air market crammed with horses, hand carts and foot traffic a thousand years ago. But now, the angular shape just guaranteed that certain groups of cars could only come and go together—you couldn't pull any one out without several others obliging.

She pulled a couple of vinyl shopping bags from the back seat and marched towards the cliff end of town. It looked like a perspective test from the Fledgling Artists' School, identical three-story attached houses running steeply downhill until they dropped completely out of sight, the view capped by a church steeple three stories below.

Our destination was, by American standards, a mini-mart—three or four aisles. We entered through sliding electric doors like the ones at the airport, except I had to duck to clear this one. The ceiling was white plaster between black crossbeams and needed painting—I had a closeup view. The flush-faced woman behind the counter gaped at me for just one second before chirping "Hello Emily" with that familiar adoring tone. Emily then stunned me by twining her arm around mine and giving me a little squeeze.

"Mary, this is my friend Paul."

"Oh Paul—we've heard so much about you," Mary said, extending the sheath of Emily adoration to cover me as well.

"Hello," I said, trying to keep up as Emily half-caressed, half-dragged me into the store. "What much has she heard about me?" I whispered.

"We have to get scones and brown bread," Emily returned into my ear, like it was a plot. "They make them in the store." I followed her pointing and found roughcut woodbins, immaculate but probably seventy years old, filled with local baked goods and produce from the Middle East and North Africa. The bananas had spots but they were really ripe, instead of being shipped green and force-ripened on the truck.

"Put them here," she said, holding open one of the plastic bags she'd pulled from the car. "They charge if they give you shopping bags." I looked around and saw all the customers brung their own. Here's a custom that would never survive America. An American supermarket chain wants its logo *everywhere* and they certainly don't want you thinking "my bag's almost full" and not buying that extra item.

"What's she heard about me?" I repeated as Emily breezed by, beelining for the rear of the store.

The packages on these shelves were simple and functional, designed by some underpaid artist in a back-room instead of an army of marketers and seven terabytes of extrapolated focus groups. The milk in the stand-up refrigerator said 'Lisheen Creamery' above a simple line drawing of the bridge at the center of town. Chrome and glass cabinets displayed fresh-cut meat and cheese. Next to these bits, American produce looked cartoonishly unnatural, inflated helium and candlewax, hype and hubris. I wondered how expensive it would be to go vegan when I got home.

"So what's she heard—?" I started again but Em shushed me off—for the third time. Three, as far as I'm concerned, eliminates coincidence. Three in a row is a *trend*.

A blonde man with glasses and a squashed-looking cap was cutting fresh pork chops at an ancient wood table—I would have sworn he was entirely oblivious to us. Then Emily said, "Hello Simon" and he nearly leapt to the counter, grinning like a pirate.

"Hello Emily, where've you been?"

"To the States for a few weeks—this is my friend Paul."

"Hello Paul. Nice to meet you finally." His expression took on that familiar mixture of earnestness butting up against resentment. I was with Emily, which was clearly where *he* wanted to be.

"Hello," I said, biting my cheek and fighting to control myself.

She ordered salmon and a small roast. Simon had it weighed and wrapped in brown paper in seconds. "Hope you enjoy your stay," he told me, handing over the package. This was rank chivalry considering the envy in his eyes.

And then finally we were out into the crisp night again. Emily set a brisk pace toward the car. It took a real effort to overhaul her but I'd had enough.

"Okay," I said, a virtual barricade, "out with it. What has everyone heard about me?" She mimed an astonishing mixture of shock and innocent denial, but I wasn't having any. "What's with our arms interlaced and the warm-hearted smiles from everyone and the envy from Simon behind the counter who wants some? No shit here, Sherlock."

Innocence dissolved into her usual brisk pragmatism, as if we were discussing winter coats or snow tires. "Okay—you're my beard!"

"I'm--?"

"My beard—my protection."

"Oh come on."

"I'm serious. This is Ireland and it's not Dublin. I'm already the Queen of gossip around here. Unmarried woman, living alone in the country—and an American—and a Protestant! I gave one of my ponies to the local minister and suddenly we were supposed to be having an affair. It was all over town. He told me he couldn't ride the horse or even have lunch with me anymore."

"You were having lunches?"

"At restaurants in broad daylight. So you see, darling—I need cover. And you're it. I've told everyone about my very tall boyfriend from the States whom I visit regularly and now you're here so I'm not making you up. All we have to do is walk around town together a few times—and it would be nice if you'd go to church with me on Sunday. The minister would appreciate it too."

"I don't know if I love you that much. You could have told me."

"I didn't think it would be a problem," she said, daring me to say it was.

I might have. I wanted to protest. I *needed* to, really. I'd promised myself *something was going to happen*, and whatever it was, I'd expected it to be about Emily and me. So what if I didn't want her that way, I'd thought, at least she wants me. Maybe, face to face, alone together, I can *make* myself feel that way about her. If not, maybe I can fake it.

It does me no credit to admit this—I was willing to take consolation in feelings I couldn't return. But it was the only consolation in sight. So I was working up to a good protest but I never got the chance. A voice broke in—a woman's voice with an unplaceable accent.

"Emily! Welcome back! Will you have anything for me soon?"

We turned to the owner of the voice and if I'd had any doubts about Ireland as a land of ghosts and apparitions, they disappeared on the spot. Tall even by my standards and everything about her elongated, stretched—face, torso, every aspect lengthened as if out of a press. El Greco would have thought her entirely ordinary.

"I have been telling several buyers absolutely the wildest tales about my American artist and I will be called to account if I cannot produce some tangible evidence of your brilliance—and soon."

This was a woman genetically bred to be a character, to be assumed an oddball at first glance—anything else would have been a waste of material. Her face was vaguely birdlike and intense, hair black and spiky like a punk rocker's. Her eyes were black and piercing and sharply judgmental—not someone to have an intellectual discussion with in a dark alley. She was wrapped in what looked like a sheepskin coat, but the fur was long, not cropped the way tame individuals wore it. She looked like some wooly bird who had just graduated with honors from Oxford.

But the thing that really struck me was the look on her face. I remembered it from Sarah Lawrence, that look Emily aroused in men and women, that look that said they'd follow her through a wall if she'd only ask. El Greco's girlfriend here had it in spades.

Em always took it totally for granted, of course. It was just the way people looked at her. At least, she always *had*. This time, when I turned for her reaction, I found her ramrod straight, cheeks bright red and seemingly struck dumb. This was all clear even in the dim light of the square.

"I—I have three...mostly finished," she replied finally. "I'll—I have to do a few touchups on the others. I—They should be ready...in the next few days." She sputtered like a Model T for a second and then added, "Maeve, this is Paul." Maeve nodded vaguely in my direction. "He...he helped me pick out some of the paints."

And didn't *that* turn me around, oh yes it did. A moment earlier, I was pissed at being the show boyfriend. Now, I was the guy who helped her *pick out some paints*.

"Good to meet you Paul," Maeve offered, in the tone one uses on the preacher's ten-year-old and returned to Emily with renewed energy. "Well, see that you bring them and soon—I have a reputation as a local crackpot to maintain, thank you."

And then she was gone. Emily continued to blush all the way home.

$$\neq$$

"That was Maeve," Emily said at the house, having spent the drive in a stupor. "I fancy her. That's how they say it here — *'fancy.'*" She rolled the word around on her tongue like it was a taste she wanted to savor.

She had emerged from her room in a soft caftan, a very un-Emily thing to wear and proceeded to cook salmon and roast potatoes for dinner. I was pretty sure heating anything several hundred degrees in a pan automatically sanitized it, so I had no problem letting her cook. But I made sure the salad ingredients, bowls and utensils were thoroughly washed.

"So what's the local attitude towards the love that dares not speak its name?" I asked. I was having a hard time taking this problem seriously at the dawn of the 21st Century.

"The town is touristy so they're probably somewhat tolerant — but it's one thing to visit and leave, quite another to live here gay. And the immediate area around here is all miners."

"'Around here' ? We're two miles from town."

"It's a small country. Two miles count. I don't think they'd stone us but who knows?"

Her voice had gone deep, a seductive octave drop. The caftan was thin and clung to her as she moved. I noticed. We were alone, alone in her house. Not visiting at Bib's house in New Jersey, fifty miles from my apartment, listening to her chatter about horses and Harry Potter. Alone. Alone together.

"Have you approached her?" I chopped onions to add to the tomatoes. I mangled them, really—better the tomatoes than my friend. She looked so relaxed and sensual. If she'd been in a movie, I'd have been hard. If she'd been some woman other than Emily, looking like that, I'd have been inside the caftan already. But she was Emily and somehow, in the room together, even prompting myself, nothing was moving, throbbing, nothing.

"I don't know if she's into it or not," she replied, swaying back and forth, singing softly to herself with the wide-eyed *I'm just a girly-girl* face I hadn't seen in a while. And from Em, never, not even in college. "I don't want to blow the friendship or whatever it is we have."

"Isn't there like a gay directory or something you can check?"

"Ha ha. And I guess I don't know if I *am* either. Doesn't it mean something, that I'm not sure?" She squeezed past me between the kitchen table and the counter, to get some lemon from the fridge. I could feel her breasts brushing my back—she wasn't wearing a bra. Her perfume had the complex scent of good cognac—Em always had all the nice stuff.

She was a really beautiful woman and I really did love her. I would have enjoyed suckling at her nipples and the feel of her hands on me and coming—a man enjoys coming, period, even with a woman he *doesn't* like very much. *Didn't it mean something that she wasn't sure?* Sure it did—it meant she was throwing me a cue.

Fifteen minutes earlier, I'd been upset that she'd brought me over simply to beard for her. Now, here was evidence that I counted. I really had to do something about it. I had to.

I found a bench in the living room to use as a dinner table and carried the serving dishes onto it. I pulled everything off the couch but blankets and pillows, which were a necessity, what with the room being dead cold. We just fit, snuggled together. She was warm, her head at just the right height to lean on my shoulder.

She looked up at me and smiled gently. We were inside but I'd swear there was moonlight. This was the moment. If I kissed her now, she was mine. It's why I'd come. It's why she'd brought me over. She was beautiful and she wanted me, when no one else did. All I had to do was take her.

I didn't, of course.

I stayed rooted to the couch, Em's head nestled on my shoulder, her breast three inches from my palm. I sat blank—no, that's not true; I sat in total awareness of a big red 'Stop' sign somewhere inside.

"Are you eating enough?" I asked finally, because they were the first words my mouth could form.

"I'm eating fine. Why?"

"You've lost weight." It seemed true and it's not like I could have gone wrong with that answer—no woman alive doesn't delight in hearing it, true or not.

"They gave me a new medicine and it had that smell—chemo smell—so I couldn't eat. Chemotherapy takes your hair and your sense of smell. All I could smell for the longest time after was chemo, chemo everywhere, in medicine and perfume, cleaning products and the dry cleaners, at the boat basin and the stables. Whenever I smell it, even now, it puts me off eating. I don't look *too* thin?"

"You look good," I said and meant it. I've always liked skinny girls. Emily was just about the ideal woman for me except for maybe being gay and not turning me on for some inexplicable reason. Tonight, she'd tried. I'd wanted her to try and she had.

"Is there any heat in here? The chill is getting to me." I actually expected to see my breath in the air, it was so cold. "Why in hell don't they insulate the houses in this country?"

"Maybe they're used to the chill," she said, returning to normal conversation. I felt accused and rightfully so. Caution is a disease.

"What are we doing tomorrow? The Dingle Peninsula is nearby—the Cliffs of Moher are maybe a few hours away."

She rummaged among the clothes and horse equipment to pull a fibrous-looking brick out of a paper bag.

"This is peat," she said, holding it up to me. "This is the real stuff—the guy down the road cuts it out of one of his fields. If you're Irish, the government gives you part of a peat field—and you can sell it to the local American." She opened the fireplace in the corner—it looked more like a Franklin stove, with a squat black iron body and an odd-angle sectioned pipe twisting to the ceiling—and tossed the brick in. "You can buy logs at the store but the home-grown ones are cheaper and burn better." She leaned back in her chair and breathed deep. "It smells nice, doesn't it?"

It did smell nice. If the house had resembled anything other than a homeless shelter after a tornado, it would have been charming. But now she'd ignored my travel plans twice in a row. Two out of two. Given the track record, *two* now began to feel like a trend.

Dinner over, I did the dishes (I insisted) while Em laid out pills from bottles and vials the size of cookie jars. Two from this container, one from that, three from another into a plastic daily divider. By the time she was finished, each day's cell was filled to brimming. She caught me staring.

"These get my thyroid to work at least a bit. These for osteoporosis—radiation does a real number on the bones. Soy—mimics estrogen—I'm hoping it's safer than hormone treatments. I have artificially induced menopause—I'm just a walking disaster.

Can't remember what these are called but they help me take the thyroid pills without throwing up. Zinc—skin. Plain vanity," she laughed.

She filled two large tumblers with water, both of which she needed to get the job done. She choked on some of the larger pills, spurting water, gagging and starting over immediately. Seeing her choke was a physical shock. The fragility of her shoulders shaking, the indignity of stubbornly fighting these things down, made some of what she'd been through—probably only a tiny amount of it—tangible. I felt a wave of protective feeling. Of course, what she'd been through, no one could protect her from.

"I'm sure we can do something tomorrow," she said, returning to the living room but lingering, not taking a seat. "I've got to check on the stupids first."

"The stupids?"

"My horses. They have to be fed and catered to, at least a bit. And there's a horse auction—I have to go to that; you just can't let me buy anything, okay? Maybe we can fit in the Rock of Cashel—it's nearby. Oh shit though, I've got to make sure I have what I need to finish those paintings for Maeve. Maeve—" She sighed in a way I thought she reserved for me.

"Why don't you just attack her some dark evening?"

"It won't work," she moaned. "She's going to want sex. Everybody wants sex but me."

"Why don't you want sex?" This is how I am—when it came out of my mouth, it sounded like an innocent question. I repented in seconds, seeing her face.

"Chemotherapy doesn't just kill the cancer," she said. "It *hurts.*"

"They have hormones to give you back some of the desire," I pursued, stupidly. "I've read—"

"You eat chocolate, you get fat. You smoke, you get cancer." This was a litany, something she'd repeated to herself a thousand times.

"If you stop eating, you'll die."

"If I stop smoking, I get healthy."

"You don't smoke."

I stared at Emily. She stared at the wall, the fireplace, everywhere, searching for nothingness without being able to find it.

"Why isn't romance enough?" she asked finally. "Why can't there be love without proof?"

"None of us is that secure. We want to hold it. Otherwise, it's empty, bloodless."

"Why does there always have to be *blood?*"

She walked back into the kitchen. I could hear her actually washing dishes for a while, though surely they were the dishes I'd already washed. I stood in the doorway helpless, hoping she'd get over it by herself.

"Alright, so just fall into unrequited platonic love," I joked eventually, when the silence got to me. I hate dead air. "Think of the paintings, the longing, the magnificent frustration!"

"What if I'm already in love?" she asked quietly, still working over the sink. And here I have to admit, my heart skipped a beat. I might not want Emily but clearly, I wanted her to want me. I wanted *somebody* to want me.

"Don't you know?"

"I don't know what love is," she said. I admired the way she said it—naked and despairing, but an honest despair. There was no false drama or self-pity in her. It was a statement of fact from a grownup who'd tried her best.

"I don't either," I replied, "but I remember what it feels like."

$$\neq$$

The alarm was going off but it was the middle of the night but I didn't *have* an alarm.

My phone was ringing but it was the middle of the night and I couldn't find it because it was the middle of the night and everything in the room was thrown all over the place because…because I was in Emily's house and everything in

Emily's house is thrown all over the place and that's why I can't find my phone because I put it away because I'm ON VACATION!

The phone was in the back pocket of my laptop case. I found it once I got the light on.

"Well—any bites?" Ron demanded.

"What time is it there?"

"Midnight. I waited so it would be the end of the day for you, right?"

"Wrong way. We're five hours *ahead*."

"Huh?"

"It's five in the morning here." My watch was on the night table. It said five in the morning so there was a good shot that was what time it was, approximately.

"Oh good then you've had another day to get something accomplished."

"No-same day—at least so far. I flew over last night. I'm letting the jet lag wear off."

"Plenty of time to sleep when you're dead," he pressed. "It wasn't Bin Laden."

"No?"

"No, the White House said within half an hour it wasn't him. That's pretty quick, don't you think? For them to know for sure, half a world away?"

"Well...yeah, I guess." I was still trying to remember if I set my watch ahead or not. It could be midnight, Irish time, in which case I'd had an hours sleep. No, midnight was if we were *behind* New York. If my watch said five and I hadn't changed it and we were ahead, it would be...

"And then later I saw a thing on the Internet where some anonymous Pakistani politician said they *did* have him but the Americans had told them to keep it quiet until after the election. That could be good, don't you think? That would give us a year-and-a-half to milk him, right?"

"Right sure." What the fuck time *was* it?

"So when do you think you'll have fish on the line? You've only got a week."

"Ron, I haven't met a single Irish person so far, unless you count 'so nice to meet you' as conversation. If you want to extend my vacation—"

"Ha ha, I enjoy your sense of humor sometimes. You know I wouldn't normally let someone take a vacation after working here a month."

"I've been working for you almost five months."

"Part-time," he jumped. "No benefits. No seniority. No vacation," he added, in case I needed things clarified. Ron was big on clarity.

The first time we'd met, he'd introduced me to his type of clarity. "Business works because it's entirely *about* Business," he said, "because it's not about anything *but* Business, about *Getting the Job Done."* This came after ten seconds of exchanging names and looking each other over.

His glass and metal desk had no paper on it—and no fingerprints. I'd had a good look before he'd come in. The thing was literally spotless. On the gleaming surface sat a dust-free calculator, Apple computer, telephone and notepad—nothing more. A perfect cliché black attaché case leaned against the desk leg, next to a 2-liter bottle of designer water Ron would refill at the tap down the hall. A stack of loose-leaf folders in alphabetized order stood like sentries on the windowsill, accompanied by seventeen prescription drug vials. Album covers dotted the walls—*Led Zeppelin, Abbey Road, Disraeli Gears.* There were chairs for Ron and two visitors, a couch to fill out the room and nothing more.

"I'm in television too," he told me. "Not the kind of television you're in—*were* in," he added, twisting the knife just enough that I couldn't miss it. "I do business video. I've done videos for Mercedes, Nike, Target and Sharper Image in the past two years."

"Nice list," I said.

"It *is* a nice list," he agreed. "It took me way too long to get here and now I have to take The Next Step. That's what business and entrepreneurship are about—taking The Next Step." He eyed me with a proprietary gaze. "What are you? A Manager, an Entrepreneur or a Technician?"

If this was a test, I was going to fail. "I'm not sure," I admitted. "What's the difference?"

"You want to know what the difference is, huh?" he said, tongue wagging about in his open mouth. "I'll tell you the difference. If Entrepreneurs run the company, it'll go out of business, because they're always sitting around dreaming about The Next Step. If Managers run the company, it'll die but everything will be really neat and organized when they come to pack everything up. If Technicians run the company, they'll burn out because they try to do all the work themselves." He paused to give me time to appreciate the logic of the problem. I tried to look appreciative.

"Do you understand?" he continued. "Each type by itself will kill the company—"

"So you need to have them all to—"

"So you NEED TO HAVE THEM ALL! That's correct. You're quite intelligent," he said. I could tell from his tone of voice this was not a compliment he paid easily to anyone other than himself. "So—which are *you*?"

"I guess I'm a manager," I said. It was the only useful answer. If I was a Technician, I was asking to do all the work. Ron had Entrepreneur wrapped up. That left Manager, and he seemed pleased with my answer.

"Melanie is on the phone," Vic announced from the outer office.

"I'll call her back," Ron answered. "I'm with Paul at the moment. Maybe you should close the door until we're finished. I don't want to speak to anyone except my Vision consultant if he calls—he should have called already but he's very busy—and my father. And call around, see if you can get me a yoga session this afternoon, okay? Not before 330 or after 6 but 4 or 5 might be okay. 445 would be good."

"Okay," Vic said and closed the door.

"Yoga is fantastic," Ron said. "You isolate the mind and spirit from the day to day concerns. It's great for meeting women too. I've tried everything—speed-dating, online, you name it."

"What's speed-dating?"

"You haven't tried it? You should come—I'm doing it Thursday night. Vic!" he yelled at the now-closed door, "Speed-dating is Thursday, right?"

"Right," returned the muffled voice.

"Call them and see if Paul can come as my guest." He turned back to me, conspiratorial. "You have to fill out a questionnaire to get into my group. It's very selective. I don't think you're making enough money yet, but once we get going with our plans here, you'll be rolling in it. Anyway, speed-dating is, you go into a room with twenty or twenty-five other singles, 20-45—"

"I'm 48."

"You'll be my guest. They won't know. You look younger. Anyway, you get into two lines. You have two minutes with each person to make a connection and then you move on to the next person. You're not gay, are you?"

"No."

"Good—that's a different group. I don't know them. At the end of the evening, you exchange business cards with the ones you want to see again. There's also speed-dancing, where you actually dance with each person. It's more primal. You think you'd be interested in that?"

"I'll have to have business cards printed."

"You'd probably like dating better—you're good with words. But none of it helps. It's hard to meet the right person. Everyone's so self-involved. It's great networking though—I've gotten three good clients that way."

The man was a fastidious mess. His hands trembled as he reached for his water glass. His shoes tapped relentlessly against the carpet. He was a tiger shark in the shallows, about a minute-and-a-half from a nervous breakdown and it was obvious to everyone but him. Yet Ron was a true believer. He had the passion that drives success. I'd seen that same obsessive, orgasmic focus in every fast-rising small business owner I'd profiled in the past ten years, after the old breed started to die out. So in my head, I converted craziness into opportunity. If anyone needed me, I reckoned, this was the guy.

"So you haven't met anyone in all of Ireland who might be interested yet?" he said now.

"To be precise, I haven't met *anyone* yet. And it's Saturday morning, so I'm not sure how much business I'm going to do real soon. But I'm going back to sleep now so I can be in shape in case I meet anyone useful. Okay?"

"That's right," he breathed. "Be watchful. *He who turns over the most rocks wins.*"

"I remember." Ron collected business aphorisms to deflect any possibility of failure. In person, they came across as a desperately-repressed certainty that he *would* fail. But at least I'd bought till Monday afternoon to enjoy my vacation as a vacation. Then the phone calls would start again in earnest. "Talk to you as soon as anything happens," I said.

He muttered "Okay" but he didn't mean it. The sound was of someone infinitely distracted, already moving on, a soul that found no sanctuary anywhere. I pulled the covers over my head and went back into hiding.

SATURDAY

It was pitchdark in the room and too damn quiet.

Nothing was going to happen. I was on vacation while Emily had come home. She'd brought me over to live her life with her, to share her tiny house full of uproar on a backroad off a backroad, on a hill hidden from the world.

I longed for an ambulance siren or the sound of some stoned wino singing to himself on the street below my window, the jagged diversions of city life. All I got was a cow lowing in the field outside. Ireland was not going to help me. It left me too close to myself for comfort.

Finally, I heard stirring in the kitchen. I sat up and willed the evening's evil flavor to melt away. It's awful waking with no memory of your dreams but knowing they were bad. It's like someone trying to warn you in a foreign language.

I stepped to the window. The room was frigid but once I opened the curtains, the view was lovely. The sky was leaking violet. Cows were stirring in the trees under the moon. They looked like bankers in clownsuits, affecting a stupid mock-dignity in a polka dot uniform with tassels.

The hall smelled like breakfast. Em scurried about the kitchen in a smock the color of Lucille Ball's hair, cracking eggs into a bowl and dropping the shells onto half-unwrapped butter sitting on the counter. A frying pan burned empty on the stove. The kitchen was regaining its normal chaos. As she worked, she continued popping an unending array of medicines from her pill dispenser.

"Didn't you take those last night?"

"Those were yesterday's," she said, throwing a little milk into the bowl with the eggs and scrambling vigorously, so globs of mixture ended on the counter with the eggshells and butter. "You want some breakfast?" We seemed to have regained our normal friendly distance.

"I'm going for a run first. Will we see some Ireland today? Meet some Irish people?"

"Not a problem," she reassured. "The horse auction is in Goresbridge—that's a drive. We'll get to see lots of country on the way. It's only the first day. And there's the Rock—"

"—of Cashel. Yes, I know. It's nearby."

Her look made me feel puckish and high-strung. I was running on New York time: *New Day—New mountains to climb! Let's get at it!* Emily was on Irish time: *We'll get there, what's the problem?* It was the difference between a Stairmaster and a shrug of the shoulders.

I headed for the bathroom. Before the door closed, I realized I could actually see my breath inside. "You may want to do this," Emily said, leaning in behind me and flicking a rheostat on a bulky box mounted high on the wall. "It's the heater. Give it five minutes and you'll be a lot more comfortable. The timer only goes fifteen, so you'll want to turn it back to the start once you turn the water on."

After five minutes, the box was humming like a generator and the six inches directly under the heater were reasonably warm. Unfortunately, those six inches were nowhere near the toilet or sink. My breath fogged the mirror as I squeezed out the toothpaste but I couldn't brush my teeth because they were chattering too hard. *Run first, then shower. The shower will heat the room and then you can brush your teeth.* I returned to the bedroom and threw on a hooded sweatshirt and sweatpants, gloves and a wool hat over my long johns. I stretched as best I could without disturbing the Emily piles on the floor and then padded down the foyer, ready to face the Arctic chill.

I got three steps out the door and stopped dead. It was the same lovely friendly neutral temperature outside as the day before. It was only frigid *inside* the house. Goddamn stupid concrete boxes. This was why no one ever bragged about Irish engineering. I returned to my room, shaking my head and dumped the long johns and sweatshirt. Then back outside to start chugging up the hill.

When I returned, Emily was humming to herself happily, dropping her breakfast plate into the sink. The frying pan, eggshells and half-used butter remained on the stove. I reminded myself to clean before we left so it wouldn't demand a chisel and blowtorch later.

"Did you know—you must—that church down the end of the road has no roof?"

"There are lots like that," she replied.

"They've got people buried inside the building, in the floor of the church itself—graves dating to 1823. And from 1643 to last year in the graveyard. But no roof."

"You don't get buried in your local church," she explained. "You're a member of the parish so they bury you on whatever parish property is available."

"But why does the church have no roof?"

"Because the English taxed anything with a roof."

"Jesus," I hooted. "No politician would dare do that now. Your handlers would be screaming 'You can't have people saying *he taxed the roof over our heads.*'"

"Remember," she advised, "the English didn't *want* them happy. They wanted to punish them for being Catholic and stubborn and independent. They taxed the windows too. You could tell a man's wealth by the number of windows in his house. If you were turning the house into a barn, you filled in the windows to lose the taxes."

"People turned houses into barns?"

"All the time. Sometimes they converted half the house—people one side, animals on the other. That's no longer the style."

"I don't wonder."

"I'll show you when we go out."

Going out—that sounded like good news. At least we were going *somewhere*. The shower actually heated the bathroom. It fogged the mirror to the point that I had to Braille-shave. But after that—finally—we were off.

We headed in yet another new direction, across the disappearing pavement, around the corner and downhill, twisting across a succession of woolly-grass knolls and fast-running gulleys. It must have rained overnight, what with all the streams, though nothing above the waterline looked wet.

At the bottom of the hill, Em pulled into a mini-mart even smaller than the previous night's, serving a small cluster of houses at the base of the hill. The cluster boasted its own newspaper (!) and banners for its rugby team, which was apparently playing the bigger town two miles away the next day. America had whole cities digested into suburbs of bigger cities, Ireland had independent mini-neighborhoods.

Emily pumped diesel into the tank, without paying or notifying anyone first. Apparently everyone simply trusted everyone else over here, or maybe they figured they knew where you lived.

A wiry little fellow, looking 65 and built like a jockey, meandered out of the store eventually and loitered at the pump, tugging on a curvy pipe.

"'Morning Emily."

"Morning, Daniel—how's your daughter?"

"Flyin' it," he said, with some satisfaction. I wrote this down immediately, without the slightest idea what it meant. Then he leaned into Em's ear and added, "He's back," in a stage whisper. I have no idea how to convey the tone of voice—pride, something close to awe and a touch of resentment mingled in it. Em's eyes darted towards me and then away. "When?" she asked, with a forced lightness. "Day or two ago," the old gentleman answered.

We went into the store for scones—apparently the Irish consider scones fresh for about twenty minutes. Once inside, Em had the same conversation with the ancient woman behind the counter (who'd heard so much about me).

I prowled the aisles browsing the wares. A lot of washed-up American brands from my childhood seemed to be living productive lives in Ireland, though often with the first letter of their names changed. I remember 'Duz' from a long time ago but now it was 'Guz.' Not much of an improvement, if any. It occurred to me there had to be some kind of trademark technicality at work here—it could be a cute business story, if I ever found meaningful employment again.

The top shelves needed dusting but I didn't offer. I was too busy trying to eavesdrop on the old lady and Em and I'm just too big to carry that off. Here was a revelation: Em was keeping secrets from me (!), however clumsily.

I'm not stupid but I'm not always shrewd about people either. I regularly overestimate my own cleverness and underestimate their guile. Apparently, I had to start applying this rule to Emily now, along with the rest of the world.

A few minutes drive found two iron gates hanging wide-open in an expanse of featureless stone wall. The Irish had left frippery to the French and monumentality to the Romans and Germans; they were the champions of premodern minimalist architecture. Anything Irish left long enough would appear to have sprung up in place naturally.

"I've been looking for the right property since I moved here," Em said. "Someplace with land and stables and a view, right for me and the horses. Until then, I keep them at this fellow's house—his man tends them when I'm away."

The long driveway ran uphill between rows of nonchalantly ancient trees—two or three trunks from the same root, leafed branches beginning high off the ground, the trunks bowing at dizzying angles. To our left lay a muddy field holding one very large cow, sheep, goats and horses.

"Those are my stupids," Emily trilled, rolling down her window and letting her hair fly. "Hello boys!"

The house stood just above the field. French—*rich* French— would call it a country house, two-stories in stone with a tile roof, old windows with new glass and ancient stone walls fanning out behind. It was plain in the Irish style but dignified, at least 150 years old and a souvenir, several renovations ago, of nobility. Not a king or anything that expensive—maybe a duke or earl or one of those 2nd Assistant Vice President nobles.

The roof tiles were missing in one corner, the path from driveway to door was all dug up and a replacement gate stood tilted alongside its aged predecessor, waiting to be installed. The owner either loved projects or never bothered finishing them—or maybe that was the same thing.

We pulled around the back into a courtyard in happy chaos. The rear of the house was a different color from what faced the street—at least most of it was. The walls surrounding the courtyard were remnants, each a different stone and style, none matching the house even slightly.

Two tractors, an old horse trailer like Em's, a Rover sedan and a horse-drawn cart were placed haphazardly round the yard, amongst piles of old brick, mismatched tires and wheels, hoes, picks, sickles and mallets, an upended wheelbarrow and a three-story scaffolding that stood waiting for construction to begin spontaneously on the spot. So maybe Emily's house just reflected normal Irish housekeeping.

She threw her jacket onto the front seat and led me to a tarpaulin-covered column, plastic-wrapped bundles of wood chips almost as tall as me. "I need two of these by every stall," she said and stalked off.

I carried the bundles into place. They were surprisingly heavy—I had to lay them against my shoulder to make the fifteen or twenty foot distance—and gave a satisfying thwack! when they hit the ground. The straw smell was a flashback to country summers at camp. By the time I got the last bundles in place, I was breathing hard. It felt good. If I felt used for a moment—I'm not saying I did, exactly—I could always look in on Emily, who was shoveling horseshit into a bucket. I heard myself asking, "What next?"

"Climb up there," she said, pointing to a mountain of hay under a two-story three-sided corrugated metal shelter. "Throw down a bale and put it on the hood of the car." I climbed the tower, finding secure footholds one bale at a time and tossed down a bundle. I set it on the hood but when Em came out of the stalls, she said "Not that way—I won't be able to see." I moved the bale to my side of the hood and she gunned the car downhill through a tiny gap in the walls.

We stopped near the top of the field. "Bring the bale," she called, "and don't touch the fence; it's electric."

"That little thing?" It was no kind of fence—two yellow ribbon cables loosely clipped to posts at each end.

She unclipped her end and held it away so I could walk through. "The idea isn't to *electrocute* them," she said. "It's just supposed to keep them on this side." She clipped the ribbon back to the post and led me over ground heaving with roots and low-tangled bushes.

Across a narrow trench lay the horse field, which was 100% pure mud. Surely no finer-brewed mud existed on the planet. I remember visiting Oxford in the early Eighties. I remarked to a groundskeeper on the green of a lawn. "It *should* be green," he muttered. "We've been tending it continuously since 1163." This mud had that feel—generations of breeding to achieve just the right consistency. The smell too could not have developed overnight—it was a potent broth of horseshit, rotted carrots and hundreds of years of old boots.

Em had warned me to bring my work boots, though she hadn't explained why. In New York, boots were an affectation; here, they were a survival mechanism. They made an awkward sucking noise as I struggled to keep up with her, carrying the hay bale—or what was left of it, as bits kept shedding with each step. At least if I fell on my face, the hay might break the fall.

Emily strode purposefully at her horses. Her legs didn't waver like mine; her boots weren't in danger of coming off every three feet. The horses saw her coming and were upon us in an instant. If I'd thought about horses before, I'd have used words like *sleek* or *majestic*; the kinds of words you use when you only see something from a distance. It was quite another thing to be stumbling around the middle of a field with them. Up close, they were massive and powerful. If two converged at the same time, they'd crush me like a tank rolling over a tomato.

And they might easily converge—their attention was all on Emily. They ate carrots from her hand and danced about on display, manes bobbing and bouncing, hind legs kicking high in the air to keep the others at a distance. At twice my size, they somehow skimmed the surface of the muck while I sank with every step. I pulled off sections of hay bale and scattered it about, as a peace offering and some kind of a buffer. When they got too close to Emily however, she just reached out and shoved them away.

"How do you do that?" I yelped as one of them bounced right in front of me, feet flying.

"You just have to show them you're the bigger horse," she said as though that meant something. Her house was a catastrophe but here, Em was the boss, earthy and grounded. Among her animals, calling them names and shoving them away when they crowded her, Emily was finally at home, knee-deep in mud and full of grace in the same instant.

I wandered back to solid ground. Emily followed after a few minutes. But as she crossed the verge from mud to grass, something behind me seized her attention. Her reaction lasted just a moment but when she turned away, it was with the same guilty expression she'd worn at the store that morning.

There was no way I wasn't looking. I pivoted to see a rider galloping over the top of the hill, silhouetted against the sunlight, framed by the treeline and the low-rising hills. Even at that distance you could see him guiding his horse over ruts and gulleys. They jumped a massive low-hanging branch and scrambled up an opposing hill, coming to a churning, fitful stop and turning way too picturesquely against the clouds.

Somehow, with all the distance between us, we clearly saw the rider stare down into the field at us—at *Emily*, to be exact. He sat up in his saddle—I realized for the first time he was wearing an emerald-green military uniform—and bowed toward her with a light formality. I wheeled back and there was Em, bright crimson—about the same shade Maeve had provoked the night before. She waved her hand lightly like the Queen Mother and then snapped her attention, dutifully, back to me.

"I guess we can get going," she gasped, stalking briskly toward the car. I had a tough time keeping up as I kept trying to wipe the shit off my boots. Then I realized the mud would never be noticed in her car anyway.

As soon as we reached the Suzuki, Em slumped into the driver's seat, hugging her knees. She sat up a moment later. "Just catching my breath," she said and I flashed on all the pill bottles on her kitchen counter.

The horseman was making his way down the hill towards the house, but taking a leisurely pace. Em glanced once more in his direction and said "Let's get going." I settled into the passenger seat and we puttered down the driveway to the road.

"So who was that?" I asked finally, when it became clear she wasn't going to mention it.

"Who?" she asked, with such ridiculous sincerity that I had to keep myself from laughing.

"Give me a break. Hi-ho Silver back there."

"Oh, that was my horse landlord."

"If he's going to wear military stuff, why doesn't he just get a hussar's uniform with the big feather in the helmet? And a sword? He'd be hell to pay with a sword."

Her reticence disappeared. "His uniform is legitimate," she said stiffly. "He's a Colonel in the Irish Defence Force."

"Ooh—heavy duty." I was being an asshole but why not? The guy was a puffed-up windbag. Just watching him ride I could see it.

"It is, actually. They've been involved with UN peacekeeping since 1958. You should be big on that. He's been in Lebanon and Bosnia recently. Armed but only in self-defense."

"And even then, you have to avoid any incident they can use against you. Okay, I suck. That's serious stuff."

"Yes it is," she said, with no small degree of satisfaction. Other people are assholes all the time and get away with it. I make a fool of myself with every glimmer.

"Let's get lunch," Em said and proceeded to drive past six perfectly good-looking restaurants, several picturesque clusters of homes, some affecting roadsigns and post offices like real towns, without even slowing, smiling all the way like she was running for office. But when we finally pulled into a parking space, I couldn't fault her. The restaurant she chose perched at the northern bank of the Lough, in a substantial town by the day's standards–nine houses, a store, a gas station, two churches, three pubs and the restaurant. Two different towns were marked on the map nearby, but nothing in the spot where we were. I showed this to Emily, who seemed neither surprised nor fazed.

The restaurant was a bit sleek modern for a small-town place but I didn't care. It was my chance to sample a little bit of Ireland—corned beef and cabbage, a pint of Guinness and conversation with Barry Fitzgerald or Richard Harris or Peter O'Toole—or Maureen O'Hara, whichever icon happened to be on duty today.

As we came in, the hostess was carrying on an animated discussion with several bulky workers behind the bar. What with music and the noise from outside, we couldn't hear anything that was said, but looking at the lecture she was dishing out, she was no wageslave.

She was pretty and tall and dark—Black Irish was my first thought. Then she turned to us and said, "Welcome. Table for two?" and my mood sank at the sound of her voice. I nodded weakly and she led us to a lovely darkwood table overlooking the water. She laid menus in front of us and described the lunch specials. She was extremely pleasant and polite, her words beautifully enunciated. But that...lilt...wasn't there.

"Is this your restaurant?" I asked when she finished.

"Yes, I wish you to like it," she said with the hopeful formality of the immigrant.

"It's very nice but off the beaten track, isn't it? I'm surprised you found it," I was groping, trying to find a polite way to my subject. "I suspect you didn't grow up in the area."

"We looked for a long time, my husband and I." She didn't seem phased by the question.

"If you don't mind, may I ask where you came from?"

"Kosovo," she said—both relief and pleasure showed on her face. "This is a wonderful country—such opportunity," she enthused.

"That's what they used to say about *my* country," I answered. Her face went dutiful all at once and she rushed off to other tasks.

"What was *that* about?" Em demanded as soon as she was out of earshot.

"I just think it's funny. I've been in this country two days and—other than to say 'hello' and 'thank you' and hear how much they've heard about me—I haven't spoken to a single Irish person yet."

"Well, they're all around you," she laughed as though that was an answer. "And what's with the crack about America? It's still the land of opportunity."

"Then why isn't she opening her restaurant in Chicago? Or Denver? America used to be the land of the rugged individualist, the home of the entrepreneur. We might still offer opportunity but we're not *the* land of opportunity anymore. *This* is where I'm a Republican—a Teddy Roosevelt Republican. Bust the Trusts. America's being overrun with monopolies. Seven companies sell 90% of the gas, one company sells 95% of computer software, another owns 70% of the radio stations and billboards and sells 90% of concert tickets, seven companies dominate news coverage, five companies sell 90% of the clothes."

"Is that true?"

"I'm making up the numbers, but I'll bet they're damn close. Seven old white guys make all the money. And the politicians they buy. Everyone else goes to work for McDonalds and two other jobs trying to make ends meet."

"But see, you really are a Republican," Em said with relish. "Entrepreneurs make everything go. And those are Republicans."

"You're an entrepreneur till you join the country club. *Then* you're a Republican."

There was no Irish food on the menu. I ordered trout in a wine and shallot sauce; Emily asked for half a roasted chicken with spinach and new potatoes. It might be *better* than Irish food, but still a disappointment. I drank wine—Em stuck to water. The bread was nutty and hot but I resented it all the same. I had a second glass of wine with the salad.

I could see it raining on the far bank of the Lough though the restaurant windows stayed dry. The moody light was getting to me and so was the wine and even the bread. I was sinking into my chair, my breath deepening. My shoulders began to ache from letting go. I told myself I was finally on vacation but there was more going on and nothing that gave me any satisfaction.

Then the food came. The hostess lingered after the plates were laid in place. When I looked up, she stammered—at me (!), "America did important work in Kosovo. It was a very good thing, what they did."

I flushed. This was damn uncomfortable. I wasn't sure what I felt about what we did in Kosovo. I wasn't sure I *knew* what we did in Kosovo. I remember reading about bombings and that Bill Clinton had decided he was willing to have a war as long as the Joint Chiefs promised him *zero* casualties. But that was all that registered. And now the hostess was making me the representative for America. If there was a more ludicrous candidate for this task, he wasn't in sight.

"It's okay with me," I said stupidly. "We did a good thing there, I guess." I wanted to be a good guest, which is probably what *she* wanted. Iraq hung over the table and I wanted it to go away. I had to admire her waiting, hovering over me, sticking to her guns— it wasn't good business but obviously a matter of passion for her. I admire passion. I'm drawn to it. "Look," I ventured finally, "I'm glad we could help. We rescued people there."

"There are a lot of people in the world who need to be rescued," she said. Why tell me? I'm no damn Ambassador. What about *Em*—why not tell her? Because she looked Irish, other than being six feet tall. No one expected the Irish to save anybody, except maybe the galloping Colonel in the Defence Force.

"We have to rescue ourselves," I said finally. I didn't know what the hell it meant—I was uncomfortable. I was resigned to Iraq—I just didn't want it to be *my* war.

She smiled politely and returned to the bar, wistful. Unintended consequences were a decadent irony to her. She was one of those people who'd stood in the rubble watched the bombers pass over, to wreak havoc on the other guy. She didn't—couldn't—fathom any limits on the power or the righteousness of America.

"See?" said Emily quietly. "The World is Republican."

"Does it comfort you that the old Communists are the only ones on our side?"

"She wasn't a Communist," Em said. "She was struggling—*your* people. Now she's an entrepreneur."

"Yeah, in Ireland. The land of opportunity."

The drive to Goresbridge was beautiful. Shafts of light cut through the clouds while dark formations advanced in the distance. Any kind of weather you liked, you could have in Ireland, and usually within half an hour. I stared fixedly at the trees and barns, sheep and cows, hills and valleys and peat bogs flashing by. Every time we reached a crossroads (which was about every five minutes), I came to, possessed by the desire to cry out, *"That* way! That looks good!" I was feeling contrary—any direction but the one we had planned. Not because I hated the horse auction—simply because I hated having a plan.

Goresbridge was big type on the map but on the ground, it was just a town perched on a soft incline. Em began shunting left and right as soon as we arrived, navigating roundabouts and spurting onto sidestreets. At each point of decision, she looked purposeful and self-assured, but after a few moments, it became clear we weren't getting anywhere.

"You don't know where it is?" I asked. Drowsily. Mildly. Very mildly. No reason to make her feel foolish. If she feels foolish *without* my making her, that's okay.

"I haven't been there in a while," she admitted.

"What's a while?"

"Ever," she said. She took a hairpin 90-degree turn onto a promising side street. "And remember—*don't* let me buy anything."

"Won't be a problem if you can't find the place," I said and she shot me a look.

I drifted off, the result of a heavy lunch and no Irish people to talk to, for no more than a minute, I swear. I wasn't even aware of being sleepy. And then Em was pulling me out the open door. "I found it!" she said. "I just followed a horse trailer and here we are."

I stepped out of the car into a muddy yard. Was there anything in this country that hadn't turned to mud? Ahead, beyond an encampment of horse trailers, a narrow walkway ran uphill, bounded by tin-roofed long sheds and concrete stalls in rows. Our reflection shimmered in the aluminum trailers as we passed. Goddamn we were old. When did *that* happen?

The paddock air was full of hay and feed and the rich manure of well-fed animals who shit wherever they felt like. Everywhere you turned another handsome huge horse in chestnut or buttermilk was clopclopping behind some teenager in a parka and riding helmet. The kids were of two groups—the freckle-faced/red haired contingent and the black haired/olive skinned Black Irish. Well, if I was frustrated at not meeting Irish people, that had to change now.

Just past were the tracks. First was a walking track, an enclosed outdoor pen, muddy (of course) and filled erratically by two fourteen-year-olds with very green hay. One or two horses at a time cantered slowly about, carrying equally young riders.

At the top of the hill was the jumping area. It was another big shed, tin-roofed and enclosed on three sides, with wooden hurdles appearing at random. At least, the placement seemed haphazard to me but the riders recognized a winding route in it instantly. They were kids as well but of a greater status than the hay patrol. They sat high and preening, not that you could blame them. The horses got up a good clip jumping the barriers and pounding around the edges of the enclosure, close enough to the fence that you could really feel them. To control such a creature had to be pretty intoxicating.

"The horses are green and the riders aren't much better," Emily said, following the progress of one pair. The animal was an almost liquid charcoal color—if I ever saw that shade in a thundercloud I'd head for cover immediately. He was ominously, thrillingly beautiful. "But it gives you an idea of their potential—of what they're worth."

Each horse circulated a grand total of maybe three minutes. "You can watch a horse for so little time and then buy him?" I asked. I didn't know exactly how expensive they were but the thought was staggering.

"Not really," Em answered. She opened the leaflet we'd been given entering the paddock. "We all know each other—you know who's got the good horses. And you can read who's the sire—hopefully he's some horse you've heard of, who's won something. And you see how many hands he is—that one's about 18 hands," she said, pointing to a chestnut taller than me. "My pony's 14 hands," she continued. "You can walk up to them when they're out of the ring and see how the joints and muscles look, how big they are and how they're built."

"And check the teeth," I said, offering my sole piece of knowledge about horse ownership.

"And check the teeth," she smiled, without explaining why.

Just then, the chestnut caught his hind legs on a jump and went down hard. The rider rolled clear and was back in saddle and circulating the ring again before the rest of us could even react. "He just lost value," Emily pronounced, off-hand.

"From that? Nobody makes mistakes around here?"

"I didn't say it was *fair*, darling. But he did it right in front of us. And look—he's still dragging the foot" and sure enough, he knocked the top pole off the jump again the next time round.

A clamorous noise rose behind us and a voice said, "I should have known you'd be here." And from Emily's face, I knew who it was before I even turned round.

He was still in his green uniform and taller than I expected, not spectacularly handsome (at least to my eye) but with the easy air that came of too much admiration. Is that sour grapes? I guess there's never too much admiration if they're admiring you. And after a second's time lag, I realized that everyone in sight, in the shed and the yard, was staring at us—at *him*.

"Paul Roget, this is Malcolm Lowell," Emily trilled. "Malcolm's my horse landlord—and one of the world's best riders." *My horse landlord* had that same uncomfortable sound as *helped me pick out some of the paints*. Malcolm smiled and held out his hand to shake, heartily of course like a real man.

"Emily exaggerates," he murmured smoothly. An extensive and seemingly color-coordinated brace of campaign ribbons gloated from his chest.

"Third in the world last year—not too shabby," Emily persisted, beaming.

"I do some riding," Malcolm shrugged. He was a celebrity—not a worldwide celebrity maybe but here, inside the boundaries of the horsy world, he was the Cheese. Everything and everyone was drawn to him like the whirlpool in the sink. It's so easy to be modest when you can count on everyone else to praise you. The guy was eating it up inside, I could tell.

"So the Army lets you out every once in a while to do a meet?"

"No, actually I ride for the Defence Force. We have a team."

"A great team," Em added instantly. "They take first or second almost everywhere."

"I'm not so sure this year."

"Oh there are always problems at the beginning—they'll get sorted out." This was Emily, supportive and positive as always. To him just as she'd always been to me.

"Do you ride?" he asked.

"The last time I rode a horse, I was pretending to be Roy Rogers." This raised not a glimmer. Either ol' Roy's reruns didn't make it over here or Malcolm had no sense of humor—or maybe he was too young to know who Roy was. It was possible, now that I was paying attention, that he was a few years younger than us. None of this helped my mood any.

He turned to the ring—which meant that every eye in the place turned there as well. It's a wonder the poor kid on horseback didn't get knocked out of the saddle by the sudden shift in attention. "See anything worthwhile?" Malcolm asked.

"There's a really nice grey—they just took him out of here," Emily answered. "Good jumps, turns well. Looks like he'll take some riding—"

"Don't they all?" Malcolm finished, mostly for my benefit. The whole dynamic had morphed in thirty seconds. Now I was the outsider in *their* world. "Intelligent but stubborn creatures."

"Oh God are they ever," moaned Em.

"Let's have a look at him," Malcolm said, motioning Emily to lead the way.

It had been dripping rain on and off. Nonetheless, the courtyard was crammed with people and horses moving between the jumps and the auction house. People circulated in clumps, some groups surely just ogling—*all* these people couldn't have serious horse-buying money—while others might as well have been discussing soy beans or oil drilling prospects.

The crowd parted magically for Malcolm and Emily, but it was thick going anyway because there was always someone who wanted to shake hands with Colonel Lowell or offer a good horse or a supposedly valuable piece of investment advice. I saw him place at least four business cards in his jacket pocket by the time we'd crossed the yard.

The auction house itself was way too small to be the center of all this activity. Surrounded by the busy expanse of tracks and stables and car park, it was almost shockingly modest and utilitarian, like a grapefruit in the center of a Thanksgiving table. Even from the five or six rows of bleacher seats around the far walls, you could make out the eye color and condition of the horse's legs as they were led one by one round the center ring. And there were more people in the walkway surrounding the ring—where you could feel the animals *breathe*—than in the bleachers.

Across a vented divider was a pub (naturally) packed with onlookers throwing down a pint or two—and bidding! The pub groups were raucous but only a few of them seemed really serious about buying anything.

The auctioneer stood at a raised dais above the ring. Without the loud haranguing I expected from movies and commercials, he simply announced the horse, the sire and breeding farm as each animal was led around and then began to take bids. A board on the wall behind him showed the changing tally in Euros, Dollars and Pounds Sterling. As we entered, a horse went for €5500—"About $7000," Emily said.

"And only 15 hands," Malcolm commented.

"Mmm," Emily murmured. "That's a good price. Who bought him?"

"Don't know them," he answered, pointing to a burly black-haired group in the pub. "They must be *Americans*," he slurred and the two of them giggled.

"Anyone pays too much around here, the Irish assume it's a foreigner."

"As though we never overpay for anything."

"There's a point there," Emily said. "The Irish don't throw money around. And you know your horses."

"And then there's William," Malcolm replied and they both burst out laughing. Emily waved a hand in my direction saying, "It's too long to explain."

I nodded vaguely and tried to smile. It's not as though Malcolm was doing anything overt, of course—he was just casually discussing horses, which coincidentally happened to be the most important thing in Emily's life. I wondered if Malcolm knew I had no horse background. Then I remembered I'd told him myself.

The grey was led into the ring. "Oh, he is very good," Malcolm breathed. "Look at the hindquarters," Emily said, without a hint of humor. Appraising looks and meaningful nods passed between them. The horse was led round the ring twice in preparation for the bidding.

Emily was practically melting in place staring at the grey. I hadn't seen this level of emotion in her since freshman year at Sarah Lawrence but since arriving in Ireland, I'd seen it repeatedly for two days. She was too old to fold up—the frustration of wanting something you can't have certainly isn't new at our age— but desire was written all over her face.

"You know them?" Malcolm asked, indicating the owners.

"I've met them."

"What do they say about him?"

She threw her hands up. "I haven't talked to them in months. I haven't got money to buy anything. You know I've got to sell one of the ones I already have."

Malcolm threw her a heavy-lidded look. "You can't part with them," he said, bemused. His voice struck a deep note. "You have such a relationship with animals. There's a real attachment...in both directions."

There was something striking here in this man among men, Hi-ho Silver on the hillside, going to mush over Emily and her horses. He didn't understand as I did that Emily's attachment to animals was the only affection in which she felt truly comfortable.

"I wonder," he said after a silent moment, "whether you would do better if the horse wasn't entirely yours?"

"What do you mean?"

"What if we went partners?" he said. "I put up the price, you train him. I'd be willing. But it'd be no good if you couldn't sell him." He looked her squarely in the eye. "The question is whether you can be detached, whether you can appreciate the temporal value in things."

Emily's eyebrow hooked like a question mark. "As opposed to?"

"Life is change. I'm talking about taking satisfaction as it comes, instead of insisting on some endless attachment, all or nothing," Malcolm said and it sure didn't sound like he was talking horses. Emily's eyes lit up.

"I'll have to think about that," she said, beaming.

What the hell was I, invisible? Where did this two-bit local celebrity come off trying to heist my girl right in front of my face? Okay, maybe she wasn't *really* my girl—but he didn't know that. This was an utter lack of respect. Emily had chosen me as her fucking beard. It wasn't a position I wanted but it was a position. She'd flown me across the Atlantic and dragged me around town to display to the miners and their wives. I'd done my bit for society. I wasn't sure exactly how much respect a beard was entitled to but surely it was more than *this*.

What I really didn't like was the feeling that Malcolm *knew* she wasn't my girl. Could that be? How come *he* hadn't heard so much about me? Why had she built me up to everyone except the actual competition? Or was this why I'd been brought here, to provoke Malcolm, to make him jealous?

Em hadn't agreed to his proposition yet but Malcolm was already bidding. This was a clever game. Even if she didn't openly agree to his terms, how could she resist once he had the horse? It was a pretty horse. At least it was a pretty color—that's all I knew about horses, other than you should look at the teeth and I still had no idea why.

Things quickly spun into a bidding war. The raucous pub groups bid lustily, cheering each back-and-forth. A squat couple on the other side of the ring and four Calvinist accountants in the bottom bleachers made restrained bids, as though juggling Renoirs at Sotheby's. But all eyes, of course, were on the estimable Colonel Lowell of the Irish Defence Force, worldwide peacekeeper, fabled horseman, signaling his bids with an elegant turn of the wrist — and, irresistibly, inevitably, on the lovely blonde woman now grafted to his side, the woman alight with the incandescence of all that attention. There was such a look on Em's face, such a torrent of conflicting emotions, during the contest. It was as though they were bidding for *her*.

Malcolm put in the winning number, beating the pubcrawlers, who outbid the Calvinists just from self-respect. When the auctioneer accepted, Malcolm and Em exchanged a handshake that traveled to the elbows, cackling in each other's faces.

In the midst of this triumph, Em glanced at me and went guilty-faced, confirming my paranoia. That was nothing, however, compared to the look on *his* face watching her. I still didn't know if Malcolm was shrewd enough to size us up, to recognize us as a sham — maybe he simply knew a good horse was all it took to split

Emily away from anyone. What I knew was, I didn't like being cut down to size—at my size, it ain't natural.

Malcolm told the sellers, "Emily will be training him—if there's information we need, please see she gets it." Emily whipped a business card out of her bag and added her email address. As we reached the carpark, the two of them chattering away about their plans for their magical horse, Malcolm said, "Let's get supper. We should celebrate."

We'd come in separate cars, of course, so we agreed to meet back in Ballynkill, at a pub Emily liked, for dinner. Not that it mattered to me what we did. I was a third arm, a fifth wheel, a useless appendage with an odd number attached.

I stewed in my seat, hunching down as far as I could go, which wasn't far. My head is always just about on the ceiling of any car I ride in anyway, but now it was closing in, oppressive, claustrophobic, agoraphobic, just plain phobic, all-sorts-of-phobic at once. I wasn't any more miserable than I was on the way out to Goresbridge, but this time I had a reason.

Em had asked me to Ireland and I thought, she wants me. There might be nothing left to me but at least I stir something in her. And now, the car hit a bump and my head hit the roof and I knew I'd got that one wrong too. Even being a beard was too weighty for me. I was a decoy, a prop, a means of provoking Malcolm Lowell's jealousy—just a convenient illusion. What point was dreaming, when you were just a dream yourself? What hopes can an illusion have, anyway? I just wanted to be a real boy.

We were on the highway for Ballynkill when Emily hesitated at a crossroads and darted across at the last second onto an uphill back road. If it was a shortcut, it wasn't one she used regularly. Why she should be trying out uncertain shortcuts on me, I couldn't figure. Let her go adventuring with Malcolm if she liked him so much.

"I've been looking at properties all over the place," she said a bit loudly, trying to prod me from my funk. "There's a really nice one here. We'll stop for just a second, okay?" I didn't want to be in a funk. I loved Emily. But I couldn't help noticing that the situation felt entirely different once it was Malcolm rather than Maeve she was interested in. Then again, maybe it was just the field getting crowded that got to me.

Em had always been there. She'd been the one sure thing, the really beautiful woman I didn't want, the one I could console myself by rejecting, if only in my own mind. In my time of need, she'd soothed me in her loneliness. I'd fashioned her in my mind as the last resort, the best available offer, the consolation prize. Watching her try to cheer me up now only drove home what a farcical notion this was—no one this beautiful was anyone's consolation prize.

She pulled up next to a 12-foot-high stone wall and leapt from the car with her usual energy. "Come on. I want you to see this."

We tracked the wall which encircled the property, threading through a line of towering oaks—this had to be one of those English estates she'd mentioned, old trees everywhere. She reached a spot where the wall had collapsed and stepped brazenly through.

"Is this kosher?" I asked, following gingerly.

"It's the only way I've ever seen this place," she said. "I know it's for sale but I keep playing phone tag with the owner."

Normally I'm not big on breaking and entering in foreign countries, especially ones where the citizens have been blowing each other up intermittently for a thousand years. But now I was sleepwalking, barely paying attention.

Our path threaded between decrepit concrete barns. A Model A vintage truck rusted picturesquely on concrete blocks. Rusty hoes and threshing equipment leaned lazily against the yellowing walls. At least that's what I took them for—I'm a city boy so my identifications of farm equipment should be considered approximate.

Then we came around the side of the barn and stepped into a courtyard and Wham! the whole place opened up in front of us.

The manor house—it was impossible to call it anything else—had to go back to Charles I. It made Malcolm's place look like a shack, but it was even more in need of rehab. Whole sections of roof had gone missing. The windows were cracked in rotting casements. The flagstone steps leading to the door were dislodged, broken stone askew in pieces.

Nonetheless, the place was overwhelming—three stories tall and Georgian, with a simplicity of line and a dignity we can't even imagine anymore. Moldering but exquisite, three wings and a central courtyard, standing at the center of an incredible panorama of hills and clouds and trees. Looking closer, I realized that the structure looked solid as the hills and there were new gutters, doorknobs and new windows on one side, so somebody had at least started updating the place relatively recently.

Emily followed my gaze. "The plumbing and electric are only ten years old. The mother died of a coronary in the midst of renovation at age 68. Brother and sister have been fighting over it ever since. Sis had an aneurism five months ago at 39 and is insisting they dump it for whatever they can get. The brother's 50 and figures he doesn't have much time left, the genes evidently being weak." There was a real sense of triumph on her face, of having beaten the competition to Sutter's Mill. "It'll be our Artist's Retreat. We could put up thirty-five people at a time, between the house and the cottages." She swept in a circle, her hand outraised and beckoning—as I followed her, the big picture suddenly came into focus.

Emily was always showing me websites and brochures for artists' retreats, where painters, musicians, writers, playwrights and wannabe's go for a week or a month to find solitude and inspiration. They exist all over the world but not surprisingly they make the most money in already-beautiful places. Who can't imagine making great art in Tahiti or Firenze or... a spectacular hillside mansion in Ireland?

It was one of our oldest manifestos over vegetarian dumplings and green tea back in New Jersey. But now she'd *found* the place.

There were three barns in a line coming in—two average Irish small, one huge and overtall. A gatekeeper's cottage was visible down at the end of the drive and another between the big barn and the main house. The cottages were in tumbledown condition but lovely just the same—slanted roofs with gables, stone chimneys and vaulted doorways with half-moon windows above the lintels.

"I figured you'd want *that* one," Emily said, pointing behind me. I turned and nearly swooned. This was not a structure for a guest—it was the master's, when he got sick of the company he was keeping at home and longed for someplace more magnificent within walking distance. It was still a cottage in size but not in ambition—hand-worked masonry skirted the doors and windows, an amazing wood-carved balcony wrapped around the roof between the bedrooms and a telescope poked through a third story glass-roofed observatory. And this cottage—not the main house—stood at the crucial curve of the hillside, the spot possessing the most magnificent view of the valley.

Yeah, that would do for me.

"I figure the staff would get room and board to make the wages more competitive," Emily continued, speaking more slowly than usual from behind me to make sure I took in every word. "We can put a drama group in the big barn, musicians in the smaller ones and use the big downstairs rooms for writing and painting studios."

"How many sessions a year?" I asked.

"I don't know—you know logistics better than me," she lied. "You figure it out. I'm guessing writing and painting stuff all year round and the others in summer—it's too expensive to heat the barns, at least until we get rolling. So, drama and music would be spring and summer, maybe early fall."

I whipped out my notepad, to write down 'Retreat' but I couldn't move the pen. I didn't need to, really. I knew everything about this place by heart already. "We could have performances for the public at the end of the summer," I said. "Drama and music festival. Should make enough money to pay for heat, if it's done right. Have you looked into non-profit or not-for-profit status here?"

She was beaming. "Not yet," she said.

"Obviously we could charge more if the tickets were tax-deductible." I wasn't working very hard at this—just looking at the place, the ideas just came tumbling out.

"The thing to remember is:" Emily said, eyebrows arching, "an artist in Ireland—a writer, for example—pays no income tax. If you wrote a book about Ireland, it would surely get published over here. And then—voila—you're tax-free."

"The plays would have to be workshops or staged readings—not full-blown productions," I continued, "because the authors will want their official debuts on Broadway or the West End. But that barn is big enough for simple scenery and lights. And one of the smaller barns could be soundproofed for a recording studio. They'll have Pro Tools studios in a suitcase in the next year or two."

"I have another spot in mind for recording," Emily said and the look on her face was tantalizing. I followed her around the far side of the house and actually gasped—I don't think I've done that since I was nine.

There was another house growing out of the back of the estate house. Actually, 'another house' is a gross understatement—there was a *castle* growing out of the estate house.

The castle was six stories tall, precisely cut and fit together of huge stone blocks, with a flat patrollable roof and turrets at each corner. A huge four-story vaulted doorway opened into a great hall suitable for Prince John and Guy of Guisborne, overfed nobility and bustling starving servants. I'd seen Aztec pyramids in Mexico but they were ruins; this was a gross, primitive prototype for modern human habitation. It was like the first computers or the first clocks—each component overlarge, incredibly strong, enormous margins for error built-in, the learning tools of skills that have now become commonplace. All it needed was windows, doors, insulation, staircases, plumbing, electricity, gas lamps or something similar. No, on second thought, those things would ruin the place.

Emily was glowing. I'd forgotten for a moment that she was there—I'd forgotten everything for a moment. "It's Eleventh Century," she said. "I can't find the name of the Lord who owned it yet. But I was thinking we could set up a stage in the doorway and have one hell of a music festival. HELLLLLOOOOOO!" she called into the archway and the echo rang like a cash register in an empty Walmart.

I was in a stupor. I could see the thrill on Em's face—she knew she'd pulled the five-hundred-pound rabbit out of the hat.

"You need a Board of Directors," I said. "Offer stock to well-known artists. They lend their names and lecture once a year or something and get endless tax writeoffs, a piece of the profits and a chance to do good work."

"Can we afford that?" she asked. I had no idea but I was back in television production mode, where it's more important to sound decisive than to be right.

"The first few names are taking the risk of associating themselves with you so you overpay for them. But they're crucial. We need real artists—inspiring—and Irish."

"Bono."

"Perfect. Part of the profits would go to AIDS in Africa— that's his thing, right? The rest of the board are business types— companies that donate to good causes and have products we could use. And government pull wouldn't hurt. You'll need a well-known auditing firm to make them comfortable—just watch the money yourself to make sure they're not cheating you." I turned back to the castle, marveling at her find. "Pearl Jam would sound amazing here," I said.

"I was thinking classical—or maybe jazz," she countered. "Think practical—we live next door."

"Come to think of it, the U2 concert to inaugurate the place," I said and her eyes opened wide.

"Unplugged," she stifled.

"Oh c'mon—let me have one blowout before you go all cultural on me," I begged and she laughed. "Does Ireland have government support for women-owned businesses?"

"Oh God I've never looked into that."

"You need a list of things to look into."

"I can't do it all on my own," she said. And let the words hang in the air.

$$\neq$$

The car radio played "Domino": *Don't wanna discuss it; Think it's time for a change.* The clouds broke up and ran for cover over the far hills. Things were rearranging themselves rapidly all over the place though the master plan, as usual, remained elusive.

"There!" Em pointed suddenly at a hillside lit up with sunshine, the whole expanse glowing like a neon tube had been placed just under the grass. "That's why they call it the Emerald Isle." It was otherworldly, an entire field gone florescent in broad daylight. In twenty-five seconds, it passed. "I've seen triple rainbows here—and you can drive up to a field and see the end of a rainbow nearly touching the ground in front of you." She stared over to make sure I was paying attention. "All sorts of magical things happen here—signs and wonders for grownups, not storybook magic. The usual rules don't apply."

She wasn't trying hard to be subtle. In a matter of minutes, everything had changed. Even after gaining Malcolm's attention and a new horse, Emily still wanted me. She'd gone out of her way to affirm that, even if the terms remained obscure.

Obscure but not opaque. The more I thought about it, the outlines were there, even if a bit sketchy. It was, in essence, the kind of offer women get all the time from rich men. Brazenly or subtly, it's money and security in exchange for sex—and looking the other way when there's competition. The only thing that made our bargain unconventional was that it seemed to be for *no* sex. I was being offered the role of Mrs. Rock Hudson without the swimming pool. And surely, this was why I'd come—why I'd teased my way to an invitation in the first place. My get-out-of-jail-free card—maybe not exactly on terms I'd anticipated, but when you're starving and they offer steak, you don't quibble about potatoes versus rice.

I can't say it felt like a triumph, exactly. I can't say I expected it to. I knew what I was in for when I took the ride— maybe it wasn't something to be proud of but in the world's litany of sins, it wasn't major league material either. Maybe not even Double-A ball. Maybe...

Ballynkill was as flat as Lisheen was vertical. The pub sat at the end of a row of attached houses next to the bridge, just where the river widened into the Lough. It was painted an impossibly deep green with a griffin on a sign swinging outside the door. Malcolm was waiting in the parking lot, smiling as though he was still in control of his destiny, not realizing the train had been rerouted through Dead Man's Gulch on its way to town. Before either of them could utter a word about their miraculous new horse, my phone rang. I knew who it was but even he couldn't dampen my spirits at the moment.

"Fish on the line yet?" Ron asked.

"Well good afternoon to you too," I said. "Or good morning, whichever it is there."

"It's noon," he said. " 'Every day is a new promise' —I forget who said that. Which is why I'm calling you early, so if you haven't found someone, you still have the rest of the day. What's our progress level at this point?"

"I've been trying to squeeze a little vacation into my vacation time," I said. "It's Saturday and late afternoon, remember?" Malcolm and Emily had stopped at the door and were waiting politely for me to finish.

"It's a working vacation, remember? Ireland's not a Third World Country—and really, there's no Third World anymore. Business works 24/7 *everywhere*. In India they're fixing our computers. In Taiwan they're making our clothes and toys and radios the size of aspirins and they don't care that it's Saturday. The guy we want is working today. Besides, it's part of your personal growth. The successful entrepreneur is always looking for opportunity. That's why we are the most vibrant force in the world for change and growth. What did Buddha say about the Path?"

" '*You can't travel the path until you become the path,*'" I chanted, Aphorism #263, like a rookie in boot camp.

Emily was rustling, ready to go inside. Malcolm was openly staring at his watch. Time is money, time is money and Malcolm was, in his own way, a businessman, which is in its own way like an entrepreneur—both types spend lots of time staring at their watches in annoyance. This little gesture was like a door opening all at once in front of me.

"You know, you're absolutely right," I snapped. "I'm sorry I slipped out of attack mode for a second. It turns out I'm having supper right now with someone who might be able to help us." Malcolm arched an eyebrow. Yes, the two of them deserved each other. This was going to be fun.

"You SEE," Ron's voice boomed across the Atlantic Ocean, "Thomas Fuller said, 'A wise man turns chance into good fortune.'"

"And Groucho said, 'I came to Florida without a nickel in my pocket. Now I have a nickel in my pocket.' I'll call you as soon as the fish is on the line." And I clicked off.

It was dark as a tomb inside, so we actually heard the room before we saw it. A swarm of notes poured out of the corner where a fiddle, mandolin and guitar were busily thrashing:

> Don't you remember when you lay beside me
> And you said you'd marry me and not deny me
> If I said I'd marry you, it was only for to try you
> But bring your witness, love, and I'll not deny you

As my eyesight returned, a wide oak bar came into view at the back of the room. Two or three patrons teetered on stools there, several more snuggled in booths on each side. Chambers no bigger than the booths clustered on the outer edges, like concrete caverns.

"This way," Malcolm suggested, leading Emily by the arm into a cave. "We're for supper," he announced to the barmaid, who barely looked up from scribbling in her journal.

"What was the phone call?" Em asked as we took our seats. Emily my friend, who always knew just what to say.

"I'm glad you asked that. Malcolm, I think this could be the opportunity of a lifetime for you."

The barmaid came in to drop menus on the table. Malcolm ordered Guinness all round and she disappeared into the darkness.

"What sort of opportunity?" he said stiffly—what could I have that might mean anything to him? Good. I'd sat through his horse palaver. Let the shoe be on the other foot for a little while.

"I represent one of the few companies to take advantage of the fastest-growing commodity on the planet."

Emily'd seen me go giddy like this before; she was already looking for a chance to dive under the table, smart girl.

"What's that?" Malcolm asked.

"Trouble," I answered. "What is there more of, and more of every day? America's been attacked by people who can live anywhere and move as soon as you get their post box. We're not going to catch them all and they're not going to give up. We're about to invade Iraq. That should tie us up for ten years in the Middle East, where they *really* know how to make your life miserable. The English are helping and at least some Irish are against it—there was a demonstration at the airport when we arrived."

"There's another planned for this weekend," Malcolm replied.

"A massive one—millions of people around the world," said the barmaid, who was now distributing the Guinness. Emily asked for water. "Protesting a war that hasn't happened yet. First time in world history." An Irish voice, a tart cutting brogue like Maureen O'Hara in the John Wayne movies except a little higher toned, more soprano than alto. Maybe even coloratura. I wasn't sure what coloratura was, but it sounded like great head. I couldn't see the barmaid through the haze, except for a glimpse of the eyes passing. Big green eyes.

"Thank you, thank you," Malcolm said, dismissing her. "Alright, so how is trouble good for business?"

"It's not just terrorists," I said, getting wound up. "Scientists are cloning sheep, the coral reefs are being depleted, the snow is melting on Mount Kilimanjaro, whole sections of icecaps are breaking off at the poles—"

"Global warming," Malcolm intoned but his impatience was muted already.

"But that's just the *beginning*," I cautioned. I'd have twirled my mustache, if I had one. The whole pitch was cartoonish, my lampoon of Ron's original. But Malcolm was already getting sucked in. I'd seen this before, seen the pitch settle even the most skeptical listener. It was scary how effective it was once you started connecting the dots.

The first time I'd heard Ron do it was at a mall in Westchester when I'd just started working with him. It was six months after September 11th and Ron wanted man-in-the-street interviews on tape to back up his pitch to a hotel chain. I was shooting and he was talking.

"You don't get just a bit nervous now when you see an airliner in the sky?" he asked his first subject, a bank officer in blonde bangs and a silver-gray suit.

"Oh, I have some pangs," she admitted.

"And you've seen the hole in the ozone layer, right?"

"Yes."

"It doesn't strike you as foreboding that new ailments arise each day that defy our antibiotics? That whole continents are being ravaged in a plague of sexually transmitted diseases? And weird climate fluctuations on top of everything else? Doesn't it feel a little like Nature itself is at war with us? Hasn't it occurred to you at some point—maybe just for a moment—that maybe this really *is* The End of the World?"

"Well, those things aren't necessarily related to one another." But there was a note of uncertainty in the banker's voice.

Ron didn't falter. "What about Michael Jackson's face?"

"You're telling me Michael Jackson's face is a sign of Armageddon?"

"Can you find a better explanation?" he demanded. "You can't, can you? It's not just him. Is there *anything* in popular culture you really like?"

"Well, I like things that maybe aren't the most popular," she stammered.

"*Everyone* says that," Ron retorted. "How is that possible? How can it be that everyone hates popular culture, when the whole point of it is to be popular?" The woman took a step backward. "If it's our world," Ron insisted, "how can everything be so distant, so out of control? If Sodom and Gomorrah was more than a metaphor, don't you think it would be something just like this?"

The woman wandered out of our little booth, talking to herself. "That's what we're all about, yessir," Ron said.

"You might want to build up a bit to the Sodom and Gomorrah part," I'd suggested to Ron at the time. But here was Malcolm soaking it all up, just like the banker, except without walking out so far.

"The End of the World," he mused. He wasn't being dismissive. I worried for a moment that he might be devout—I like starting trouble now and then but only a little.

"The End of the World," I repeated pointedly. "We can sit on the sidelines and leave this whole market segment to irresponsible terrorists or we can take it for the profit-making opportunity it is."

"And how do we profit? What's the product?" he asked. Even Emily looked interested in a disinterested sort of way.

"Well, there's two components to a sale: you've got the commodity you're selling and the concept you're marketing." Malcolm looked confused. As a business journalist, it was at least a familiar concept when Ron started hammering at me about it.

"Do you know who Charles Revson is?" Ron had asked.

"Revlon?"

"EXCELLENT!" he boomed. "You're the kind of person I want to be associated with. Do you know what he said?"

"No."

"He said, 'Cosmetics are my commodity—what I sell is *confidence.*' You SEE? If you sell a commodity, anyone can sell it cheaper. They can steal your market share by undercutting your price. But if you sell Confidence, no one can cut into it. You transcend the Commodity. You must Transcend. You must Dominate. *Dominate or Die.*"

This might have been a bit much to repeat to Malcolm—he began to glaze over a bit. It was of course standard American business but maybe this approach hadn't migrated the Atlantic yet. The barmaid returned with Emily's water but her back was to me so I couldn't see any more of her eyes.

"Anyway, the point is that we're marketing The End of the World," I continued. "This is *It*. Armageddon, Apocalypse, Meggido, Zarathustra, whatever name you like—that's it. Collapse, anarchy, madness and confusion. Not overnight and not next week but inexorably and inevitably over time."

"Alright," Malcolm said. "I get that. It actually is compelling in a way. But what are we selling?"

"It's a mattress."

He blinked, twice, like a red blinker signal—a full stop. Not that I could blame him, really. "A mattress?" he said.

"Well, it's not really fair to call it a mattress," I cautioned.

I remembered the first time I'd seen the thing, five minutes after being hired and twelve minutes after entering Ron's office for the first time. The Getaway Bed glowed under a bank of spotlights in the outer alcove of Ron's suite. Clothed in a thousand-threadcount Belgian damask ticking with a handstitched border and titanium edgeguards, it shouted technology and ambition and profit motive. A thick bundle of cables ran to a multipaneled computer monitor mounted above the footboard.

Vic, Ron's majordomo, laid down on the mattress and the monitor flickered bright. "The graphics read his muscle tension, blood pressure, heart rate, respiration and perspiration, receiving data from twelve hundred sensors embedded in the ticking," Ron intoned.

Bladders in the side of the mattress expanded and contracted, adjusting as Vic squirmed around, air whooshing from the side panels as he settled into place. The gauges slid smoothly over to the side screen and the larger middle screen pulsed footage of cloud-shrouded mountains in the Andes and waterfalls in Kauai, accompanied by natural sounds and New Age ommmm music in six-speaker Dolby Surround. Vic's Relaxation Index rose and his Tension Index dropped according to the screen readouts and who could argue with Science?

"Are all the readouts too distracting?" Ron asked. "Does it make you think about your body too much when you're supposed to be relaxing?" He stared at me earnestly. "You're part of the team now—I want your opinion."

"I'm getting little shocks," Vic said. Ron continued to stare at me, awaiting an answer.

"Make it an optional extra," I suggested. "Some people definitely don't like thinking about their bodies."

"It's shocking me," said Vic.

"You're imagining things," Ron snapped. "Good answer," he told me. "But then optional which way? See the charts first? Or not?" This was a test, not a question.

"I'm not imagining anything. I'm getting zapped."

"You're not letting off smoke," Ron insisted. "You're not twitching."

"I didn't say I was being *electrocuted*—I'm getting shocked from somewhere inside."

Ron ignored him, staring at me, awaiting his answer.

"The default is to show the meters," I said. "Even if they never use them, they'll be impressed with the technology. They paid for it—they should see it."

This apparently was the right answer. He turned back, finally, to Vic.

"Well, is it a ten-volt shock? A hundred? What do I tell them when I call to complain? How am I supposed to confront a cutting-edge technology firm without facts? Why are you still lying there if it's shocking you?" Vic hopped up and the whole whirring, Ommmm'ing, flickering, medical feedback circus faded to black and silence.

"Okay," said Malcolm. "So you're selling a mattress that helps people relax... Is that it?"

"This isn't just relaxation. The bed reacts to your body sixty times a second, warming or cooling the surface where necessary, massaging where you're tense. It learns which videos cause your blood pressure to drop and whether you like up and down or side to side vibration to sooth your muscle tension. This isn't just relaxing—it's a refuge in a world that's going to hell in a handbasket. It's a way to regain control of your environment. With a monthly subscription for new videos and music, of course."

"Of course, if there's a real crisis," Malcolm said, "you might lose electricity. What good is the bed then?"

"We offer a home generator option," I answered, fast as lightning.

"How much is it?"

"Retail?"

"Yes."

"Eleven Thousand. Dollars. Don't know how that converts to Euros."

"Uh-huh." I could see a certain skepticism on his face, but he wasn't jumping ship.

"That's why the End of the World. Most consumer items become less enticing in times of stress and crisis—people lose motivation to buy. This one will become more and more of a necessity."

"Unless Iraq solves the terrorist problem," Malcolm drawled. "Just because people are against it doesn't make it a bad idea. Saddam truly is a bad man and sometimes force is the only way to deal with bad people." The words were spoken with the certainty of someone who'd dealt with bad people, who'd seen what they could do. But I couldn't help thinking that those bad people woke up looking at themselves in the mirror and saying 'I made the hard decisions. I did what had to be done. Sometimes this is the only way to deal with bad people.'

"Would you like to order now?" asked the barmaid. She was standing over my shoulder. I turned to get a look but the pad was in front of her face. Who knew if she was cute? She was certainly elusive. When she left, I got a trailing view of a compact backside, nice legs and chestnut hair that lit up red in the light.

"Well alright," Malcolm said when she was gone, "it's intriguing. Do you want to know why I'm skeptical?"

"Of course."

"America is the center of the western world—it's Rome, if you will. So when there's a terrorist attack there, it takes on a new *gravitas*. The End of the World makes sense if you're thinking that way. But everyone who can vote in this country remembers when we were blowing each other up on a regular basis. The terrorists lived next door and our parents were on their side. We remember this country in wracking poverty. Now we're building computers, we're the most globalized member of the European Union and we haven't bombed anybody (he crossed himself while saying this) in several years. If the Irish have a problem these days, it's that life seems *too* good."

It was a convincing argument, or it would have been if his heart had been in it. Instead, somehow, the speech came out dry, almost theoretical—more like defense than offense and in business that's a bad sign. I hadn't expected Malcolm to actually buy into this idiotic scheme. I was just hoping to blow his mind and get Ron off my back for a while. But now I realized one last push might actually get me over the hump, whatever it was.

"The Irish might feel fortunate but they're not blind," I attacked. "Unlike Americans, they're aware of their place in the world. Whatever problems you grew up with were your own—America's problems, on the other hand, are everyone's. America sneezes and the West catches cold. And now that the Irish are doing well, they have something to lose. I would think that anyone who marches in that demonstration tomorrow would be a potential customer for the bed and I get the feeling they're expecting a crowd." I knew nothing of the sort but after the buildup from the barmaid it seemed credible.

Malcolm considered this for a long moment, nursing his Stout. "What would you want me to do?" he asked finally. Bingo! Fish on the line!

"You're a celebrity," I said, "at least among the horsy set." Might as well get my little digs in while I could. "I get a commission if I come home with an Irish distributor. You can open doors—introduce me to someone. If he ends up the man, I'll split the commission with you 80/20."

"You'll get nowhere without me. 50/50."

"Emily knows other people around here. I wouldn't have even thought of talking to you until Ron called. 75/25."

"My contacts are far more extensive than anyone else Emily knows," Malcolm said though how could he know that? "70/30 just for amity." He held his hand out and added, "Just business. If we have other issues between us, they remain separate."

It was a pretty bald statement for an action hero like him. Emily's face lit up—that was annoying. But I took Malcolm's hand and we shook, both of us working our firm manly handshakes. Amity meant shit to me—70%, being on the high side, was all I cared about. When you've gotten used to losing, there's no such thing as an insignificant victory. So I grabbed this one and squeezed the juice out of it.

Our dinner came, without the barmaid. The two of them started in on their new horse again. I finished my food quickly and got up from the table. Em shot me a look and I said, "I want to check the band out. They're not bad." She nodded and I was off to the races.

I would sound less stupid—though possibly more reckless—if I pretended I knew what I was after but I had no clue.

I'd hit bottom and had somehow bobbed to the surface again. This left me swooning, cocky and a bit dizzy at once. I felt the need to *move*.

A barmaid but not ours—no green eyes, heavyish, dirty blonde, probably not a coloratura—was standing in front of the band singing another sad song. Did they know any other kind in this country?

> *She was coming from her uncle's in a sharp shower of hail,*
> *And under a green bush herself did conceal.*
> *Her true lover been a-fowling, he mistook her for a swan,*
> *And to his misfortune he shot Molly Bawn*

She wasn't much of a singer but the song was haunting, like the ones on the Irish station on the radio. This was a music of ancient hurts and endless daily tragedies, for women in particular. Couldn't Em have moved to France?

The band were young except for the leader, the mandolin player. He was closer to my age, hulking and intense, lost in the intricacies of the music. He played tight phrases across the melody while the barmaid sang. The other players were competent while this guy filtered all the feeling of the song through his skin. He pulled them through the arrangement with nods of his head and pointed glances.

As I stood watching, I noticed a small but steady stream of people trickling through the side caverns toward the back without returning—and others appearing that way that I'd never seen before. After twenty years reporting for a living, I don't hatch questions without seeking answers. So eventually I stepped out railroad-car style through the caverns. There were several more of them than I expected—the bar seemed to go quite a bit deeper than it looked. The music faded as conversation welled up from the back.

I paused in the doorway of another dining room, the mirror image of the one I'd just left, save for a few significant details. With no band hogging the attention, this room had the feel of a cozy club, but there were actually more patrons here, smoking, drinking, passing familiar conversation and tossing darts at a board in a corner. This bar was also enlivened by a lazy, crackling fireplace—and a dog.

The huge black creature lumbered out of the smoky haze like the Hound of the Baskervilles and clamped his jaws over my hand. I panicked until I realized he wasn't biting down. Nonetheless he had me firmly in tow—I followed him to the bar without argument.

"Let him go Rudy—he doesn't look like a terrorist," said a voice in the far corner. To general laughter, the dog released me and curled up in front of the deep fireplace. "Rudy's our social director," said a sandy-haired man hiding behind a tall glass. His hair grew straight out of his head in several directions. "As long as we have him, we'll never be lonely."

The others snickered as I took them in. Two boys of about fourteen were playing cards in a booth. At the bar, I counted a rail-thin gent of at least 80, a 60-ish woman with a wire brush of silver hair, a thick-waisted fellow in a sailor's hat who seemed joined with her at the hip and a thirtyish Liberal Arts professor beneath a thick beard and cable-knit sweater. The rest were wearing coats inside despite the fire. Apparently, all Irish heaters were as effective as the ones at Emily's house.

"What'll you have?" said the ancient gentleman, stepping off his stool.

"He'll have a Guinness."

"Let him speak for himself."

I usually drink wine but this really didn't seem like a wine kind of place. "Guinness sounds fine," I said.

"What' I tell yeh?" Sandy-hair pronounced, to resounding murmurs from the rest. The place was a pocket of white man's gospel—every phrase requiring affirmation, echo, call-and-response, accompanied by quality beer at a reasonable price. The old gent worked his way laboriously around the bar—his gummy hips reminded me of Dyson—placed a glass under the tap and began filling it. He took it halfway and popped the tap, letting it sit until the head went down.

"Where're you from?"

"New York," I answered and they all hushed.

"Sorry," someone said and I nodded in thanks. The old lady pointed to a corner next to the fireplace. I walked over and discovered the Shrine. A glass case held two NYFD firefighter helmets, an NYPD cap, a yellow emergency jacket, axe and several front pages (NY Daily News, Irish Times and NY Times) from 9/12. A veneer of dust coated the top of the case, but someone had spent a good deal of time arranging the items inside and securing them in place.

"Some of our boys went over to help in the cleanup," someone said. "Johnny Regan's boy was over there for three months."

"Thank you," I said, again the ambassador. "Thank him for me." We all spoke in hushed tones as though it had happened the week before. A year and a half, I thought, and it hasn't disappeared here any more than at home.

"And to whom does this orphan belong?" came the voice from behind the bar, that Maureen O'Hara coloratura. I turned and the barmaid was there with those big green eyes and a mischievous expression on her lips, one that suited the voice perfectly.

I knew she had to be striking, just from the sound of her and she was. She had a face out of an Irish portrait gallery, a face that had surely appeared in Ireland for 10,000 years in an unbroken line. An upturned nose and a narrow mouth, auburn hair with blonde streaks for modernity, skin opaque white between freckles. Her face was a riot of laughlines; her shape curved nicely but without advertising itself. She was attractive rather than beautiful, if you were being objective. But I never had a moment's objectivity about her. I wanted her instantly, without a moment's attempt at understanding. Actually, I knew at that moment that I'd wanted her *before* I'd ever laid eyes on her.

"He's mine—I intend to adopt him," I answered, a bit dizzied. She filled the glass slowly to keep the head from stealing too much of the drink.

"You'll provide him a good home?"

"With your help, I'll at least provide him the company of his own kind."

"You seem suitable," she said, pushing the glass in front of me.

"He's an American."

"I've got ears. Doesn't look like an American, though. Where's your guns?"

"Left 'em home. Ran out of bullets."

"Where's your bag o' money?"

"Don't use money anymore. We're going to conquer the world on credit."

We were both grinning—this was fun. Suddenly, I was having *fun*. Hell, I was on my *vacation*. I almost swooned at the thought.

The barmaid stepped out into the room. "How's my little lover?" she cried, her voice rising two octaves. The Hound of the Baskervilles roused himself instantly and jumped, his paws to her shoulders, licking her face. They could have been dancing. Emily was right—the whole country was animal crazy.

Of course, this also gave me—and any of the others who cared to—a chance to admire her shape and a nice one it was too, the kind of sleek curves that always make me aware of my breathing. She popped back behind the counter for a moment and returned with a dish shallow with beer. She laid it on the floor in front of the fireplace. The dog lapped it up, then settled in front of the fireplace glassy-eyed and began to snore lightly.

"He has a condition," said sandy-hair.

"A condition that responds to beer?"

"We don't want him to respond," the bristly-haired woman said and everyone laughed.

"Does anyone have a cigarette?" the barmaid said. "I need a cigarette." No one moved.

"We're not helpin' her," said sailor hat to me, taking a drag on his own.

"I smoke the organic ones—they don't have so much chemicals," she explained. "But the store doesn't have them today. So I need something." She picked up a cocktail twizzler, stuck it between her teeth and sucked hard. The others tittered.

A man a few years older than me hobbled in from the front on crutches. "Hello Bill," the barmaid piped.

"Hello Jilly m'girl. Where is it?"

"It's settling," she said, inclining her head toward the tap. "Just a minute." I don't know how the pint got there—either she knew he was coming or she always kept one waiting, which wasn't a bad idea, actually.

"Anyone know what won the 2 O'clock at Mallow?"

"Mister Memory."

"Ooh that smarts," said Bill, taking a stool and flapping his arms like a pelican. "It's brass monkey weather out." The group shivered in sympathy.

There were lots of glances thrown at the fire but no one willing to leave the bar to get closer to it. Jill (this was apparently the barmaid's name) set the beer in front of him and Bill slurped it down in a few gulps.

"Thank you m'dear," he said and started clomping his crutches out toward the front.

"Making progress?' Jill asked as he disappeared.

"Please God."

"He'll be months yet," said Sweaterman, once Bill had rounded the corner. He was leaning across the barmaid now, who didn't seem to mind.

"He fell," she explained, turning to me. "No, that's not so. A wall fell on *him*, to put a point to it. He was building a wall and it came down all at once. And he's not healing right for some reason. He should have been off crutches in September. And him a man who likes to move around."

"Don't we all?" said Sweaterman.

"Not all so much as you—or Bill," Jill answered, eyes flashing.

She was flirting with him and flirting with me. And over the course of the next ten minutes, I watched her proceed to charm the room. Five new men came through the doors in that time and, with the exception of the boys in the booth, who remained glued to their cards, Jill kept us all in line, lost in her wide eyes and insinuating voice, the way she sniped at our stories and took us down a peg—but just one or two, like a spirited girlfriend would.

Every glance she threw me made me puff up like a blowfish. The look in her eyes said I was *special*, that I'd touched her, that she looked forward to my little glances far more than the ones she was sharing with every other man in the place. And somehow, knowing—seeing—that they felt exactly the same didn't diminish our connection one bit.

There was a lull as the place thinned back to the original group. "Why is the building divided up like this?" I asked. "It's a strange arrangement, all these little rooms and everyone in the back."

"It's a very favorable arrangement," said Sweaterman.

"When the boss starts looking for ya," added the old lady and they all cackled. And I got it, looking around. The place was a labyrinth. If you wanted to sneak a pint during the day and you just kept moving from room to room, it would be nigh on impossible for anyone to find you. Alcoholism as architecture. I wondered what *Russian* bars looked like.

I finished my drink. The other barmaid was behind the counter. "I should get back to my friends," I said, pulling five Euro from my wallet.

"It's paid for," the ancient gentleman said.

"No please," I stuttered.

"You wouldn't insult a man your grandfather's age," he told me and I wouldn't. My grandfather didn't buy anybody drinks, not even beers at Mets games. I took my money and made my thanks and goodbyes. Then I headed around the side of the bar. Halfway forward, the master plan came clear—there were doors to this place on two streets, with the bar itself cutting through the middle. The private club opened onto a small side street instead of the main drag and that made all the difference.

Jill the barmaid sat between rooms, at the midpoint of the thick bar, writing emphatically in her journal. Her hand jabbed at the page under a narrow shaft of light, staccato slashing, while the rest of her hid in shadow an inch away. I actually took a step backward at the sight. It felt like I'd stumbled onto her swimming naked in a pond.

"What do you write?" I asked. She slammed the book closed.

"It's poetry," she chimed. "I don't show it around."

"I'm a writer too," I said, like it was the password at a speakeasy.

"I can imagine: *How to Profit From the Coming Apocalypse.*" Ouch. She'd been listening!

"I was just making trouble. I have to earn a living."

"Ah, that's why Americans make so much trouble? To make a *living*? Nothing more dignified than that?"

I sighed without a thought. "Dignity's archaic in New York. Your bank account's flush or it's lean. Dignity doesn't enter into it." I threw up an eyebrow. "You offer Dignity here? Is it the name of a drink?"

"The next time you come, everyone will know your name. If the rest of them are livid at Mr. Bush for his oil racketeering, they'll keep it to themselves."

"The rest—but not you."

She smiled with a twist of lemon. "I'm poorly-mannered and a bad host. The Tourism Board will be after me as soon as you complain."

My turn to smile. "Complain about what? I've no dignity to lose."

"I'm Jillian," she said, offering her hand. I took it and the shock shot up my arm like I'd stabbed a light socket. My breath got sharp and—shockingly—so did hers. It was a wonderful, scary adolescent moment.

You get older and you think you're past having your feelings jump up and swamp you like a leaf in a tsunami. You tell yourself you've caught on to love and passion, its distractions and delusions, that you understand the only position the firm offers is 'dimwit' and you're not interested. And then you find yourself lying on the rocks watching the wave recede into the ocean, hoping your back is only broken instead of shattered.

I wanted her like it was the only way to keep breathing. I wanted every inch of her skin, I wanted to know everything about her and to tell her everything that ever happened to me that mattered, to take her everyplace I'd ever been, to explain how I was too old for this kind of stupid stuff so she could tell me I wasn't.

"Paul," I answered, even though it felt like twenty minutes since she'd given me *her* name.

"I know," she answered and oh hell, did *that* let the air out of the balloon. At least she didn't say how much she'd heard about me.

This was Em's favorite place to eat—that's why we'd come. So of course she'd talked me up here the same as at the market and the corner store. And, for all I knew, the national media: *Paul Roget, giraffe-like American, arrived at Shannon Thursday to begin his reign as official boyfriend to Emily Ormond, American Protestant living in Lisheen-Ballynkill. Ms. Ormond, who is now demonstrably* not *gay, looked radiant in her winter parka. She has asked that her privacy (prih-vah-cee) be maintained and that paparazzi be restricted to a distance of 1000 meters. Mr. Roget immediately began hunting women closer to the age of consent.* Changing the subject seemed like a good idea.

"Can I ask about the poetry?"

And now the flinty barmaid's face went ruddy as she stared urgently at the counter. It wasn't that any vulnerability suddenly showed, more that the thick shell she kept around it suddenly did. For the second time in two minutes, I felt like I'd stumbled onto her in the bath.

"The poetry's—well, all sorts of things. Every man I get involved with gives me at least two—one when we become entangled and one when we sever. I have *volumes* of those. I'm working on one about the man who repaired my stove the other day. Arms like tree limbs and a tattoo of Jesus. He looked me over once or twice like men do and told me—without prompting—that I was a good girl." She laughed and shrugged. "Doesn't sound like much, does it?"

"Stories are in the telling," I said. "I couldn't describe mine to save my life."

"But what sort are they? Surely not the destruction of Western civilization?"

I had a thousand answers to that question—well, not really answers. Catchphrases maybe—*pitches*, to be precise: *The Dignity of*

Work got me my first published articles and a television career. *Neurotic Jews and their Wacky Sex Lives* — that was the novel I hoped to write when Em invited me over. But when I opened my mouth, something different came out — I said what I didn't know I meant.

"I'm not sure what I care about anymore," I heard myself say. "Of if any such thing exits, for that matter. I've spent so many years on what people would pay for and wanted to hear... I've been banging on the laptop since the moment we got on the plane — you know, writing in hope of getting in touch with myself — but I haven't really met anybody yet."

When I looked up, there was a new look in her eyes. It wasn't the professional charmer of the back bar or the combative poet wielding sharp tongue. There was something unguarded, almost innocent in her expression. She would never be a girl again but there was a bit of a girl behind her eyes. And that girl, for just a moment, was soaking me up, like it mattered. I started floating in place a bit.

And then her expression stiffened and she said softly, "Don't you think your *girlfriend* might be wondering what's become of you?"

My girlfriend. She was talking about *my girlfriend* Emily. I straightened like a Republican in a gay bar. "Oh. Right. Uh...sure. Uh. See you later." And. I. Stammered. And. Stuttered. off into the darkness.

≠

Malcolm was holding the door open for Emily as I reached them. It had gone dark outside while we ate—the whole town was lit up on the hillside across the water.

"I have a few thoughts for your fish on the line. I'll let you know," Malcolm said. We fought our way through another handshake. Then he pulled his nice new Mercedes out in a hail of pebbles, waving out the window. Em watched him go, smiling and humming, way too comfortable with us fighting over her.

This interlude lasted just a moment. She looked across the river and started at the sight of Maeve's gallery, her face bright red.

"Maeve's paintings—I've got to finish them!" she moaned. She stalked across the parking lot. "Three paintings shouldn't take that long, right? I'm almost finished anyway—I just have to figure out the stragglers."

She was unapologetically talking to herself, clearly not caring if I was listening or not. This was probably what she did the fifty-one weeks a year I *didn't* visit.

"Where are my car keys? Ah, in my hand—good move, Emily. Anyway, I have to stop thinking and just *do*, right? That's what you always used to tell me."

It was the first interest she'd shown in her paintings since we'd arrived, not that this proved anything—anyone who managed to be a painter/MBA/horse trainer had to have *some* sort of attention deficit.

"The problem is, they're a progression, a group, like a slideshow. I can't just stumble on without a plan like I usually do. It's not just coming up with the right light or the..."

I rolled down the car window going up the hill, while Emily streamed painterly rhetoric. I felt warm all of a sudden; I wanted to let everything outside in.

The night bugs were chattering like traders at the Chinatown market. The moon was brilliant in a mystical Turner sky. The great English landscape paintings always seemed phantasmic to me, otherworldly. Now I saw that they just recorded what they saw outside the studio window. Life is miraculous and smart artists accept sublime gifts when offered, thank you very much.

We reached the house and Em plunged down my hallway, threw open the last door and disappeared inside. And then emerged ten seconds later.

"Where are those paints we bought?" she yelled.

"Unless you've unpacked, they're in your suitcase," I answered for no reason—she was already hurtling past my door, heading for her wing of the house. A minute of clanking and clunking and she returned with a handful of tubes in hand.

I pulled out a book and started turning the pages. Furniture and canvases were being dragged across the floor of the studio but I ignored the din. Sure, we were due for another conversation, but I would wait to see if she came to me.

I was thinking about the retreat—I was trying hard to concentrate on the retreat. Running the place would certainly be work—government forms and the kind of maintenance a house older than my country demanded, massaging creative types from playwrights to plumbers. But it was dignified, unhysterical nineteenth century stewardship, dealing with people on their vacations when most would be fairly reasonable most of the time. And surely I would make connections that would help me publish my novel. Not that I had a novel or even an idea for one but in the last hour or so I'd started feeling something coming, maybe even close if I kept my eyes open.

Of course, there was another tune humming along in the back of my mind, one I was relentlessly trying to ignore.

Business is the World, as Ron made me chant six times a week. Life was opportunistic. I had offers now, plural—and I had a favorite. Naturally, my favorite wasn't the glaringly great one right in front of me, but the one that promised smoking rubble in every direction.

"Can you help me?" Em called. Down the hall, I'd heard her grunting and groaning. When I reached the studio, she was on hands and knees, squeezing bits of paint onto a palette, fitfully narrating to herself.

"Never mind—I found it," she said. I pulled a yard of tarpaulin off a loveseat and settled in with my book. The studio was a wreck, though no more than any other room in the house. Splintered easels and half-stretched canvases stood in stacks against every wall. Paint tubes open and capped spread like shell casings underfoot. You could cut four-foot sections out of the floor and sell them for Jackson Pollock's.

On an easel near the window stood a canvas of a brokendown shack on a windy hillside—purple morning haze, dappled stone and grass—painted in the photorealistic style I remembered from Sarah Lawrence. In fact, I'd swear it was the *same* damn shack on the same hillside she'd shown me there 25 years earlier.

Dyson had hated that painting. Em had worked on it for months before showing it to me, but Dyson swore it had bottled her up. "Some artists create more than one work in a lifetime," he'd grumbled. It was amazing for what it was: a picture of a tumbledown brittle hovel, the planks gone to termites or rainsoaking or mold. You could feel the wind blowing through the gaps. It could have been a photograph, which was the problem. It was so realistic, so detailed and distanced and objective, that nothing appeared to have been chosen. And choice is the essence of art.

"Leave something out," I'd told her when she asked for criticism—we took each other seriously, held nothing back. "Or add something that jars. Do something to tell us we have to pay attention. Because right now, it's so deadpan that any viewer who's not inside your head will just onceover and out."

Emily mixed two precise shades on her pallet. She stood hunched before the easel, creaking back and forth for the longest time. Then finally she held out the brush and added a fleck of precise color—just a dot, a short slash—in two or three places, a few glints of light off the barbed wire fence in the background and the sky above the trees. Ten minutes of deep consideration followed and then she cleansed the paint from her pallet and started mixing another pair of precise shades to be added.

I'd seen this ballet now on both ends of a twenty-year span. Lengthy brooding consideration leading to tiny additions to the canvas, none of which markedly changed or deepened the story. With art, more precise can mean smaller and Emily's paintings years ago seemed to have become studies in diminishing return.

She continued to mix colors, tight pockets of color dotting her palette. "So," she said finally, "what do you think of the retreat?"

About time she'd asked but I knew she would. This was another way we were alike—once there was a question on the table, we had to have an answer. By waiting her out, I was in control. I was winning. At least, that's what I told myself.

"It's astounding," I said, getting it on the record. "You've found our dream spot."

"Yes," she agreed, though she seemed almost wistful about it. "It's right there and I don't think anyone else has put a bid in."

"But what's my job really?"

"Run the place. You know me—I'm not an organizer." Somehow, we both kept from laughing among the debris. "Choose vendors, make sure we get what we need when we need it. Anything philosophical, we should discuss. Practically, I trust your judgment. I won't be an intrusive boss—more like a backer, except I'll have an apartment in the house."

This was not the answer and she knew it. "And—the personal side? Between us? The fine print?"

She shrugged. She didn't pretend to be offended by the question. "Be what you already are. Watch TV with me at night. Pick me up at the hospital when they've finished poking and beating on me. Like you did for Dyson. That's about six times a year so it's not a small thing. Live with me—let everyone think we're lovers. We love each other as it is."

"But we're *not* lovers. And you're not proposing that we become lovers."

"No." Her voice was quiet but there was no hesitation.

"So you're asking me to give up love and sex."

"Have affairs," she answered immediately, without drama—clearly, she'd thought this through. She pulled a large brush out of the bundle and tapped it against the edge of the easel. "The word'll get around you're cheating on me and that's fine. I'll be a perfectly ordinary cuckolded woman; there are a million of them around here—and once I'm safe and normal in the shadows, maybe I can find someone on the side to make me happy."

"What about Malcolm?" I asked.

"What about him? You heard what he said: Can I *take satisfaction as it comes*. He wants an affair. Surely he's had a million already and I'm another notch. But he won't stick. He certainly won't take me to the hospital."

"So you wouldn't want an affair with him?" She sure had *looked* interested.

"I don't know," she laughed, trying to shrug it off. "Maybe."

"I thought sex *hurt*."

"*Not* doing it hurts too," she answered, tart. "*Life* hurts."

She was ready to paint, tapping the brush against the easel. I stood to leave but saw all at once that she wasn't done.

"But you can't leave me in the lurch," she cautioned. "I don't really have to say this, but I will, just to have everything on the table. We've always been completely open with each other."

"Yes," I nodded. We had, mostly.

"If you say 'yes,' you've got to stick with me. You can have all the women you want; just don't get involved." She laughed. "God, I sound like an idiot. I'm offering you what men dream of—

affairs without consequences." We shared a smile, but it felt, even at the moment, more like hiding what we felt than showing it.

I hunkered down in the couch, attempting, for minutes or seconds or God knows how long, to get the feel of the ground under me.

It was an insanely good deal. I'd come over—I'd wangled an invitation—because this was just what I'd wanted. At least, I *wanted* to want it. I felt like I *ought* to want it. I wanted the retreat and I wanted Emily happy. If it was possible, I wanted to be happy myself.

Four hours earlier, I'd been desperate for any sort of clarity or purpose. Now the house was dense with things unsaid, as obvious as a shrieking teakettle no one will take off the stove.

When I looked up, she was cleaning her palette in the corner. The air stung of turpentine. She rolled up her sleeves to clean the brushes and I saw the red marks—nasty bulging scars— up her forearm.

"What happened?" I asked, pointing. I would have been afraid to touch them, afraid the contact would hurt her.

"Oh, they're just cuts," she said. "They're old."

"What do you mean 'cuts'? Who cut you?"

"I did. It was a thing I used to do. In high school and college—and when I was married." She continued cleaning the palette and I continued to stare, totally unsatisfied with this answer. "Lots of women do it," she insisted, still not looking at me.

"I've never known any."

"Sure you did. Several of our school friends. You just didn't know it."

She stood and walked down the hall. I heard the television go on and knew I should follow, that she'd expect me. But that teakettle was getting deafening.

I grew up in a house full of Holocaust survivors. My father, his father, my great uncles and aunts were all in the camps. The numbers were on my father's arm when he shaved in the morning. The photos were mounted in the foyer, all the family members whose names I was taught but never knew—their spouses and parents and brothers and sisters who hadn't made it out. There were a lot more dead than living in that house—their spirits crowded us in. No one talked about it, ever. I learned at an early age the power of things left unsaid—and the chatter that covered what no one could bear to say.

I barely remember my mother, those few years before she died or disappeared or whatever happened. I remember her voice reading me Golden Books and her Victrola filling the house with Sinatra and Tony Martin, Doris Day and Rosemary Clooney. I remember a feeling I only identified long after she was gone, the relief the others felt having her gone, no longer hearing her romantic songs, no longer having to remember the one optimistic impulse in my father's life.

My father and grandfather only listened to ballgames — the Mets, the halfwit stepchild of the traitorous Dodgers. They would lean back in their wooden porch chairs with the thick green cushions, drink Rheingold (The Dry) beer and debate the statistics and nuances of the worst baseball team that ever played the game. It let them feel, for hours at a time, like real Americans.

America was my father's hope and I was raised to embody all that gawky energy and optimism he could never really share. The family spoke Yiddish but they didn't teach and didn't want me to learn. My mission was to grow beyond the Pale, to move into a larger world, one that would hopefully render moot the lessons they couldn't forget for a second.

That house taught me guilt and longing, taught me to find them indivisible everywhere, to know them the way you can only know something that's been in your bed and the toilet, carried in all your pockets and worn behind your eyes. They were the motive for everything I ever did and the reason I ran from that house the first chance I had.

And so it was in that familiar state that I awoke after two hours of snatches of sleep on the loveseat in Emily's living room, full of unsourced guilt. The TV flickered in front of me but Em was gone, probably reading in bed or sleeping the sleep of the innocent. I stalked the living room and the kitchen but my legs needed to stretch, to keep moving. I found myself throwing on a coat and stalking out into the night and down the hill toward the lights.

By the time I hit Lisheen, the night crowd was out. The guidebooks say Ireland's pubs close at 11:30 but the ones I passed at 11:15 sure didn't seem to be winding down. The doors were open and swarming with patrons. I would have sworn I was randomly circulating the narrow streets but somehow every turn led in the direction of Jillian's pub. The place must have had a proper name but I never found out what it was or thought of it in any other way.

I wavered at the door a moment before reaching for the fatal handle. And then it opened without me and Jill was on the other side, coat in arm, the music just about pushing her out the door. She didn't look a bit surprised to see me, which only made me guiltier.

"Is this closing?" I asked.

"We're not serving anymore but they keep playing a while. They'll sneak themselves a few before cook locks up. I must have part of the evening for myself."

Hers was a modern woman's smile—previous generations would have found it immodest; a man wouldn't attempt it. We stood staring at each other for a moment, until I realized I was the one who needed an explanation for being there.

"I thought maybe I could... walk you home? Or..we could just...walk..."

She threw me a quizzical smile. "With me, it's all uphill," she warned and led the way.

There was a time I was brave with women. I was young and onair and there were no stakes yet, none that I felt. Divorce makes you feel *everything*. The anger is pain and the pain is anger and on the rare occasions you feel good, that's painful too. You mourn the things that were good and the things you hoped would be good, even if they never actually were. Anything that reminds you of the good times also reminds you how bad they turned out and that raises the internal stakes forever after. After the divorce, I'd taken a vacation—from women and from big parts of myself. Now I was full of feeling and scared to death of it. I wanted nothing more than to be with her and to find some excuse to run in the other direction, both at once.

The bridge stood at the edge of the parking lot. It was a stumpy, primitive stone bridge, old enough to be the town's identity, short enough that it was hard to imagine it meaning so much. An exoskeleton of scaffolding glowed in the moonlight. Ballynkill ran in layers up the hill ahead of us, bright-colored houses like rows of candy drops.

She kept glancing over at me until I realized I kind of owed her conversation. "I'm trying to figure out what to do," I said. "Not much point offering a barmaid a drink, is there?"

She smiled indulgently—surely she'd heard the line a thousand times. "I don't drink at work," she answered. "But I'm not in the mood anyway."

"Tea?"

"Why don't we just walk for now?"

"'For now'?"

"Until I decide if I want tea."

You could actually hear the river moving under the bridge. A car—not a particularly wide one—rolled by and we had to crowd the stone wall. Her hair fluttered against my cheek. Her scent was fresh even after a day in a bar. She smelled smoky good; the thought sounded like a commercial.

"You're deciding about tea—or me?"

That bold smile reasserted itself. "I'm fairly centered so far as tea is concerned," she replied and I had my answer.

Of course, it was me. I was Em's boyfriend. The word was all over town. Not that it stopped her from walking with me, however. We came off the bridge and mounted the hill, passing fifty metal placards pointing out distant towns in every direction.

"I'm in kind of an odd situation," I said, trying to back into real conversation.

"What's odd? Your being here?"

Birds swarmed just off the surface of the river and up the funnel-like street in squadrons. A swirling windswept leaves and bits of paper uphill into walls and the dark overhead. I didn't notice anything coming down. It would rain soon, the taste was in the air.

"I don't feel like myself. I've always been pretty transparent..."

"An honest man?"

"A simple one, maybe." She laughed, thankfully. "But ...right now I...can't be."

Em's price was for me to lie. Cheat on me, she said, just don't humiliate me with anything real. So now I was confessing, without the details. Was I hoping Jill would just shrug off my guilt and laugh at it? 'Who cares? Girls just want to have fun.'

No, that wasn't it. The thought rang off-key, a clanging note, instantly—I knew better. If anything was to happen between us, it would be real and consuming. That's what I wanted, too, whenever I wasn't too scared to want anything.

"I don't know if I believe in transparency," she said, setting a leisurely pace uphill. "People aren't open creatures, really. Transparent usually means you just stick to your story."

"Maybe I haven't got a story."

"*Everyone's* got a story. We all count the cards at the table. We all worry how we look—to others, to ourselves."

That cut closer than I felt like acknowledging. "If you take advantage of someone, but they *want* you to, does that make it better?"

"If that's really true, at least you'd only be disappointing yourself. But it can't really be true, can it?"

"Why not?"

"If they really wanted you to, you wouldn't feel you were taking advantage, would you?"

"Phfft! Well, then..." and I fizzled out.

"There you are," she shrugged. "So what's transparent? What's it mean?"

I had no idea for a long moment.

"Is this a schizophrenia issue?" she snapped.

"No, a practical one...between you and me."

"Ah!." The smile returned. "Well, why don't we just keep walking?"

"What will that do?"

"Sometimes things just work themselves out." She flashed that smile at me again and I felt myself smiling back.

Nearing the top of the hill, she stepped into a store. I didn't notice until the door snapped shut behind me that it was the mini-mart, the place Em had paraded me the night before. Jill pulled soap and a box of loose tea off the shelves and headed for the register.

And now Ballynkill showed its other side to me for the one and only time in my stay. I have to say I saw it coming—the woman at the counter was the same one who'd greeted Emily with such worship the night before. Now, here I was with Jillian and her disapproval was toxic.

"Hello Mary," she said.

"Hello Jillian," Mary replied stiffly and added, "Hello Paul."

I reddened; it was clear this comeuppance pleased her. There'd be gossip in the morning.

Jill's eyes flashed. She stepped back among the stacks and returned with a jumbo box of tampons, rapping them sharply onto the counter.

"Will that be all?" Mary asked after a startled moment, her face reddening.

"Thank you," Jill replied and handed over her money.

A moment later, we were out, crossing the square and cutting through the graveyard behind the church. I was sheepish and apologetic but Jill was on a trajectory that couldn't be altered in mid-flight.

"You were saying," she prodded, hurtling through the gate of the churchyard into another mini-neighborhood, "about your situation being...awkward?"

"I did."

"Point taken," she said, coming to a halt against a gate between two squat concrete houses. She was breathing hard, though it didn't seem physical exertion as much as controlling her feelings.

"I'm sorry—".

"Don't!" she spit. "Don't you even *think* of defending yourself against these narrow-minded gossips! They've no place to judge us…whatever we might turn out to be." Her face was red in streetlamp light; her finger wagged in my face. "They draw lines in the sand for other people. Real life," she concluded with a cluck of the chin, "happens *outside* the lines."

There was a little boasting in it; I found myself swelling, from being momentarily included in her gang. But there was a challenge in it too, to jump the barriers I'd been mumbling about.

"I won't make your life easier," I said and she laughed, which was about the best I could have expected. "I've been going through the motions a long time. I'm used to having a quick line and a slick excuse, even talking to myself. Maybe it's good that I don't have that now. I want to know you. You make me feel things. You make me *feel*. Which scares the hell out of me. And that's all I know." She was listening—the snarky smile was gone. "And I'm saying it to your face, so I can't take it back or pretend otherwise, even though it makes me sound like a raving idiot."

Her eyes were wide now, swallowing me up—it was way too soon to feel this engulfed. "I vanished for a while," I muttered, "which, when you're my size, is a good trick."

She regarded me now like a butcher regarding a roast. It felt like what I deserved.

"Eejit," she said finally.

"What?"

"That's how it's said over here. You're not a raving idiot, you're a raving eejit. When in Rome..."

"I see," I said and almost giggled from the release.

"That place with the garden?" she pointed to an overflowing stone courtyard behind an old foundry. "They make a decent cup of tea."

"Tea that cures vanishing?"

"In Ireland, tea is an accepted cure for vanishing, heart disease, bad marriage and compulsive gambling."

The place occupied a quiet corner looking down on the hillside, the bridge and the Loch. It served a mean tea with lemon and some very good cakes. I picked at mine, watching my figure, while Jillian devoured hers in seconds and stared at me in triumph. A liberated woman indeed.

"Okay," I said. "Now tell me one thing about you. One thing that matters." She just stared back at me. "It's only fair—I've told you all about my vanishing personality."

"I didn't ask you to."

"I'm buying the tea."

"I thought that was payment for listening to your tales of woe."

"I thought you did that out of kindness."

I couldn't help noticing how much smiling we were doing. I felt a bit lightheaded and it wasn't the tea. She sipped hers as I watched in complete contentment.

"I grew up here, in this town. And here I am," she said finally.

"And?"

"That's all there is to tell."

"No, it's not. There's more. Lots more."

"How do *you* know?"

"I have eyes."

"And very nice eyelashes. Why do the boys get all the long eyelashes? One thing, eh? Well, when I came back to Ireland, this was the last place I wanted to be."

"Home usually is." I said and she sighed.

"I suppose so. I had gone to England, writing girly articles for the glams—'How to Make Your Man Stand Up and *Fetch*!' that sort of drivel. Anything to escape Ireland—the poverty here, you can't imagine. There was a recession all through the 80's but it felt as though there had never been anything but recession here."

"I was in England in the late 70's—I loved it."

"You wouldn't if you'd been Irish. I could bring a party to a halt simply by opening my mouth. This was the time of the IRA bombings in London. They heard an Irish voice and the whole place went silent." She stared into her cup, as though the world was there, her past among the dregs. "And then I got a call that my mother had taken ill. I told myself I was visiting, that it was simply an obligation. Visiting my mother was not pleasant, on any level. But I met Matthew at a pub in town the second night and he dragged me out to his farm in Connemara and I stayed, for two years. I fed the chickens and sheared the sheep and mended his clothes and smelled his smells on everything because it was his home and it had been his father's and you weren't getting their smell out of the place."

"And then you realized you hated that narrow life," I guessed.

"No actually I loved it," she laughed at herself. "I loved every minute of it. I submerged myself in two-hundred-year-old floorboards and how to tell the really good eggs from the ordinary ones on sight and installing the electric light that would trick the hens into laying them out of season. And knowing exactly when a ewe was ready to give birth and what to do about it. I loved fixing the well and having my own carrots and potatoes and my herbs growing on the windowsill. I could march out onto the peat bogs, fields of long grass, with water from the rain a quarter-inch below my feet. The grass was so thick I could hear the water lapping underfoot with every step but my shoes never got wet. It was just the two of us together all the time, doing everything together. I loved folding myself into him at night—he was round like a bear and furry too. I loved every second. I loved it too much. Matthew couldn't suffer me after a while, all my womanly fluttering about every little thing."

"You? That doesn't seem like you." Her eyes fluttered now, wavering under scrutiny. It was another glimpse of the girl who wrote in such a careful hand, who thought long and carefully about every word but shared her poetry with no one.

"I've learned my lesson, sir. *You care too much about too much,* Matthew said. Mister Yeats says the Irish have fanatic hearts and I'm Irish to the core. You're not the only person who's vanished — at least a part of me vanished out there, and I was shocked to find I liked it that way. I gave myself up to a greater cause, to the bigger thing that was 'us.' This is what women learn from the cradle, you see. So I didn't read the signs. I wondered why he never spent a punt on the place, patching things long past repair instead of replacing them. I knew things weren't going well but I was a woman — I figured they'd right themselves. He didn't have another woman, so we'll work it out."

I laughed. I couldn't help myself. "That's what my ex said. 'Men don't leave unless there's another woman.' "

She offered a curious look at this, waiting for me to add on but I was done. I don't talk about the ex unless you make me. "So I came back from visiting a friend in Dublin for a weekend," she continued after a polite moment's wait. "He was gone and the place shuttered, the animals sold and me out on the street. He'd been waiting to sell, since before we'd met, you see and when he got the chance, he took it. Sold the whole parcel without a word, sold it right out from under me. My clothes and costume jewelry from London, my books and music, he left neatly packed in town, as though those were the things I would miss. He left them at the pub here, the pub my father had bought and my mother had sold."

"Where you work now?"

"Where I work now." She lifted the last of her tea in salute. "My mother's gone, my father's long gone but I'm working at the old place now and it's alright in the way that real life is. But I miss that farm. I miss that shared solitude." And she smiled her Jillian smile at me again. "I don't think I've spoken about that to anyone since I moved back here. So now you know something about me. More than I meant to tell. More than you wanted to hear, probably."

"No," I murmured. "I love it all." I felt mired in story debt, actually. And a thought came to me which I blurted out without the thought of censoring myself.

"Actually, the only one being taken advantage of here is *me*. She's getting what she wants, I guess. I wish I understood better what she wants and why but she has to have her reasons, right? I can't make myself responsible for other people's choices, now can I?" I sputtered to a stop.

"What's got you in such a twist?" she demanded. "Life's about now, isn't it?"

"I...just want to be fair," I said, without being even slightly sure I meant it. "I want to be fair to everyone."

"I've never thought that possible. Fairness is a trap; choosing and living with your choices, that's freedom. Maybe that's where you started to vanish." She seized a wedge of cake on my plate and began scarfing it down. "Do you want to go for a drive?"

Six minutes later, I stood in the middle of her block watching her wrestle the locks of her car. This was an affectation—anyone could have pulled the doors off without half-trying. It was an English Ford, at least fifteen years old. The fenders looked like papier-mâché; the engine clattered like a Brooklyn radiator on the first day of winter. The back seat was filled with placards: "No War for Oil" "Power without Limits is Injustice"; "Not Anti-American; Anti-Bush" on top of the pile. In *this* car, my knees were in my chest and my skull nestled in the headliner, or whatever was left of it. I hoped she would be a gentle driver.

"I see you're the chief anarchist."

She laughed. "I'm driving the lot of us to the train in the morning, so I have the propaganda. The Gardai will surely impound my computer eventually—I'll burn that bridge when I come to it."

"I didn't vote for Bush."

"You all say that over here," she replied, smiling.

She barely missed the car in front of her pulling out and jumped the curb rounding the corner. She drove like Mr. Toad all the way through town, across the bridge and out to the north. My head smacked into the roof beams every time she changed direction.

"I'm the *other* America," I persisted, "the old America, the one everyone liked—Freedom of Speech, Habeas Corpus, no Double Jeopardy, all that stuff."

"Oh really?" she said. "Yet you're guiltily taking advantage of someone—either Emily or yourself, you're not entirely sure." She was enjoying this quandary way too much. "Or is that just what comes of power?"

"What power?"

"Men control relationships."

"Honey, you're fighting the last war. Women hold the reins now."

"It always seems to be the men who are leaving."

"Maybe it's the only way we can still feel in control. We're acting out of panic." She laughed at this though I didn't see what was funny in it.

Her headlights were dim; she struggled to make out the curves ahead. The car probably never got above forty but that seemed more than it was made for. Jill's foot stayed pressed to the floor and her conversation never flagged. This careering tumult was the way she traveled; if you were with her, you grabbed the handle over the door and breathed deep.

A second later the car burst out of the trees into a Stanley Kubrick wide-angle. The road carved its way across a lush hillside, the Lough a tureen of dark water glittering below. The engine whined a jig, the narrow tires screeching and hooting at every near-miss. A ghostly monastery glowed on the far bank. I swear you could hear the London Symphony Orchestra swelling in the background.

We rolled down the windows and hung our heads out. The wind whipped through our hair and we burst out laughing, from the buoyancy of the view and the night air.

Five minutes later, she pulled onto a dirt path that wound to the banks of the lake alongside another roofless church. She was out of the car as soon as it stopped moving, wandering to a grove of willows at the water's edge. The Lough rolled in patient swells, gleaming like someone had buffed the surface.

"This is one of my favorite spots," she said, skipping a stone. Headlights appeared on the far shore like moonbeams. "I swear the car would come all by itself if I took my hand off the wheel."

"Like one of Em's horses," I said and knew it immediately for a mistake.

"I *like* Emily," she said with obvious discomfort. "She came into the pub on September 11th and sat watching the telly with us. We all adopted her that day."

"I *love* Emily," I answered and saying it out loud actually seemed to help. "But she tells me what she wants and who can tell if she means it? I'm not sure she knows herself."

We wandered the lapping bank. The grass grew right to the waterline. Trees burst in clusters from the grass and hung over the edge.

And then all at once a rowboat materialized out of the darkness, roped to a fallen tree, crossbeams glowing and spectral. It was a supernatural moment, if only because, speaking practically, whose boat could it have been? The only structure nearby was the crumbling church. Jill noticed it at the same moment I did and, without thought or consideration, stepped off the bank into the stern.

She held out her hand to me, beckoning like a cop directing traffic. I surely weighed more than two of her and the water was already nearing the gunwales. But she was having no second thoughts or first ones either. Come hither, her eyes said and if I'd had sailors to tie me to a mast, I'd have given the order.

I stepped in and the thing dipped right to the brink. I settled onto the center bench and made out a wooden oar at my feet.

When I reached for it, the boat almost upended, swaying like a cocktail shaker. Jillian cackled, bent for the oar and produced another alongside I hadn't seen. Then she untied the line holding us to the shore and we floated out onto the Lough.

"So Emily not knowing what she wants—that makes this okay?" I couldn't tell if it was accusation or just heckling. She'd led me here in the moonlight, after all.

"Emily as much as *suggested* this."

"So what's the problem?"

"The problem is, I don't believe her." That really was the answer, the answer I'd been avoiding the whole night. Now it came tumbling out of me.

"Meaning, she's lying?"

"No. She's probably telling me what she believes. But I'm her friend—she might expect me to see through it." I raised an eyebrow and Jill did the same, in response or mockery. "Women do things like that."

"We do," she murmured, smiling.

"So I don't want to do evil to someone who cares about me—doesn't that make sense?"

I took a few pulls on the oars and we drifted into the middle of the vast blackness. The couple of villages close by twinkled like Christmas lights. I could hear a car chugging a mile away along the far bank. Jill simmered but she came to a bubble quickly.

"First of all," she snapped, "the likes of us don't do *evil*. Evil's too grand, it's keeping life at a distance, dealing with abstracts rather than people." She smirked. "Like America. Or maybe just ambitious men."

"We're not splitting hairs a bit?"

"Ah well, *you're* no Catholic. We're schooled in evil our whole lives. Of course, they're all advocating against but you know by the time you're ten all the thrill's on the other side. You just haven't been properly educated."

I bowed graciously to the curse.

"Don't worry about evil," she continued. "Just make a decision. Decide that she means what she says or that she doesn't. Or suspect she's lying and do what you want anyway."

"Those are my choices?"

"I suspect I'm leaving out several of your favorites but I don't care."

"My favorites? Like, for instance?"

"Like avoiding life because it scares you and blaming Emily for it. Like denying your own desires because they make you guilty."

"*How* long have you known me?"

"Ha! All my life."

She opened her arms and raised them to the sky. "I mean, all this worrying, and we're just a mote in God's eye—look!" I followed her gaze upward. Every star I'd ever seen now had a million brothers and sisters, the whole firmament rim to rim freckled with constellations.

I drifted, lost in that sky, for several minutes. Then I took a breath and started over. The problem wasn't Emily. The problem was, cheating wasn't enough for me. I'd never have the energy to hide someone from Emily and I'd never want someone I was willing to hide.

I wanted Jill to be crazy about me the same way I was about her. I wanted to be wanted. That was what I couldn't get from Emily, because somehow, she couldn't give it and because it wouldn't mean anything if she did, because I couldn't return it.

But anything less than that wasn't worth cheating for.

Jill leaned over the side and trolled her hand in the water. The ripples fanned in all directions undisturbed. It seemed entirely reasonable to imagine someone discovering them hours later at the far end of the Lough.

"I act on what I feel. You just think too damn much," Jill said. "I won't be a hypocrite. If we want to do evil, let's do it and enjoy ourselves."

That was the moment when everything in me surrendered. I bent to kiss her and the boat jerked immediately, first in one direction, then the other. I gripped the rails fast and hunkered down as low as I could. After a fit of rocking, the thing settled back in place, still upright. Jill was hunched in the center, breathing heavily with surprise. We were so close together now, so close. I made a tiny movement towards her and the rocking commenced again.

She burst into a cackle. She threw her arms out wildly in both directions. Of course, the boat didn't move an inch.

"You've been the big man all your life," she said with glee. "Now you can't do a thing."

I touched the oars to the water and took a few ginger strokes back toward shore.

"You're having too goddamn much fun with this, thank you," I said.

"I'm certain you've had women simply because they could see you above the crowd. Now you're nullified. And I can do whatever I like." And she proceeded to sing nonsense sounds and swing her arms back and forth, splashing me obnoxiously.

"Where's your bag?" I asked.

"In the car. Nobody comes here this time of night," she said lazily. We were nearing shore now—I pulled the wallet from my pocket and flicked it onto the bank. She flashed me a look, like what was *that* about? And saw the answering look on my face.

"Ohh don't you dare!" she spouted but too late. *Nullify me? Nullify yourself.* I leaned the tiniest bit in one direction and then the other and that's all she took. The boat went over like it had been hit by a cannon shell.

The water was only about three feet deep but it hit like a blast furnace. My entire body went prickly hot in violent reaction to the icy water. I grabbed Jill to carry to shore and every place we touched stung like needles. It didn't help that she spent the whole distance punching me vigorously about the head and neck. "Are you crazy?" she yelled. "*Jaysus!*"

My teeth were chattering like the bird house at the zoo. I was hauling the rowboat, still upside down, behind us, the rope stinging my frigid fingers.

The bank was a dirt wall a foot above the water—no shoreline of any kind to create a transition. I lifted Jill with one hand while righting the boat with the other; that shut her up for a second, though she was still shivering like a cat. I waded back out to retrieve the oars and then sprung out of the water. My clothes weighed a ton.

Hers were clinging to her. She had a sleek shape, athletic and girlish. She saw me staring—I didn't pretend not to--and despite her shivers, pulled herself up, giving me full value on every curve. Proud of her body without apology, the way women are now and it's a glorious thing. They call themselves goddesses, these modern women and they earn the title in moments like these. But if they're goddesses, we have to be Gods to measure up.

I tied the boat to the stump again and retrieved my wallet. When I turned around, she'd disappeared. I headed for the car—it would be just like her to leave me there freezing. But it stood in place with her nowhere in sight.

"Over here!" I followed her voice to the church-hulk. It was definitely eerie in the moonlight, like a silver-gray picture frame with no picture. I stepped down carefully through the doorway and wandered past several huge marble crypts. The light was streaming in where there should have been a roof and through the empty window casements. I cast shadows in several directions at once. With all that light, I still didn't see her. "In here!" she said again.

She was *inside* the crypt of Lord Charles so-and-so, next to the ancient pulpit from when this was a working church. The lid of the crypt, which looked like stone but wasn't, was propped against the side. There wasn't an awful lot of empty space inside. She had squeezed the water out of her blouse and hung it over the edge of the box; now she was peeling away her skirt.

She smiled up and nodded for me to join her and I panicked. What with the cold and the exertion and the jet-lag, I wasn't at all sure what I was capable of. Suddenly this all seemed to be happening very fast.

"I might be a bit taller than Lord Charles," I warned, trying to find an out.

"Oh, come on," she said. "They had him in here with a broadsword, a shield and a suit of armor—you'll fit." Finding no alternative, I climbed over the side. The thing was larger than it looked and surprisingly warm.

"Is there a heater?"

"Eight-inch stone walls and a 400-year-old bed of moss underneath," she explained, beginning to unbutton my shirt.

"Well, not just moss," I said, wondering where Lord Charles' sword had gone, just to try to keep myself from thinking. *Don't think, don't think. Don't think about not thinking.* "You're sure Lord Charles won't be offended?"

"It's a little late now," she said, pulling off my shirt and unbuckling my pants. "Sorry to burst your bubble, but you're not my first," she confided.

"In *here*?"

"We've only recently developed co-ed schools in this country and I was an early starter. This is just far enough out of town and it had a lid so if mourners showed up, we could just wait them out—and have a lovely time at it."

"You've done it with the lid on?"

"You think they buried him in 1124 with a fiberglass lid? We pushed the thing off one night after the visitors left and the stone split to rubble. Thankfully, they never found us—my Mam wasn't paying for *that*." My pants and shirt were now squeezed out and hanging on the sides.

"I have to tell you," I said. "I'm not all that sure what I can do. It's been a while. I might be entirely harmless." This was the last thing I meant to say but somehow, I had no control in her company. She wasn't forcing anything out of me—I offered up my entire inventory without being asked.

"Don't worry about it," she said. "We'll fool around. We'll have fun."

She held her arms out to me and I pulled her close. Her body was ripe—she had filled in to the peak of her shape. Her pores were tight from the cold and damp—I kissed her shoulders and ran my hands over her. She put her hand between my legs and began to warm the cockles of my heart. And to prove that prayer isn't totally worthless, I felt myself responding at a brisk rate.

"I think you've misled me about your helplessness," she accused.

I took a little swipe at the moss with my hand and moved it across her breast. It left a little green stain, which I kissed away. I swiped at the floor again.

"You're going to get dirty," I warned her.

"Uh-huh" she nodded and her eyes got wide.

About two hours later, we sloshed our way into her apartment. She took a quick peek through the door before dragging me the length of the place into the bedroom.

We peeled our clothes off—she'd stashed the underwear in a plastic bag in the trunk of her car, Em not being the only person who refused to pay for grocery bags—and she drew a bath.

"We're doing so well dirty," I said.

"There's a limit," she replied.

I tumbled in immediately—the warmth was wonderful. She deliciously, tortuously kept me waiting while she hung everything up to dry. It allowed me to marvel at the sight of her, her freckled skin, the story written in the lines of her face, the play of light and shadow across her folds and curves. They say beauty is superficial; I'll admit it's fleeting but as far as I'm concerned that only makes it more profound. It touches us on a level we're defenseless against.

Let me put in a word here about breasts. Men are accused of obsessing over them but it's impossible not to. Each one has its own personality, like a face. Actually, bobbing in the water once she settled in, they seemed more like pets. Hers were lovely—not large but beautifully shaped and sensitive all over—she oohed and aahed at every caress and kiss and tug.

We spent a few minutes getting clean—but not long. Then we were sloshing around, unloading enough water that she complained about her next water bill. I pulled euros from my wallet and began throwing them into the air. "I'm a socialist," I said and she laughed.

We made more of a mess transferring—after a halfhearted attempt at drying off—to the bed, but she was laughing and yelping and not complaining. I trusted my every impulse to be right now, to be her impulse as well. We shuddered together and anticipated each other's changes.

Two big talkers but almost no words now. Mmm-okay. There. Yeah—there. Oh yeah, oh sweet. Yes yes yes. Ooohhhhhmmm...

She was a free-range conductor. A magnetic charge shimmered between us, looping from her skin through my fingers and tongue and cock back to her. And tongue—she loved to be tasted and I loved her taste, lemons and fish, salt and spice. She was pierced down below—the first woman I'd ever had with a piercing. It felt like a provocation, a challenge to dive deeper and longer, to be more intense, to drive her to her limits. We started out sweet and ended in violence, pounding hard until the wave broke.

Around 3 in the morning, she lay with her eyes closed, mouth slightly open. I caressed her shoulder with one finger and she followed the movement without awareness. Her breathing began to mirror the movement of my finger on her—wispy and drawn-out. I continued to stroke her skin, lifting lighter and lighter with each caress, rhythmic and hypnotic.

Finally, I actually lifted my finger totally off her and held my hand open a millimeter off the skin—and as I moved the hand upward, she bent at the neck following. Her eyes were still shut. I started laughing. She opened her eyes and smiled that lovely heavy-lidded smile of the contented lover but she had no idea what she'd done, no sense of the place we'd come to together.

"It's not an answer," she said out of nowhere.

"What's the question?"

"Anything."

"Okay," I said but I didn't mean it. If it wasn't an answer, it was at least the beginning of one. It was at least the comfort of a strangers' touch, that temporary grant of absolution that comes with a new body. And maybe it could eventually be more than that.

She shrugged and smiled. "That was nice. Thanks."

I caught an odd note in her voice. "Are you throwing me out?"

"I'm offering you a graceful exit. I don't want you staying out of politeness."

"What if I wasn't going anywhere?" I asked. "What if I was quite comfortable?"

"Well, that would be different," she grinned.

"And what's with 'that was *nice*' ? I thought we both did a little better than 'nice.'

"We did," she sighed, running her hands through the hair on my chest. "We were…" In a few minutes we were both sound asleep.

Around 5:30, one of us rustled and she said, "Shouldn't you be going?" Her smile was soft but there was something unyielding in her eyes this time.

"Now you *are* throwing me out." She didn't deny it.

"I'll sleep well, on the train to Dublin, thanks to you," she said. "And I'll remember that I'm not protesting every American—only the one most of your countrymen voted for."

"Al Gore?" I said and she kicked me. Which led to a bit more tussling and giggling and surely the sexiest moment in history actually inspired by Al Gore.

SUNDAY

I spotted the signs before reaching Jill's front door. Alongside the radical's library—Marcuse! *Das Kapital* with pages thumbed and notes scribbled in margins!—two pair of jeans way too big for her perched atop the laundry bin; a pile of music magazines sprawled across the cheap coffee table. I wasn't checking—they were just there. There was another man who made himself comfortable in this apartment. It was the reason she'd dragged me through the living room when we first came in.

I held back the protest inside—what was the point? It was just one more place in life where I had no say. She was funny, lovely, uninhibited and skilled at charming and juggling the attentions of all things male. I'd had my romantic dream; now here was reality. I pulled the door closed and marched up the hill toward Em's house.

Violet light seeped through morning fog. Cars appeared out of nowhere without a sound but thankfully not moving very fast. The air was crisp. If I hadn't slept much, what else was new? I'd had three sound, maybe even contented, hours. I understood all at once that my bad sleep started long before stepping on the airplane.

I spotted him first in a garage doorway near the taxi stand, then hovering in the alcove of a bank a block further on and finally in an alley across from the churchyard at the top of the hill. It wasn't till the third sighting that I recognized him as the mandolin player from the pub. Not a likely candidate for hiding in broad daylight, he wasn't quite my height but broader and a bit sinister from the scar across his forehead from eye to ear.

If this was the boyfriend, why was he hanging around outside? The skulking about seemed seriously forbidding, appearing and disappearing out of the fog. When I finally saw him move, bulky and ungainly, even his awkwardness seemed menacing, as though there was too much force in him for elegance.

By the time the town ended in a line of stone walls and broken fields, I was altogether unnerved. I had no idea what Hulk Jr. had in mind but I was not ending up in an open glen somewhere, lying around for months before they found the body. I took off, hoofing uphill at a decent clip. I haven't been running all these years for no reason. When I looked back, after a hundred yards or so, he had already turned back to town.

Em's house was dead quiet when I arrived. I threw on the heater in the bathroom and gathered a change of clothes. Pulling my old ones off, I caught Jillian's scent on my fingers and kept them jammed to my nose all the way to the shower. I could tell Em

I'd had an early run and continued jet lag—that would feel pretty much the way I felt, except for feeling so damn good.

I nodded off for an hour in the same couch I'd slept in the previous night. When I woke, there she was—Emily, paint limning her smock and jeans, hands face and hair. But she was coming from entirely the wrong direction, from the hallway leading from the studio—the hallway running right past my bedroom door. Had I left the door open or shut when I went out? Had she been working in the studio all night? She didn't look angry but I couldn't remember ever really seeing Emily angry.

"They're done, I guess," she said, sinking into the chair opposite me. It took a moment to realize she meant her paintings. "It's like you said—eventually I've just got to decide they're finished, so they're finished." When did I say that? I tried to focus—how could she possibly have stayed up all night? It's miserable to sleep for an hour when you're exhausted—it only reminds the body how tired you are.

"Congratulations," I said but all I felt was queasy inside.

If she'd been in the studio all night, I'd passed her window coming and going. If she hadn't caught me missing, it was just dumb luck.

I felt terrible about lying to Em—although of course, I hadn't said a word yet, so the lying was merely implicit at the moment—and about having sex with Jill right after she'd told me…well, actually, she'd *encouraged* me to have affairs, hadn't she?

This whole situation was very confusing. I knew I'd done something reprehensible but all I could find at the moment were loopholes. If there's anything worse than feeling immoral, it's feeling like a lawyer.

"Why don't you collect the paintings and I'll get cleaned up," she bounced out of her chair, tensile after just a moment. "Then we'll go show them to Maeve."

"Will the gallery be open?" It was, after all, 8:30 am of a Sabbath in a rural town in a Catholic country.

"I don't know. If not, I know where she lives."

That was a hook. Even in my dizzy, guilty state, longing for 42 hours of sleep to add to the three I'd just had, the idea of visiting the roost of Maeve the birdwoman was tantalizing.

And of course, it came to that—forty-five minutes later, we stopped on a residential street overlooking the Lough and mounted the steps of a two-story gabled purple house—royal purple, deep purple, plum-color, the same shade covering window frames and gutters, lintels and banisters. Emily pounded a severe elongated-V doorknocker against the one exception to the color scheme, a brushed aluminum door.

A gap of almost a minute followed. "She doesn't answer quickly," Emily said, fidgeting.

"You've visited her before?" She'd been so nervous meeting Maeve on the street—she was trembling now—that I couldn't imagine her alone in Maeve's house.

"No," she said. "I just know."

A different location might have made this more plausible. But Maeve lived at the farthest edge of Ballynkill, a block from where the street ended on account of running out of hillside.

I had a sudden vision of Emily stalking the birdlady, following her home after work, staring through lit windows with binoculars. It was a comical image, but a week earlier I wouldn't have accepted the concept of Em juggling Malcolm and Maeve and me either. I'm convinced I know people until they prove me wrong but they keep doing it.

Finally the door opened and there was Maeve. I'd wondered in the interim if I'd made her up, exaggerated her in memory a bit. Well, maybe a bit, but only just.

She still looked like a latex sculpture stretched after setting, wearing an apricot robe over a deep purple silk dress—or was it a nightgown(?)(!)—culminating in a swirling tube skirt just above the ankles. And furry slippers. The shade of the dress exactly matched the house paint. This for a Sunday morning in sweet little Balynkill.

"Emily! How delightful! Care for a drink?" Maeve didn't seem even *slightly* surprised that Emily knew her address.

"I've finished them—" Em said, gulping in breath, "—the paintings."

"Wonderful news! When can I see them?"

"They're in the car."

"What? Omigod—well, bring them in! Of course, bring them in!"

I carried the ten paintings disguised in paper and twine up the winding stone path to Maeve's house, ducking to clear the ancient vaulted doorway. This was another of Emily's mysteries— she couldn't keep eating utensils clean but could painstakingly wrap ten paintings for a drive of fifteen minutes.

The inside of the house was gutted—stark modern surfaces, Chinese partitions for walls and the sparsest decoration. Art magazines on the coffee table had clearly been selected—and placed—for color and contrast; you wouldn't think of disturbing the tableau to leaf through the pages.

Maeve had me space the paintings in a pool of carefully placed track lighting alongside a spiral metal staircase. She supervised while Emily stood by in near-panic, arms trembling, legs quaking. Once they were all positioned, Em near bursting, Maeve said, "Alright, *I'm* getting a drink." She threw me a look. "Would *you* care for a drink?" I was the 6'7" guy huffing and puffing so I guess I was hard to miss. It was all of 9:20 in the morning.

"Water?"

She wrinkled her nose at the suggestion. "I have whiskey."

"Anything else?"

"I have two *kinds* of whiskey."

"I guess I'll take the second kind."

"Good choice," she answered with a smile. "And then we can proceed with the unveiling."

She brought the drink, which I wolfed down without thinking. Didn't taste it either. When Em seemed unable to take action of any kind, I began unwrapping her paintings one by one. Maeve stalked back and forth taking them in.

"You say they're a grouping?" she asked finally.

"Yes," Em managed to answer.

"What's the unifying principle?" Emily just stood staring at her, like a schoolchild called on in assembly. "I'm not asking you to wax poetic. If we needed artists to speak, we'd never have progressed past cave paintings. But do you see my concern?" When Emily just remained rigid in place, she turned to me. "Do *you?*" she asked and I nodded.

I was staring at five landscapes, five totally separate scenes. The familiar cabin stood on the familiar hillside. Water frothed through a stone streambed. A crushed beer can lay in the gutter of a cobblestoned street. Snow blanketed the ruins of a castle, tiny against a range of surrounding hills.

They were astonishing likenesses, perfectly, insanely clear and detailed. Detailed to a point no human being could see without psilocybin. But they were strict, observational *pictures* — no emotional overlay, no viewpoint. If there was something here that mattered intensely to Emily, I couldn't have told you what it was.

"I'll take them and I would think I can sell them," Maeve said with a tone that was almost protective. "Are you certain you're ready to let them go?"

It was hard to miss the clanking note here. I wondered if Maeve hadn't overestimated Em; I doubted she was prepared to be as ruthless—or exhibitionistic—as art required.

"Well, yes, let me..." Emily flushed and began replacing the wrapping around the first of the pictures. She fumbled repeatedly. I finished four in the time she did one. As we padded downhill, carrying them back to the car, it was hard to miss the panic in her eyes. The paintings had achieved her vision. Adding more tiny dabs of color wouldn't change a thing. And she'd actually gotten up the nerve to show them. Any next step would be miles out of her comfort zone.

She sat slumped in the driver's seat for a long moment, collecting herself. She seemed really shaken and I couldn't bring myself to disturb her. Finally, just as she reached for the gearshift, a silver Jaguar—the same color as the doorknocker—pulled into the spot in front of us. And then we didn't move for some time. Emily painstakingly adjusted her rear and side-view mirrors, reorganized the chaos of compasses, Q-tips and ballpoint pens in the instrument binnacle and started rummaging through all seven compartments of her bag.

"What are you looking for?"

"My sunglasses."

"It's raining."

"I just want to make sure I didn't leave them at Maeve's," she insisted. If she'd worn them into Maeve's gloomy house, she'd be going in for laser surgery.

And then the door to the Jaguar opened and a tall very elegant woman emerged sheathed in black leather. Em stopped instantly, transfixed. The woman crossed the street and mounted the steps to Maeve's house.

We now abandoned fixing the car, looking for sunglasses and all other pretexts and stared blatantly after the new arrival. "She could be a customer," I said just before she opened Maeve's door with her own key.

Emily put the car in gear and headed back toward town. I kept my silence—was this another blow after the failure of the paintings? The thrilled look on her face gave me the answer.

"She's *gay*," Em exclaimed, smacking her lips like she was working a sucking candy.

Em hummed all the way to Malcolm's, simmering some plan or other. Watching her, I marveled at the blinders we wear with even our closest friends.

How did she know the location of Maeve's house? Was she really a stalker? I was used to thinking of Emily as predictable and benign, as incapable of surprise as a teacup. Things were changing so fast I was getting whiplash.

As we pulled up the tree-lined drive to Malcolm's, we could see a horse trailer carefully backing into the courtyard. "Hmmph!" Emily snorted. "They're on time. No one's *ever* on time around here."

It was the grey from the auction. Emily bounced up onto the truck as soon as it stopped moving and laid her hands on the grey, caressing his head and neck, speaking lightly to him as she did so. She ordered me into one of the decrepit trailers nearby for blankets and we laid them over the horse's back. The truckers wanted their papers signed and the thing taken off their hands, but Em made them wait for Malcolm, the new owner, who had surely noticed the convention in his back yard. He arrived a minute later in a Lord-of-the-manse-type citified suit and cap, accompanied by the bulky sandy-haired fellow from the pub, the owner of the Rudy the Hound of the Baskervilles. Today he was wearing a hat way too small for his head and a vest that left his muscled arms bare in the crisp morning. He nodded at me tightly as though we were members of a secret sect.

"John here will help you settle our new arrival," Malcolm said.

"You're not helping?" Em huffed.

"I'm not interfering with my trainer. Besides, I may have a pigeon for our friend Paul and his mattress but we have to see him today. I assume you'll have enough to occupy you." John started leading the grey out the back of the trailer.

"I suppose," Emily mooned. A moment later, she was briskly directing John up and down the courtyard, happily watching her new grey prance around.

"This way," Malcolm said. I grabbed my laptop and two minutes later, we were in his Mercedes, cutting a stately pace into town. "We're going to visit Seamus McCarthy. I spoke with him last night and he's interested."

Easy for him to say. I wasn't even slightly prepared for a real negotiation. I was coming off three hours of sleep in the last four days and an evening of horizontal rhumba dancing with Jillian. More to the point, Ron and I had never even ballparked a figure for the rights. We'd talked the subject to death without ever coming close to a price.

"McCarthy can market this thing? He has money?"

"He has a variety of interests. Hotels, bed n' breakfasts, a construction company and several topless clubs."

"How'd topless clubs sneak in there?"

"I asked. He said, 'A man has to have a hobby.' He's a busy fellow but available this afternoon." We circled a roundabout and landed nimbly at the train station.

"Where are we going?" I asked, following him to the ticket window.

"Dublin."

The trip, according to schedule, would take almost three hours. Malcolm sat by the aisle reading an investment magazine; I stared out on long green fields and peat bogs, sheep and cows grazing, all that country tranquility. God don't make no back sides, so the farmland didn't seem second class by virtue of laying adjacent to a railroad.

But as we segued into towns and then suburbs, that's what we got—the railroad view of the world; the *back* of everything— warehouses and stores and intersecting clotheslines behind dingy rowhouses in not-very-exclusive neighborhoods. My mood sank with the view.

As we approached Dublin, a growing band of antiwar partisans filled the back of the car. The *demonstration* was in Dublin! They bristled with signs and buttons and nervous chatter, like children off to an amusement park. Absurdly, I wondered if I might somehow meet Jillian amid the throngs.

And then I noticed a couple of real children—two boys, maybe six and eight—staring at us from across the aisle. Staring at Malcolm, that is. I pointed them out and he beckoned them over. The parents looked on enraptured as he signed his picture in some horsy magazine for them.

He was very natural with the kids and I recognized something childlike in him, in his earnestness, the older brother, the leader at school, the one who looked after the others and set the pace. He'd have fallen to such a role early and taken it at face value. They'd eat him alive in New York of course but that didn't feel like a mark against him at the moment. Everything I was dreading about the day was coming from New York.

"I was surprised you were so taken with the bed," I admitted once the boys had returned, triumphantly, to their parents.

"Actually, it's a subject I've been considering quite a lot— the End of the World, that is, not the mattress part. You can't go to the places I've been without the thought occurring to you, that this could be it, that life in those places is… quite like the biblical prediction. Of course, those are not places you'll sell the bed."

"No, I suppose not," I said cautiously, wondering if I should remind him of the home generator option.

"We're selling something," he concluded, "to allow Romans to forget the Goths and Huns and Jews just outside the walls."

Goths and Huns and Jews, oh my. All this foreboding just made me more nervous. I hoped Malcolm wasn't spiritual; It wouldn't be good for him to take this thing too seriously and even a little seriously was more than it deserved.

But our conversation reminded me to call Ron. He would want to be in on the pitch and I *wanted* him in on it. I couldn't really imagine it going well—less and less with every mile—and I didn't want it thrown in my face when it went down in flames.

The retreat still stood in the back of my mind like a castle in the clouds but with about the same odds of my ever seeing it in real life. Emily running a real business—had anyone ever done less with an MBA? Until she put together a real budget and real backers—or at least an ability to focus on a project for more than ten minutes at a time—I had to keep my day job. Which, at the moment, meant Ron—but not yet. It was just 8am Sunday morning in New York and we hadn't yet reached the outskirts of Dublin.

I settled back, listening to the rails click and the crowd buzz, growing lazy for a moment, as though I was on vacation.

I swear I only closed my eyes for a moment.

And then Malcolm was pulling me from the compartment, fighting the tide of dense moving crowd.

The vaulted-roof station was crammed with protestors streaming off ten trains at a time, routed by local coordinators with bullhorns and clotting around makeshift information tables. The stores and booths were doing a landmine business in scones and watches, CD players, books and chocolates. A line of cabs stood politely at the side gate—we stepped into one and Malcolm gave the address of McCarthy's office.

Dublin felt like a workingman's city. The thick brown Liffey uncoiled like a snake through ten centuries of closepacked plain structures, plaster, brick and concrete clustered low and modest around the crouching hills. Architecture threatened at the self-conscious center of town, but most of the place was filled with buildings that didn't even hint at such dandyism. Churches and construction cranes capped every view, the past and future in feverish competition.

Five minutes from the station, we were snarled in traffic that barely crawled. It felt uncomfortably like home. A corner clock tower read 2 pm. I somehow got Ron on the second ring and explained we had a presentation in ten minutes. He was eating breakfast and sounded as dazed as I felt. He hung up to jump in the shower. Malcolm surveyed the crowd and finally told the driver, "We'll walk from here, thank you."

Easier said than done. Lord Edward turned into Dame Street (same continuous road—only the name changed every several blocks) and a quarter mile of widening square opened ahead. A truck just in front of us held speakers already declaiming loudly as the crowd filtered in from all sides. It might not have been the biggest demonstration I'd ever seen but it had to be one of the densest.

"This is not good," Malcolm said, throwing his hands up.

"Where's his office?"

"Right where the crowd is thickest," he replied. McCarthy couldn't have been more inaccessible if he'd set himself up at the South Pole.

We ducked onto a sidestreet for a moment but the march was there too, winding towards the square and leaving stragglers everywhere in its wake. There were families carrying kids on their shoulders or leading them by the hand. Two street bands were in noisy competition, the first in shiny aluminum-foil toxic waste suits dancing to a bagpipe, drums, whistle and kazoo and, twenty feet away, another in facepaint and garish-colored knits twirling flaming sticks. Everyone we passed carried a sign or placard. The feeling was buoyant and hopeful. But all I felt was claustrophobic.

They were chanting all over as we regained the square: 'No War—Don't Attack Iraq.' The shouts rebounded off the nearby banks, insurance headquarters and pubs (of course). Malcolm kept shouting into his cellphone, trying to raise McCarthy. "I can't hear a damn thing," he growled, clicking off.

"C'mon," I said. "Pretend you're a New Yorker."

I put my shoulder down and plunged into the crowd. "Comin' through, comin' through—make some room here," I said, affecting that lovely singsong inflection the beer man has at the ballpark.

People turned at the sound of my American voice, found me half a foot taller than they were and got the hell out of the way. I barreled on, Malcolm in my wake. I threw in a few antiwar chants and peace signs to keep things friendly and we made steady progress. But the crowd was crushing tight and it was like moving through a wall of noise, the chanting coming so loud from every direction.

McCarthy's building showed a curved marble fascia with windows wrapping around the corner. The Dame Street side was lovely and spotless; the other showed a hundred years of city grime. We rang all the buzzers continuously, Malcolm shouting "We're outside!" into his phone, until the door opened and we fell out of the crush of democracy in action.

Seamus McCarthy was red. Fire-engine red, beet red, blood red, a vessel of blood and oxygen, a paragon of ignition. His cheeks were as bloodshot as his eyes, his hair cranberry where it hadn't gone snow white, his freckles had freckles, his gums were the shade of Superman's cape. He was a winner.

I said at the beginning I hated stereotypes and by that score, McCarthy was a complete walkover—just a glimpse of him led inevitably to visions of four-leaf clovers, castles on windswept peaks, the Blarney stone and Guinness. A lot of Guinness. He was surely the face of the drinking man's tour of Ireland. His nose looked like Dresden after the Royal Air Force had finished with it. But stereotype or no, it was impossible to dislike the man, even for an instant. Before we'd said a word, he was already having too damn much fun.

"So boys," he said, first words out of his mouth, "let's get the business over so we can start drinking." The music of his accent only confirmed the first impression—the man was a masterpiece of typecasting.

"We could do both at the same time," I offered. McCarthy clapped me on the back while Malcolm's face accused me of pandering. I was just getting in the spirit.

"No no, a bit of self-discipline is a fine thing," McCarthy continued. "Gives you something to measure yourself against." We crammed into a tiny elevator he operated by hand, throwing over the lever just before we reached his floor.

He had the top, of course. We stepped through empty outer offices to his expansive space overlooking the corner. The place looked largely as it must have in the Fifties: ponderous mahogany furniture, ledgers in stiff sleeves lining the wall shelves, a computer on his assistant's desk alongside a typewriter(!).

We all walked instinctively to the cupola, the corner turret overlooking the demonstration. Speeches echoed off the truck platform. Every inch of the square was packed with the hopeful, cramming the road, the sidewalks and hanging off an iron-grate fence across the way. Placards bobbed up McConnell Street in the sunlight, still crossing the Liffey. The papers reported later that the march monopolized the bridge for an hour and a half.

"Big crowd," McCarthy mused, staring down. I moved to the desk and began unplugging cables to connect my laptop to the big monitor on the assistant's desk. "We like America in this country. Sorry we couldn't give you a better reception."

Was my discomfort that obvious? "It's alright," I said, snaking cable. "They're probably marching at home too, for what it's worth."

"For what it's worth? Not much—dreamers!" Malcolm muttered. "Good intentions don't change the world."

"Jesus preached about the peacemakers," McCarthy offered.

"And look what they did to him."

"My friend, you're a heretic, a gentleman and a celebrity," McCarthy clapped him on the back. "Proof of the simple sophistication of the Irish character."

"And you're a luddite, a crank and a tycoon. Proof we like our powerful men with their warts exposed."

"Which suggests we suspect everyone to have warts and prefer them visible," McCarthy said, settling into a chair to take in the show. "Paul here, on the other hand, is the sensible one. You see he's already hooked up his contraption, which I couldn't do in a hundred years. He may doubt his country's course, but he simply does his job. Sensible and faithful."

Did I say I doubted anything? The foreboding grew in me with every chant rising off the street. "I'm not strongminded," I muttered. "It's a character flaw." I booted the laptop and saw the first page of the presentation appear on McCarthy's big monitor.

"Nonsense," he said. "You have a heart. America has heart, the hope of the world."

Every word of praise only made me sink lower. My stomach was gurgling to the point that I worried about them hearing it.

"Alright," I proclaimed, rushing to work mode, "let's talk about the End of the World."

I ran through the pitch for McCarthy as I had for Malcolm at the pub, though this time using the laptop to illustrate the package of mattress, video screens and music. Malcolm joined in, even repeating some of the lines where I'd misquoted Ron verbatim. He was sincerely enthusiastic. "It's bringing comfort to the afflicted," he told McCarthy and I went dizzy.

McCarthy *loved* the pitch. Ten seconds in, he was guffawing like a five-year-old watching Charlie Chaplin skittering on an icy lake and finished redder (if such a thing was possible) than he'd begun.

"Oh this is wonderful," he stammered between seizures of laughter. "This is the most wonderful foolishness I've ever heard. It'll help you sleep through the Bomb! Terrorist kidnappings! I love it!" He pounded his hand on the conference table in delight.

"Seamus, I think the subject deserves a bit more seriousness," Malcolm muttered.

"Don't worry Malcolm. When we sell the thing, it'll be as though we're selling 'em their own casket, we'll be so reverent." He turned to me, lighting a stogie and puffing away happily — another proof I wasn't in New York.

"This is quite a contraption," he announced. "I want to do something for my daughter. She doesn't go for building things — she likes yoga. She's desperate for the stuff and now she's got me doin' it."

"You're doing yoga?" Malcolm asked — he had no trouble finding *this* amusing.

"No, I'm building a spa is what I'm doing. I've been building bridges and hotels and buying property since I was sixteen years old and that's to the corner and back a few times if you hadn't noticed. I've always followed my own instincts and it's got me here with a corner view and a very pretty secretary and no time to meet anybody but Sunday afternoon in the middle of a riot. And now I'm about to open the biggest spa in Ireland and I think the biggest in Europe — a center with indoor waterfalls and meditation nooks for Irish Hindus or something and I don't know if I like the idea or not but please God, it'll make money. My daughter can run it so it gives her something of her own and I'm having a little fun making it happen which is what I like. Your whatsit'll fit right in — I'll distribute it in Ireland but I want an exclusive the first six months. I'll build a first-class operation and advertise the hell out of it but for those six months, if someone wants it, they have to go to the spa."

I nodded but I saw dark clouds gathering. And then my phone rang.

"I had to check with my vision consultant, just a tuneup," Ron gasped, as though he'd run up six flights of steps. "When does the meeting start?"

"We've started," I said, turning on the speakerphone and placing the cell in the center of the table in front of McCarthy and Malcolm. "Ron Levine, you're on speaker. Colonel Lowell of the Irish Defence Force, who made the introductions, is here with me. We're in the office of Seamus McCarthy, who's about to open the most advanced relaxation spa in Ireland so he's an ideal candidate to represent us here. I've briefed him on the product and the pitch—" I was rushing, speaking as fast as I could. I wanted to lay out the six-month exclusive and that McCarthy was basically sold already. But as I feared, I didn't get the chance.

"Paul, I expected no less," Ron interrupted. "Mr. McCarthy, an honor to meet you. I think we've got a tremendous future for the Getaway Bed in Ireland. The Irish know terror—I think they'll accept the End of the World faster than any other nation in Europe." I held my breath a bit, knowing he was only warming up. "Seamus—may I call you Seamus?"

"You already have," McCarthy grinned.

"And please call me Ron. Seamus, the wonderful thing about the Getaway Bed is that the whole operation is turnkey—we provide the merchandise, software, promotion and scripts to cover every word from first to last. Anyone off the street can follow the script and succeed."

"Don't worry," McCarthy said with confidence, "I can assure you the best sales force in Europe. I'll hire nothing but the finest." I stiffened at this—I knew what was coming.

"Oh *no*," Ron sighed. "No Seamus, that's exactly what we *don't* need."

"Excuse me?"

"The weakest link in any business today are its people," Ron intoned solemnly.

"I understand," McCarthy said. "My people will be second to none."

"No, good people are the *problem*," Ron explained. "I see you're not up on the latest thinking. Seamus, good people cost a lot of money, whether in salaries, commission or benefits. You're always competing for them. Competitors lure them away and use this weakness to cripple you. And when the economy is good, good people start expecting things and that's bad for business."

McCarthy had his fingers on his cigar as though he had something to say but it took a long time for him to get the thing out of his mouth. "Isn't it *good* business for our employees to have things? Doesn't that motivate them?"

"You SEE?" Ron thundered. "You're so perceptive. You appreciate the subtleties. Of course, it's good for our employees to have things—they just shouldn't *expect* things."

The room went silent for twenty seconds. McCarthy looked dumbfounded. Malcolm had found a pencil on the table and was turning it over and over endlessly.

"Ron, perhaps you could explain this a bit more precisely," I suggested. Not that I thought it would help. I'd heard this rap before—oh, had I heard it. I understood it through and through. It was the reason I hated coming to work for the first time in my life.

"Of course," Ron said. "Seamus, when talented employees *expect* things, you lose control of them. They become convinced their talent has value—that *they* have value. The company's profits get siphoned off to the employees instead of stock options, bonuses, retirement packages for the people at the top—you, myself and of course, Paul here as he works his way up.

"But at ground level, the best employees are the ones who know they'd never find this kind of job on their own, who know *they don't really deserve it*. We create a system and *that's* what counts, not the employee. If they make demands, you pick the next idiot off the street, plug them into the system and make them a success. But it's *our* success, not theirs. We're not threatened by their needs and wants. And since they live in fear of losing their job, they never have to be motivated."

I'd been staring at the table while Ron spoke. It was old wood that someone had sanded and stained, that showed the scuffs and gouges, the stains and scratches of real people doing real work over forty or fifty years. I liked the table. I liked what it said. I liked it a whole lot better than anything Ron was saying. I looked up. McCarthy's mouth was open. The stogie dangled at the edge but amazingly didn't fall off.

"This—this is nonsense," he croaked finally.

"Oh, it's not nonsense," Ron responded smoothly. "Look at the big successes today—Marriott, McDonalds, the Gap, Disney—all run by idiots at the retail level. Obviously."

"I've been to America!" McCarthy sputtered. "I've been to Disney—and Marriott! Nice college educated people running them."

"Well, they're not the most up-to-date," Ron countered. "Besides, in America, none of this is an issue—we've got the workforce trained. Since Ronald Reagan, big business has been laying off thousands and thousands of workers at will every year. American productivity goes up and up because we lay off half a department and the people who are left work twice as hard to avoid being next."

McCarthy looked at me now. "Is that really the way it is?" he asked in a hushed voice. I fixed my eyes on the wood of the table and pretended I wasn't there.

"The Irish," McCarthy said after a pause, "are a nation of storytellers. I've been in business in this country my whole life. Business here is conversation, one by one, man to man."

"And woman to woman," Ron added, ever politically correct.

"I'm not up on the latest business theories," McCarthy continued, ignoring him, "but you've got people in this country who could talk the birds from the trees. You really want to make them work from a script?"

"Ohh they MUST!" Ron sounded stricken. "Good people fatally weaken the business plan. Nothing is as efficient as idiot labor. "

I wandered to the window—it was at least a couple of feet away from Ron's voice. 100,000 people crammed the square, waving placards and chanting slogans against an American war that hadn't started, trying to spare a people we hadn't yet attacked.

Malcolm was right—they were dreamers, the lot of them, possessed with an absurd faith in the power of their opposition, believing that 10 million people around the world leaving their homes and marching in the streets mattered. Even McCarthy, up here in this suddenly-stifling room, had spoken of America as the hope of the world. Maybe he knew better now. I looked down wistfully on the crowd, wishing I was down among the innocents.

"The problem, Seamus," Ron continued, "is the global economy—it's cut-throat. You can't make a living any more in America—you have to make a *killing*. Can't leave a penny on the table. Destroy the competition. *Dominate or Die*. If it hasn't reached that point in Ireland yet, it will soon. Paul, tell them what you've been doing these last few months."

I gave the window another glance, checking to see if there was any simple way to just open it and jump. But no. I faced my friendly, seemingly-decent companions and began reciting.

"I've been documenting and flow-charting every pitch, phone response, question, answer, objection and counter for the sale of the Getaway Bed, from first contact with the consumer to selling them supplemental warranty coverage to scripts for technical support in India. Every word is on cue cards and computer screens, flowcharted in succession, so no employee will ever have to think or feel or respond in any genuine way to a customer no matter the situation." I improvised a bit at the end but it captured the spirit of the thing.

In the course of this speech, any resistance I had left drained right out of me. I hated my job, I hated the man who hired me, I hated the grotesque, lowest-common denominator system that rewarded this kind of thinking and the world that allowed such a system to flourish. I hated the whole thing so much I couldn't even hide it from the people in the room with me anymore. That was five strikes. I knew Out when I was it.

"You see?" Ron crowed. "Our purpose isn't selling beds—it's making *Profit*. And Profit isn't innovation, it's control. The Product is just a rationale—Profit comes from relentless, robotic execution. Divide all the work into small tasks, execute them with acceptable quality in the shortest possible time and make the maximum profit. You eliminate self-worth, inspiration, all the distractions and just count the money."

McCarthy had jumped up somewhere in the middle of this speech. He circled the table slowly, lost in a haze of cigar smoke and meditation. He was apparently wearing a pair of suspenders beneath his jacket and sweatervest. Nothing showed but he kept snapping the things as he paced the floor.

"Mr. Levine—"

"Please, call me Ron—"

"Mr. Levine, what you're talking about here is not a business plan but a dream of conquest."

"EXACTLY! And you'd be in it with me!"

"The problem with dreams of conquest," McCarthy twinkled now, "is that all the fun's at the end. I've made myself rather a tidy fortune doing things that gave me satisfaction *while* I was doing them. That way, if things don't work out, you still had a good time."

"That doesn't work anymore, not in business," Ron said, affecting a mournful tone. "Some people hate their jobs for a lifetime. But they can be empowered employees."

"Empowered by fear."

"We're *all* empowered by fear," Ron answered and the whole room went quiet. I wasn't sure he meant to say it but now, the words were in the air, mingling with the chants echoing up from the street below.

"Well, you have me there," McCarthy admitted. "And if you're right, we should be prime territory for you. The Irishman for a thousand years couldn't expect anything worth a damn unless the English or Normans or Vikings were willing to grant it. By your definition, we should be the world's great well of idiot labour."

"Well, I think the system applies to all people," Ron sputtered, finally having caught the scent of the room getting away from him, "regardless of race, creed or ethnic origin."

"*Mr.* Levine," McCarthy boomed, snapping his invisible suspenders faster in time to some tune in his head, "the ultimate laborer, by your definition, would be a hamster. He'll run the wheel until you let him off or he drops dead. Wouldn't you rather be a man?"

"I'm not talking about you and me."

"You're talking about the man I was when I started. If I've become anything more, it's because someone gave me the opportunity—more than once, for that matter. I'm an old man, Mr. Levine. I have a few years left to shape a little bit of the world to come. I prefer to use it building men, not hamsters."

He grabbed the cell phone and clicked it off. "And now," he said, "let's not let bad business keep us another minute from our drinking."

We had to push the door open onto the street. The demonstration was at its peak, the speaker on the truck forecasting a million war dead, the crowd responding with groans and protesting cries. There had to have been ten speakers by this time; the fierce early cheers had dwindled to a wilted, dutiful anticipation, waiting for the end, for *something to happen*. Of course, something would eventually, but nothing this crowd was hoping for.

Exchequer Street, a block away, was just about empty. The wandering clusters here had a slightly dazed expression, as though having difficulty locating themselves outside the hive. Placards lay forlorn and abandoned all over the street. McCarthy herded us to a black-painted pub two blocks down.

It was a labyrinth like Jill's, a cathedral to booze compared to her humble country parish. Intricately carved wood staircases with fluted banisters joined a three-level maze of landings and obscured nooks. Fireplaces appeared in odd corners, primitive frescos spattered the walls, plaster sculptures adorned landings and doorways. You could get dizzy just finding a table.

Or, you could follow McCarthy. He loped directly to the second-floor landing, where a sash marked 'Reserved' sealed off a table with a panoramic view. McCarthy flicked the sash free and we took our seats.

"A million dead," Malcolm fretted. "It isn't likely to be any such thing. The Americans will hit them with a few cruise missiles and the Iraqis will desert by the division."

"Well, they're probably counting civilians as well. It might not be a million," I said.

"My family kept chickens when I was a boy," McCarthy said. "There were always a few of them chattering 'round the yard. I had to feed them and we named them and threw things at them and laughed at them when they clucked at us. And then come the holiday we'd choose one for supper. My daughter thinks this is barbaric but we never thought twice about it. I think it's barbaric to kill something *without* knowing its name."

"Is that your picture?" I asked him, pointing to a shot mounted just above the table.

"It is."

"Who's that with you?" It was a successful face, full of self-regard but not quite handsome enough to be in the movies. Malcolm immediately flushed and McCarthy got louder and blustered a bit in response.

"That's Charlie Haughey. He was the Taioseach here—for three terms, I'll remind you (this pointedly at Malcolm)."

"He was a thief," Malcolm said flatly. "An embarrassment to the nation."

"He stole from everyone he met, without regard to race, creed or background," McCarthy nodded. "He owes me 153,000 punts and we don't even use the currency anymore."

He turned to me. "There was a politician in America when I was a much younger man named Adam Clayton Powell. He was a congressman from Harlem I believe. And he embezzled a lot of money and kept getting re-elected and nobody in the American press could understand how he did it. But an Irishman could answer the question in a second. His constituents were saying, 'Sure he's a thief—but he's *our* thief. You've been stealing from us right along—at least one of ours is getting his own back now.'"

"A poor excuse for dishonesty." Malcolm again, staring militantly out the window.

"Charlie—like a lot of us—started with nothing. And he eventually had houses and the best cars and the best women and the best food and drink a man can have in this world. And, coincidentally, about €1.7 million in debt."

"There's my point."

"But he never intended to pay any of it back," McCarthy added, the twinkle returning to his eye.

"Are you suggesting that as a *defense*?"

"Well at least he was direct about it. He's a charming fellow, Charlie is and I'll tithe a bit for entertainment in this world. And mischief. Politicians are always a tetchy investment but you've got to have them."

There was something genuinely appealing about McCarthy. Anyone who could smile about being cheated out of 153,000 anythings was okay by me. I thought about nominating him for Dalai Lama. Several threads had been raveling under my skin since we'd left his office—days in this country seemed to be weeks in dog years.

Malcolm went off to the bathroom, possibly anticipating the pile of Guinness to come and I took advantage of the opportunity.

"Now isn't this a shame?" I said, staring out at the crowd chanting their slogans below. "All those anxious people seeking world peace and serenity. All those potential customers for a relaxation bed."

"Well there's a point there," McCarthy mused.

"And think of yourself—the father of a generation of Irish."

"How's that?"

"Seamus, c'mon. Don't tell me you haven't thought through the implications of the Getaway Bed. If it'll comfort you in times of terrorism, holocausts and natural disasters, what'll it do if she's simply nervous on the honeymoon? Or the third date? Or *he* is?"

"Men don't get nervous about such things," he said immediately.

"These days they do. Twenty-years old take Viagra because they know they have to perform. Women hold the reins."

"Don't know as I like that much."

"Well, get yourself a Getaway Bed and you can find out. Maybe you won't mind as much as you think."

He laughed at that. He was watching me now, thinking this through. "But there's still your Mr. Levine and his idiotic scripts."

"You've hung up on him now. That should have gotten his attention."

"I did give him a talking-to. You think he might bend?"

"The deal I'm offering you—at the moment with no authority to do so—is you get the rights to the bed and to figure out how to sell it in Ireland. You would have to fit into the general gist of the marketing plan but you could decide how best to accommodate local conditions—and traditions."

"You'd have to insure I won every argument," he laughed but after that faded, he stared at me with a wary look in his eye. "Alright, I'll tell you straight-out: I think this is the silliest contraption I ever saw. I don't think it'll do a thing or help a soul. But that makes it a fine match for the rest of the stuff I'm buying for the spa and at least *this*'ll attract some attention. If I have an exclusive for six months and an interest in what's sold after that, what I gain at least stands a chance of being more than I lose."

"I'll take that as a 'yes.'"

His eyes narrowed. "But what do *you* get out of it?"

"Me?"

"Oh, I'm sure you'll get a commission. But I've been doing this a long time. I've got eyes, boy. You can't stand the job or the man. You think this contraption's as comical as I do. If I'm to trust you, I need to understand your payoff."

"It pays the bills."

"It's a shameful thing if that's all you're thinking about." He gave me a direct look—I would almost say fatherly, though we were both too old for that. "Understand—if I come back to it, I'm coming through you, because of you. Which should give *you* some leverage." It was an odd moment. I barely knew the man and he was conferring his influence on me. It was a big gift—the biggest he had to offer—and it raised questions.

"Not to be ungrateful, because I'm anything but," I said, "but let me throw your test back at you: What do you get out of helping me? You could surely get the same deal out of Ron yourself."

McCarthy lit another stogie. He offered me one but I don't smoke. "I've been the low man in the room most of my life," he said quietly. "I poured the concrete myself until recently. That's all changed the last ten or fifteen years—Charlie Haughey had a good bit to do with that, for a lot of people—but I haven't forgotten what it felt like."

"My father and his friends all had their own businesses when I was growing up," I answered back. "Shoe store, clothing store, supermarket, lady's handbags. My father never seemed to get satisfaction from anything—but his business was more than a job. They didn't feel like modest men, none of them—they considered themselves titans of industry. They were content with their 1500 square-foot empires."

"There's dignity in work," McCarthy said. "Unless you're a robotic stooge reading scripts out of a book all day. I don't know anybody in India but I wish them better than that." The first round of Guinness was laid on the table.

"Should we drink to modest ambition?" I offered and we clinked glasses. "Seems kind of silly."

"I'm not a philosopher," McCarthy lied, "but I don't like bullies. Your Mr. Levine's a bully. You seem like a decent fellow and, with me backing you, you'll make a bit of mischief, I suspect. I like mischief if it's not too serious, and I'm at an age where I can indulge myself in these things."

"Well, I don't want to be a hamster."

"So there's Step One," he said, looking satisfied. "If something more concrete occurs to you, let me know."

"Done," I replied and we shook hands, like the old days, when a handshake was enough.

$$\neq$$

I called Ron three times and hung up on him twice before he actually started listening. By then, pacing back and forth outside Heuston Station, I had worked out a plan.

"*Think globally but act locally*, right? You have to bend, Ron, to make international business work. They had to tweak EuroDisney. Middle Eastern voicemail have men's voices. German cars are geared different for America—more acceleration, less top speed. Remember: '*It's not the strongest who survive, or the most intelligent, but those most responsive to change.*'"

"That's good." Ron demanded. "Who is it? Drucker? Jack Welch?"

"Charles Darwin."

"I know who he is. You think he'd cut it today?"

"We remember his name a hundred years later and the man worked with fruitflies."

"Hmm."

"And McCarthy's the perfect man for us. He's in the hospitality and construction business. He owns politicians. He's cheerfully corrupt. The trick," I said, reeling in the net, "is to make sure he doesn't go completely off the tracks. *Trust but verify*—"

"Ronald Reagan," Ron offered. "That's good thinking. But I don't know anyone over there."

"You know me."

I don't know where the thought came from. No, that's a lie—it was pretty obvious where the thought came from. What was a shock was my willingness to jump so fast, without mulling and wringing hands over it for the rest of the week. It was Jill's influence, not the influence of anything she'd said or done— simply the influence of her inside me, of an attitude inside me that had come to me by osmosis or one of the other natural processes we'd tested the night before.

"I'll stay three months—no more. Just because I have international experience doesn't mean I'm willing to lose all my contacts in New York. I absolutely refuse to stay more than six months, even worst-case scenario. That should be enough."

It had come to me after six beers that if I insisted I wouldn't stay, Ron would have to make me, if only to remain in control.

"You'll stay as long as necessary," he said decisively, like night follows day. "Never base your plans on 'Enough.' *If you want more, you have to require more from yourself.*"

"Charles Darwin?"

"Dr. Phil. I'll have the lawyers get you paper Tuesday or Wednesday. Let's try to get this signed before the end of your vacation."

"Well, that's not really a deadline anymore."

"You can't let the trail grow cold," he replied but it was an awkward moment. I might have outmaneuvered him for the moment but I hadn't fooled him—he knew I wanted to stay. It was like the moment after the woman says 'It's not you—it's me'. Ron could never understand how anyone found him resistible and here was another example to ponder.

I'd done my best to distance myself from Malcolm during the conversation but he was curious—understandably—how I'd managed to resurrect the deal with McCarthy in the time it took him to take a piss. So he ended up closer than I'd wanted.

"You're staying in Ireland?" he said, eyes narrowing.

"Just till we get the kinks worked out," I answered, trying to put off further discussion.

The train was full of protestors but we got seats when a family got off just outside Dublin. Malcolm fidgeted and frowned in all directions but mine. Eventually, he pulled his magazine from his attaché and went back to the same article he'd read on the way in, ignoring me. God, there were so damn many threads to this ol' gang o' mine. It would take weeks to separate them, to see them for what they were. But now, at least, I would have the time.

"I need to stretch a little," I told him and wandered to the half-dropped window between cars. The rails clack-clacked and the wind gushed through the narrow passage. The train resonated to a million nervous striations in the rails, a tremble from legs to trunk to eyes, while the trees along the trackbed created a shutter effect, rendering the world shimmering and miraculous.

We were skimming a flat plain filled with long grass, trees in clumps bowed in the wind. Blunt treeless hills glowed under a sky going purple from the West like ink diluting in a glass of water. The darkening sky seemed to bind all the little effects into some greater whole. Something was awakening in me, something with a vivid bit of hope to it. I tried not to mess with it, to dilute or complicate things in my usual way. Even the thought of hope was unsettling.

And then I heard music ahead, the twinkling of bright strings through train drone and conversation. I wobbled down the corridor through the chattering satisfied crowd.

I can't say that I heard her voice. It's absurd to think I parsed that sound out of the din, but somehow, I stopped just before reaching her, knowing exactly where she was.

"But this will force them to adjust," Jillian declaimed to a crowded table including Sweaterman, a biker type I recognized from the band at the Pub (spiky hair, tattoos, six piercings on his earlobe, the one I could see) and two or three others. "Three million in Rome, two million in London—who knows how many in New York! They simply can't ignore that."

I'd found her. It was a ridiculous coincidence but somehow, I'd counted on it all day. The thrill was all over me before I had a chance to deny or mute it.

"They can ignore anything," Bikerboy said. "It's their world. They let us live in it."

"Oh! Here comes a speech!"

"It's the Imperialist conspiracy—I like that one."

"Laugh all you want. Blair and Bush want permanent war, to expand their power. Afghanistan went too fast. They need something that'll buy them several years."

"Liam, that's a problem for the Americans and British," Jill said. "Our job is to keep the war out of Ireland."

"You won't do that with a march, is my point."

"Right—then we'll do more. But peacefully."

Watching unobserved from a distance, I saw that no single emotion ever appeared on Jillian's face. Sadness cut piercing through bright shiny eyes, laugh lines tangled mischief with worry on her forehead. Every emotion instantly summoned its counter. I was happy to see her, to hear the lilt of her voice. Hell, I was just happy. For the second time in 24 hours, I fell small and addled in the face of real feeling.

"Symbolic measures didn't get us independence," Liam raised his voice. "You've got to be willing to take it to the end."

"In a hurry to martyr yourself? Or just others?"

As they debated, Liam kept reaching—for her elbow, her shoulder—while Jill kept dancing imperceptibly out of range. Sweaterman watched with the same intensity that I'm sure was on my face. I found myself sizing these guys for those extra clothes in her apartment.

She's a vacation romance, I thought, *whether you like it or not* but the words just bounced off, not convincing me for a moment. At this age, I'd remember every day of romance the rest of my life. That was a new thought but it felt right—and there was no comfort in it. I walked into the breezeway before the next car, just to regain my bearings.

There was a loud party in progress ahead. The band from Jill's pub was holding forth, augmented by a couple of fiddle players and a guitarist with a deep old-timey voice.

> *Said I, my dear Sergeant*
> *We are not for sale*
> *We won't take your bargain, your bribe won't avail,*
> *We're not tired of our country*
> *We don't care to sail*
> *Although that your offer is charming*
> *For if we were such fools as to take the advance*
> *It's right bloody slender would be our poor chance*
> *For King George wouldn't scruple to send us to dance*
> *In Iraq where they shoot without warning*

The car roared and whooped. The singer beamed and the rest of the band basked in the response—all except the mandolin player, who remained hunched over his strings, oblivious to all else. The one who'd followed me from Jill's that morning. What was that about? Could *he* be the boyfriend? Certainly, she had several candidates on a string. Counting the cards indeed.

The play between verses was intricate counterpoint, mandolin and fiddle, bouzouki and guitar pushing the tempo, repeating and varying interlocking riffs to near-frenzy. It was a small wonder, the miracle of white men getting off. The song ended with whacking shillelaghs and soldiers being tossed in the ocean, to great cheers.

And then the guitarist missed a chord. He fumbled and then stopped. One of the fiddlers got crossed-up and gave up as well.

It didn't matter to the rest of us. But the mandolin player was clearly infuriated. He continued his fury of notes until the song ended. Then he put down his instrument and bolted for the corridor. Straight for me.

I had no chance to move or even think. He barged into the breezeway, red-faced and livid. His fists were raised; the tunnelvision he brought to the music now focused on walls, doors, targets of opportunity. He looked entirely capable of putting a fist through something—or somebody if they happened to be standing in his way.

And then he looked up and saw my face—and froze. He recognized me instantly but either couldn't remember from where or wasn't sure what he wanted to do about it. I just stared him in the eye as calmly as I knew how—nothing better occurred to me.

"Why do I get so mad?" is what came out when he finally spoke. It was a tiny buried voice, so out of synch with his appearance that I had to convince myself it was his. His fists were still raised and I kept an eye on the doors. My usual response to touchy situations is to get defensive or flip, but somehow now I responded the same way I had to Jill: I said what I felt.

"I get like that too sometimes," I answered, watching his reaction. "I get mad but I don't know why. It's like something I forgot long ago and something sets it off without bringing back the memory."

He wavered for just a moment. And then the deluge hit, from both directions. His bandmates poured out of the front car while, from behind, came Sweaterman, Liam the punk—and Jillian.

"I heard the music stop," Jill said. "What happened?"

"I blew a chord."

"We tried to cover it but—"

"Are you alright, Denis?" she asked the mandolin player.

"Yuh," Denis muttered, resentful, as though caught off the school grounds.

"This one *talked* to him," one of the players said and she turned and saw me. The broadest questioning smile broke over her face and she fluttered back and forth between us a few times.

"Can you play?" she prompted and Denis shrugged. The others surrounded him protectively and ushered him back into the car. The music started up in seconds. Sweaterman and Liam lingered in the doorway, throwing competing covetous looks at

Jill. She followed my glance to them. "I'm fine, thanks," she said and they grudgingly returned to their car.

"Denis doesn't like being talked to," she said, staring up at me. "It seems to make him worse. Did he talk to *you*?"

"He asked me why he got so mad."

Her eyes grew even bigger. "What did you tell him?"

"I have no idea what I said. I just didn't want him to hit me."

"You're *bigger* than he is."

"I don't care—I *still* don't want him to hit me." She giggled and I joined her. And then she answered the question in my head, as though I'd asked out loud.

"He's my brother."

"You...take care of him?"

"Hah! As though he'd listen to anything I say. He was the same with Mam—Denis was too much for her by ten. My father took him to Dublin when he was eleven—I was six. They stopped to get him a haircut though why he should get a haircut in Dublin, I don't know. Da was outside having a ciggie and the bomb went off in a car right across. He was blown to bits and the barber was killed in front of Denis, standing between him and the blast. Denis has scars all over his left side. He had six operations. They said last rites four times. Yet here he is."

"The bomb was IRA?"

"They blamed it on the IRA. We found out since that the British set bombs here to stop us sympathizing with the Republicans. So who knows whose it was? I care about Denis. Did he actually hit anything?"

"He didn't get a chance."

"That's good," she said, fingering a dent in the wall. "This might be one of his old ones. How he keeps from breaking his hands, I don't know. You'd think he'd care, if only for the music. If he couldn't play for ten minutes, he'd go croaky. Sometimes he stays out playing till morning—I don't know who keeps up with him. *I* can't." She arched an eyebrow, playfully suspicious. "What are *you* doing here?"

"I had a sudden business meeting in Dublin."

"Business? On a Sunday?"

"Malcolm said it was the only time McCarthy was available."

"Not Seamus McCarthy."

"Might be—is there only one Seamus McCarthy?"

"Lord I hope so," she replied. "He's a vicious racist."

"I don't think it's the same fellow."

"He is. Owns a chain of hotels and resorts and backs politicians who stir everybody up against immigration and such. Awful man. End of the World should suit him though."

"He does back politicians. There was a picture of him with Charlie—?"

Ted Krever

"Charlie Haughey—"

"Yes."

"Ha! That's a perfect pair. Heckyl and Jeckyl."

"You know Heckyl and Jeckyl?"

"You think we didn't have cartoons? I'm ashamed to be old enough to remember them, is all."

She smirked—we were a bit smug but it was hard to help it. The look in her eyes wasn't vacation romance. They were those eyes you get in the first days, when you feel everything all the time and all the world comes to you through your lover.

I held out my arm—she came over and nestled inside. It was a bit calculated on my part, after watching the table dance between her and Liam but it was also all I wanted at the moment.

We moved into the doorway to watch the band. Denis was in the forefront as always. He didn't seem to have any awareness of how compelling he was to watch. Even when someone else was singing, you couldn't take your eyes off him.

"This is a language he can communicate in," Jill said. "When they're playing, he's the leader. When they take a break, he plays solo. It's the only level on which he functions."

"He was outside the house when I left this morning," I told her. I had to let her know. "He followed me a few blocks. I wasn't sure what he had in mind."

"Oh Lord, " she sighed. "He insists on meddling with things he can't understand. He's threatened men who weren't doing anything I objected to. He's never actually hurt anyone but I try to keep things simple—out of his way—if I can."

Now her face was weary.

"I'm sure I should do better by him but I don't know how. Is *everyone* a disappointment to themselves?"

I answered "yes" immediately. I knew it was so.

Her head settled against my chest and she looked up at me the way women do when they want to be kissed. So of course, I kissed her, several times—it's not like I needed prompting. These were not the previous night's carnal kisses, kisses to kindle sex. There was a tenderness now that was new and an ancient memory all at once.

And then I saw movement at the doorway and there was Malcolm staring at us.

"I tired of holding your seat," he said, tossing my parka roughly at me. "We're coming into the station."

Passengers began crowding the breezeway, pushing toward the doors. When we groaned to a halt, Malcolm shot me a look and bolted into the parking lot. I wandered onto the platform and watched him go. The contempt on his face was no shock—he'd never been far from it and now I'd given him reason. What surprised me was the sadness there, as though he'd caught me cheating on *him*.

Jill stood next to me when I turned around, looking resigned and unshockable, though my conscience told me there was no such thing.

"What do you need?" she asked.

"I need to reach Emily before Malcolm does. At very least, she should hear it from me."

A minute later we were in her Ford careening through town. My stomach was turning cartwheels, my leg twitching to move move move. I burst halfway out the window as it was just to avoid hitting the roof.

We hurtled up the main road toward Malcolm's, where Em was presumably still working her new horse, the source of her happiness—reliable, loyal, faithful, all the things I was not. As we headed uphill out of town, Malcolm was still in sight but barely.

"Where's his house?"

"I don't know—Em drove the one time we went there. Just follow him."

She kept peering through the windshield but we slowed at every turn, hesitant. This was monumentally out of character and I wondered if she was trying to make me crazy until I saw *how* she was peering—squinting, actually.

"Give me my bag," she said finally. I pulled it off the back seat; she reached in and retrieved a pair of glasses. Very fashionable but prescription lenses nonetheless. Immediately after putting them on, we began to gain on Malcolm.

"Why didn't you wear those last night?" I yelped, remembering the cliff road alongside the Loch.

"I don't *need* them," she snapped. "They just help a little."

Malcolm was a decorous careful driver and Jill squealed through every turn. We caught him at the mouth of his driveway and started up the hill paired but he pulled off to park in front of his house. Jill sped past at my urging into the courtyard. I saw Emily turn in the doorway of a stall, startled first by the noise of the car and then by Jillian and I tumbling out of it.

"Hi" I said, rushing up to her, stomach churning and chest pounding. "Remember Jillian?"

"Of course," she said, nodding in that friendly distant Emily way. "How are you?"

"I'm alright," Jill said, nodding tensely.

"We've—" I wagged a finger back and forth between Jillian and me and stalled right there. I'd had this idiotic hope that I might find some elegant or at least nonhurtful way to explain—or explain it all away. But now, faced with Emily's total blank innocence, my courage crumpled. "We—" I continued stuttering and finger-wagging until finally, she caught on all by herself. A wave of painful recognition rolled across her face.

"We've...become entangled," Jill said finally and the air got thick, carbon monoxide where oxygen might have been better.

"Malcolm…came across us on the train," I added, dropping the other shoe. This one made no sense—I was supposed to be traveling *with* Malcolm—but nothing made much sense at this point. "I wanted you to hear it from me first."

Now the ambiguity drained from Em's face. What remained was a mask of pain and anger. Being Emily, she struggled to keep these unseemly feelings under control, but she was clearly having a hard time of it.

I heard a car door slam and, a moment later, saw Jillian full-throttle around the nearest stone wall, racing away downhill.

That's when I felt my cheeks flush. I turned to Em burning.

"Okay, I screwed up. I'm truly sorry you're hearing it now and that Malcolm knows. But you gave me the green light. You told me to have affairs."

She stood rock-solid, not a blink. There was nothing charitable in her look, nothing yielding.

"You can't just assume that I know when you don't mean what you say."

The truth, of course, was the opposite—I knew she didn't mean it from the first. But that was the smallest of lies between us. We'd been playing these games since she showed up at Dyson's shiva. Emily wanted me but didn't know how—or she wanted me but not really, not that way, not as a lover—or she wanted me but maybe she was gay too—or she knew I didn't feel the same way about her—or she'd counted on that—or all of the above—or some combination of the above. How could anyone know if *we* didn't?

"I said don't get involved," Emily muttered bitterly. "You agreed you'd be discreet."

"You brought me over here as a beard without a word of warning. You know I hate my job so you offer me the world's greatest gig—all I have to do is stop *feeling*. Or stop doing anything about whatever I feel. You really thought I could do that? Who's kidding who?"

So now, naturally, Malcolm appeared in a gap in the wall, approaching reverently, like the High Priest entering the Tabernacle. Emily's face pulsed watching him come and all at once, I saw vividly where I'd placed her: vulnerable to him, to his advances. She'd brought me over as a buffer, to take her money, keep her company and keep these messy complications at arm's length. Okay, she was demanding I remain forever as isolated as she was—why not? Since she'd come back into my life—since Dyson's shiva—had I ever been anything else? If I was entirely honest, had I been any different before that?

"I need to know that Paul's been entirely honest with you," Malcolm asked with a look of self-satisfied pain, completing the circuit from moral compass back to asshole in one quick spin.

I was about to respond 'I'm always honest with Emily,' because it's the kind of answer he deserved but I couldn't get the words out of my mouth. And then I heard Emily say, "Paul's always honest with me." Emily my friend. My true and trusting friend, who deserved better than me in return.

This clearly threw Malcolm. In truth, it seemed to throw Emily as well, who'd answered from instinct and wasn't at all clear where it left her.

"Emily's known my nature a long time," I scrambled. "That's...that's why we've never progressed further...no matter how many times I've asked her. Her only concern, when I told her, was that we involved you in our private issues." Okay, maybe I laid it on a bit thick but it served him right for the phony moon face.

He stood stiff for a moment, as though waiting for the simultaneous translation. Then he threw me a poisonous glance and said, "I'll never mention this again, certainly. But there are men in the world who wouldn't *require* your forgiveness." He was gone around the fence in seconds. We waited until we heard the backdoor slam shut.

"Thank you," I whispered.

"Please don't say that," she groaned. "I don't think I can bear it. You can't help but fuck things up, can you?"

I had the illusion for just a second that I couldn't go any lower. Then I realized I still had one more level to sink.

"Em—I have to go. After Jill."

"When did you meet her?" Did they teach that look in women's studies? I'd never cheated on my wife—she couldn't say the same—but I'd seen that look on her face more times than I could count.

"At dinner yesterday." Em winced—it was another spike with my fingerprints on it.

"So what do you want me to do?"

"Help me. Drive me to her place. Tell her you said I should have affairs. Put things right."

Any level below this would require scuba gear. Em had survived cancer and divorce and her ex-husband's death but only now did she seem truly worn-out, shell-shocked. Her shoulders drooped, the hair fell across her face and she made no effort to right the errant strands. The grey had nibbled about half a bale of hay while this scene played out, having wandered as far as his rope would allow.

"I don't know if I can do that," Em croaked, voice old and parched. "At least not now. After I've had a chance to think. Maybe later. Tomorrow."

She knows me too well, I thought. She was relying on me doing what I always did— juggling, keeping all the balls in the air, refusing to commit while I waited for the best offer. In the past, it would have worked. Two *days* ago, it would have worked.

The light was going red across the valley. A tractor casually circulated the field on the far side of the road. The pressure in my shoulders was pushing me faster and faster while the world kept slowing down.

"The Rock of Cashel," I said.

"What?"

"Every morning, we're going to the Rock of Cashel. Except we never get there. I have to go after her, Em. I'm sorry but I have to take your car."

I walked to the thing as if possessed and dropped into the driver's seat. Then I sat like an idiot until she came over and handed me the keys.

The instrument panel was on the wrong side of the car but the pedals were arranged normally below it. The stick shift was on my left though the pattern of the gears was the same as I was used to: 1-2 on the left, 3-4 and then 5 on a dogleg to the right. The difference was, I was shifting *toward* me instead of away and with the left hand of course instead of the right. I had to drive on the left side (*Remember—the LEFT side*) of the road, gaining a really good view of oncoming cars but only the vaguest notion of the position of the stone walls on the verge.

If I'd thought it was scary being a passenger... now everything was *immediate*. The ditch lining the road would rip the suspension out of the chassis if I drove into it. Oncoming cars skimmed around corners at alarming speed without warning. And *forget* the guessing game involved in picking a lane whenever I reached a turn.

It took ten minutes—the whole trip into town—to stop feeling I was sure to kill myself or someone else with every turn of the wheel. Once that bled off, a kind of peculiar humility took over. I'd managed to screw up *everything*. No helpers, no mitigating circumstances other than my own confusion and confusion was a good excuse for getting lost but not for dynamiting everything in sight.

I drove by Jillian's house first but she wasn't there. I headed for the pub but it proved almost impossible to reach by car—the slit-narrow streets in that part of town went one-way in conflicting directions, passing through disconnected pieces of old town wall (old as in around 1000 AD)—it ended up taking me fifteen minutes to reach the bridge and finally her parking lot.

The band was apparently on break when I arrived. Denis was still on the bandstand, tuning the instruments and playing for himself. The place was packed and buzzing.

"Is your sister here?" I asked and he pointed to a door up a staircase above the bar. I ran up the stairs and threw it open.

Five heads swiveled to me as I came inside. It was the revolutionary cell from the train, grouped around a big oak table in the center of the room. Their body language and the crumpled papers in front of them (quickly covered up) suggested it wasn't a symbolic discussion.

"Excuse me. I—I need to speak to you," I told Jill.

"There's nothing to talk about," she answered. When she stood behind the table, it became clear she'd misplaced her bra somewhere—her nipples were adamantly poking through the blouse. I felt my cheeks flush as though they'd been slapped. Liam and Sweaterman both crowded around her instinctively, as though she needed protection. Liam leaned over the table in my direction.

"We've a meeting in progress," he said. "If you wait, you can talk when it's over."

He was being perfectly reasonable but what hit me at that moment was that he knew I'd come to grovel. It was news to me and I guess it doesn't sound like a good thing but it proved what she meant to me, the strength of my feelings. That was unexpected. It had been a long time since I'd had a feeling I couldn't overlook or over-rule.

So I wasn't arguing, just standing like a lump, but Liam apparently took it as a challenge. He drew himself up to his full 5'9" and took on that I'm-the-man-in-charge-pose we all know, even if we know better than to try it in public. "It's a closed meeting," he said roughly. "You're not invited."

"Oh bollocks, Liam," a female voice called from the far end of the table. "We could take a break."

"Yeah why don't you take a break, Liam?" I said, baiting. This almost guaranteed he wouldn't, of course, but I couldn't help myself. It felt like a National Geographic documentary (*Watch the male stags butt horns on the hillside while the female eats the grass and tells herself they're idiots*) but evolution will out, dammit.

"We'll take a break when we're ready," Liam replied and of course the female voice down the table called out, "I'm ready now" to laughter all round. I saw Jill trying to suppress a smile behind Liam's back.

"We'll do things *in an orderly fashion*," he snapped and I retreated out the door, knowing they'd be following in seconds. And they did, the crowd filtering immediately to the bar. Liam followed at the back, Jill behind him. He shot me a filthy look at the bottom of the stairs.

"I just wanted to talk to her."

"So we had to stop for you, naturally," he said, getting in my chest about it. "We Irish should know our place."

"You can stick that one. Someone five-two can hit me with a club and everyone feels sorry for him. If I lift a finger in response, I'm a bully. The US got attacked by eleven green cards with boxcutters; so much for the helpless underdog. When Ireland has power, you can tell me how pure your country is. Your politicians just haven't had American-sized opportunities."

"That lot don't represent me."

"Any more than Bush represents me. Nor wants to either, not me or anybody else unless we can buy our way in. You filled the streets of twenty cities today—you really think their policy's going to change?" His face went slack. "Me neither. If the world has doubts about democracy, it's because they're paying attention."

Jill stepped between us, offering another gratuitous view of her breasts through the blouse, and that, of course, did nothing to calm things down.

"At least," Liam persisted, "we're not running around the world stealing from innocent people."

"And what in particular," I asked, "have I stolen from *you*?" This brought a few trickles of laughter and I realized we'd drawn a crowd. Jill went a shade redder but she was still smiling. Independent woman or not, they don't mind being fought over.

"I *need* to talk to you."

"Then let's talk, dammit" she said, pulling me out the door. I followed her to a grassy walk along the river. The lights of Balynkill glowed in her hair. She stalked back and forth along the wall, shoulders thrust forward and arms folded across her chest like a barrier.

"What do you want to say?" she demanded.

"Emily *told* me to have affairs. That's what I told you and that's what she said. If it was a lie, it was *her* lie, not mine."

"You said you didn't believe her."

"And you knew that before you took me home. So let's neither of us pretend we didn't know what we were getting into. We just don't like the way it turned out."

She gave me the schoolmistress look but I knew better. I've been married—silence just means you don't understand the irrelevance of logic.

"I don't love her," I said, taking a different tack. "I never have."

"She's in love with you."

"She's got seventy candidates—I'm not on the list."

"You're the one she loves," Jill stated, as though she had the blood test to prove it.

"Well, I don't feel that way about her. I've told her over and over."

And now Jillian stood staring at me for ten endless seconds, staring like I'd grown horns.

"Why *not*?" she burst finally. "What's *wrong* with her?"

My first impulse would have been laughter but I knew I'd never survive that. It was a stunning moment on a host of levels.

I'd seen the resentment Emily provoked in women before but this was different—Jill wasn't envious, she just didn't understand how she could compete. All at once, her breezy self-confidence swept away, she even *looked* different—plain suddenly, a creature of insecurities and concerns like the rest of us. Emily really was prettier than she was. That had never occurred to me before.

"How could she be so wrong about you?" she continued. "After knowing you all this time?"

There it was: if Emily was the ideal, the easy lovely companion she appeared to outsiders—and I already had her—and I was going after Jill, that made *me* suspect; inherently fickle, suspicious, unreliable, insatiable. It made me a *man*. The notes that rung deepest in me—the real feelings Jill had awakened—were simple proof to her of my superficiality.

I stood dumbfounded, watching the river glide past, regal and serene, proof that, if you just kept moving, you didn't need a purpose or a plan. At least not if you were a river.

"Maybe she thought I'd come around—or that she could buy my affections," I said finally, leaving out the fact that I'd *hoped* she'd buy them. "Maybe she was a modern American and only thought about results. Jill, nobody knows what anyone else feels."

"That's the dearest rubbish," she answered, face ignited. "If we can't know, how can we trust?"

This night was not like the last. Jill was fragmented, volatile. I was a mess, lost in my desire for her and my fear of my own need. I had a sickening sense of déjà vu, watching the pattern of my marriage reasserting itself—the more I wanted my partner, the more distant she got.

The night before had been lust and hope. Now both were tempered by expectations. We had been champagne in fluted glasses; now we were nitroglycerin in the back of a pickup. On a bumpy road.

"How could you not know what she felt? It was all over her," she asked, teasing me on the couch.

"She could be gazing at me with blind worship and I'd still think of her as good ol' Em."

"Women aren't that blind."

"No, you know when a guy's paying attention. Of course, you might pretend not to notice if you're not interested." No response. "You might even get mad at him for paying attention if you don't feel the same in return. But you're not blind."

Everything was sour. We were kissing but nothing was igniting. If that had happened the night before, we could have tabled the matter and started over later. But now, the night after the night before, it was a suspicious, discomfiting follow-up. We eventually did have sex but all it did was accentuate the space between us, the way our planets had gone retrograde.

When we finished, she rolled over the other direction. She hadn't shown me her back before. Certainly it's possible for a person just to roll over but this wasn't it.

"Hey," I said, running my finger along her shoulders, "come back to me."

"See, this is where you go wrong, you boys" she said and just being grouped stung. "That's as much of me as you get. It's my bed—I'm in control here."

"This isn't about control—it's just you and me."

"Ah but it isn't," she cooed. "It never is. It should be just the moment, the way we feel right now. But greed always gets in the way with men. You have to control us."

"Sorry, but that's the pot calling the kettle black." She had me riled now. I just wanted her to want me back. What was complicated? Why was everything a battle suddenly? "You knew I was going to show up. You leave your bra home and Liam and I nearly have a fist fight. And you were soaking up every minute of it. You and the leftie Irish coffee klatch."

"We're doing important work," she sniffed, though I knew she was just mad I'd called her on her nippleage. "We have to keep Ireland out of the hands of the war machine."

"Well, good luck with that." I was being an asshole but it was her fault.

"These are matters that concern all people of good faith," she said stiffly. "We may not be in the front lines but we do real support work in Tibet and Sri Lanka—"

I nodded sympathetically. I knew about that.

"—and Darfur—"

Yup, knew about that one too. That was good work. Maybe if I just kept nodding, things would heal a bit.

"—and of course, against the enslavement of the Palestinian people."

My hands were in the air, waving the subject away, before I had my first thought about what a suicidal move it was. By the time it hit me, it was already too late—I could see the dismay on her face.

"What?" she demanded.

"Well—you know..." I stammered. If we'd been in the kitchen with anything to stick down my throat to choke on, I'd have gone for it. " 'Enslavement' is...kind of a tough word..."

Her eyes grew wide and not in a good way.

"You mean...you support...the Zionist entity?"

"What? No, I mean—the *what*?" I'd replayed the phrase three times and still didn't understand it. Or maybe I did and didn't want to. All I could do was ask.

"The Zionist entity. The apartheid regime in the Palestinian territories, oppressing the dark-skinned indigenous population."

Okay. Now I got it.

"You mean Israel."

"The Zionist entity," she repeated stubbornly.

And this was where things had to go, like night follows day. If there was an absolute worst path for us, we were dutybound to visit, if not take a lease. I wasn't sure Basque Separatists had a good brief but couldn't she have been for *them*?

"Don't tell me you support that regime," she said firmly.

A lengthy—for us—silence followed. A kind of peace was settling over me, the kind of peace I'm sure is common while they're tightening the noose around your neck.

Here was my punishment for almost fifty years of never figuring out what it meant to be a Jew. I'd slid through services, ignored *kashrut* and any holiday that didn't offer latkes, I'd dated and married non-jews in exclusivity. Among my friends, I was the radical self-ignoring Jew. And now I was going to be offered up on the altar of the foreskin? Surely that was the only thing to separate me from the goyim.

"I can't believe you have nothing to say to defend yourself," Jill sputtered.

"To defend myself? For being a Jew?"

"You're Jewish?"

"I was raised by Nazi-bait," I nodded. "Everyone in my family who was old enough, they either killed or just missed."

Now, I have to admit this wasn't a virgin speech. My family had come up at odd moments in my history and the Holocaust reference had never failed to summon the appropriate hushed reverence. Until now.

"You don't *seem* racist," Jill mumbled to herself, as though I wasn't right there across the bed from her. "But how can you justify the killing?"

"*Racist*?! Both sides kill."

"The Palestinians kill three in a disco and the Israelis bomb a neighborhood and kill 250. And no one says a word."

"That's true."

"Don't patronize me."

"I'm not—"

"And don't give it the back of your hand. Remember, we talked about this—treating people as abstractions, *that's* the evil in the world."

"Okay but let's back off a little, okay?" I said, trying not to resort to begging. At least not yet. A million feelings were elbowing for space in my frontal cortex and none of them came close to the part that just wanted to hold her and stop thinking so damn much.

"I just came from a city where 'freedom fighters' killed 3,000 of my fellow citizens. I went to work past funerals for a month after September 11th, I remember it real clear. As to Israel, I haven't liked an Israeli government since Begin came to power. I liked the old Labor boys—kibbutz's, worker's collectives, 7000% inflation every year, you should like that. Abba Eban, Ben-Gurion. The closest to real communism there's ever been in this world."

I left out Golda Meir despite the feminist angle—she went after the Munich terrorists and that seemed like shaky ground at the moment. "I'm against the killing on both sides. I'm a Gandhi man m'self."

She was staring at me, wanting me to clarify, wanting me to find some position she could accept. Jesus, she really wanted me but this really really mattered to her. I tried to remember a time when I believed in something in the outside world that much. If I could, I had a chance to get out of this.

"I don't give a shit about the Israeli government. I think there has to be a Palestinian state and I don't know what the fuck is taking them so long getting there. I've got one bottom line, which was set by the history my parents lived through: There has to be some place in this world for Jews to go where their own government can't kill them because they're Jews. Period."

This to me was the killer point, obvious and self-evident, like Freedom of Speech or the Right to 250 channels of cable. But Jill ignored it without a tremor.

"I suppose it's reasonable considering your background. You can't be expected to...we're all human, we all have weaknesses and prejudices."

She appraised me now like a Ming vase with a crack in the side. "You're not a racist," she offered, giving this postulate an Oliver Hardy tuck of the chin. "I know you're not."

"Gee, thanks," I answered, combative. Considering my *background*? "Okay, now hear this. You want to say it was dumb to give Palestine to the Jews, no sane person could argue with you, though where else they could have offered us, I don't know. And the Palestinians, by the way, have no better right to that land than we do—they moved in after we were kicked out by the Babylonians or the Romans or Sumerians or whoever the hell kicked us out last, I don't remember. Kicked us out *illegally*, not that anybody cares.

"One way or the other, the Jews are there now, millions of them—and not going anywhere without a bloodbath. And the Palestinians have been their own worst enemy—they've never had a leader who could deliver when a decent peace deal was on the table."

"That's because a decent deal's *never* been on the table," she spit. It was amazing how good her articulation was, considering the speed she was talking. She was *focused*. "The only truly fair deal is a single-state solution."

I had to run this one over in my head—twice—before I admitted to understanding it. "You mean one state with Palestinians producing three babies for every Jewish child? Following on sixty years of 'Kill the Jews-roll them into the sea'— and the Israeli government giving them every reason to hate them? That's the *fair* deal?"

I looked at my Jill, sitting up with her bedclothes strategically drooping over one lovely breast. The girl who forced me to the genuine, who brought out the real in me, preaching this fantasy like it was the light from above. She was talking genocide and simultaneously teasing me with her boob. At least the Nazis didn't send Leni Riefenstahl out naked at the gates of concentration camps to entice the Jewish guys to enjoy the hot shicksa.

"No, I've got it," I said. "I got the problem—Jews are just too *bourgeois* for you. We're westernized, uppity and middle-class—no fun to sympathize with. The Palestinians give great value—they're poor, helpless and exotic. They're a disorganized band of freedom fighters and the Israelis are super-robots with laser guided missiles and nightvision. But remember, sweetie—they're no more dark-skinned than we are. Would you bring me home if I showed up wearing a yarmulke and praying three times a day facing East? Because I have Jewish friends who do."

She looked stung but I didn't care anymore.

"I went through a whole fracas because of the guy who sold coffee on the corner by my office—the FBI was all over him September 13th, wanting to know where his son was, because the kid drove around in a Toyota with a Palestinian flag hanging from the rear-view mirror and he'd been back to visit the family a couple times in the old country. I knew the kid—he was dating a black girl with very expensive tastes and trying to get a hip-hop gig, good luck. He was a dreamer, not a bomber.

"His father and I don't agree on the Middle East but neither of us thinks a one-state solution is a possibility. And he'd laugh if I called it the Zionist Entity."

I shot her my most sarcastic face. "How many Muslims you got in Lisheen? Or Jews, for that matter? It's real easy to be certain when nobody's going to confront you, isn't it?"

She lifted the sheet up to cover everything worth seeing. "Well, you have a temper, don't you? You really could shoot yourself in the foot, that's sure." She pulled an old nightshirt off a chair over her.

"You haven't told me I'm wrong yet."

"You're wrong. Of course, you're wrong."

Maybe I was. Maybe she was. I didn't see that it made a damn bit of difference. I couldn't for the life of me see why she cared. This was about the world, not us and I only cared about us.

But sitting there, I could see that, for her, it *mattered*. Jillian was not an American girl, satisfied with and corrupted by results. Jillian was Irish. The Scots built bridges, the French perfected wine and cheese, Americans automated everything. What did the Irish do? They *resisted*. Resistance in Ireland was history, virtue, morality, dignity, being. *I resist, therefore I am*: If Descartes had been Irish...

"I think it's time for you to leave," she said. I'd seen it coming and it still hurt.

I started locating my clothes. It was raining against the windows, a nice stiff breeze working up outside. She stood against the glass lighting one of her stinkweeds. "What makes a woman a whore?" she demanded.

"She has sex for money?" It was obviously a trick question but I didn't have the energy to come up with something clever.

"No—she has no control over her sex life. If I sleep with a man because I think he'll pay enough to make it worthwhile, I'm an entrepreneur—because it's my choice. A whore is a slave—to a pimp, to her feelings of helplessness, her fear that she has no other way to survive. Control is freedom. Control is choice. All those things America is supposed to favor, coincidentally."

"My bad—I just thought there was more to this than politics, sexual or Palestinian. I thought there was something *real* here."

The drops were collecting on the window in front of her; she traced lines between them on the damp surface.

"You boys connect these things in a way we don't," she said quietly. "You're not the first. A man once said he'd marry me if I would just tell him my name. Great sex isn't love. We're modern women. It doesn't mean as much to us as it does to you."

MONDAY

Middle of the night in Jill's room, that middle of the night feeling all too familiar by now. Coming to, all groggy in dim light, the room tilted and wobbly and my ears ringing with noise.

We'd gone a couple rounds after I refused to leave—alternately angry, sullen and plaintive, searching for common ground that grew more inaccessible as the night ticked away. I was still in her bed but we were miles apart. And now, at the hallucinatory end of things, a voice—if it was a voice.

"Come out and talk to me." It was a moan, an animal cry, nothing that would issue from a human being. No, a child's cry, innocent and unrestrained. Denis. Denis without a doubt, though I woke as his voice was fading away.

"O God—someone's given him something to drink," Jill whispered. "Don't say anything; he'll go to his room."

The clock read 4 am. "Talk to me or I'll beat the door down," Denis bellowed.

"It's not like you can pretend you haven't heard him."

"That's not the point," she said. She didn't suggest what the point was.

I lay a while, staring at her back, listening to rain, the soundtrack of Ireland. I like the sound of rain, actually, just not all the time.

After a minute, Denis stopped stalking back and forth in front of the door. The whimpering moved to—the living room couch? There, it grew again, louder and desperate. Hopeless. Utter unbuffered misery.

I've never been able to handle the sound of a child crying. When adults get sad, we know there's someone out there worse off than we are. And we protect ourselves from our deepest feelings. But Denis possessed no protections. His pain was without limit. Listening to him suffering was unbearable.

"Go talk to him. Please."

"There's no talking to him."

I cringed another minute. Maybe it was ten minutes. Time lumbered by in knee waders. Maybe it was ten seconds. Whatever. Denis' wailing was approaching Sufi funeral intensity.

"You can't—" That was all I got out.

"Nothing," she hissed, the covers over our heads and her finger in my face, "will make this stop. If I go out, I spend the rest of the night listening to his misery, for which there's no cure. Or I stay here and ignore him and he'll wear down and go to sleep."

"But he's in pain."

"Denis is *always* in pain. Or in ecstasy about a bird outside the window or angry over something I've done or not done. But all feelings full-on, clapped-out, all the time."

She pulled her legs up into her chest and her face into them. "When I was twelve, the doctors wanted to lobotomize him. My mother was useless—after Da died, she folded up. There was a father in town—I don't believe in God but I say a prayer for his soul whenever I pass a church—he helped us. He made Denis' case to people who wouldn't listen to a country girl not of age. Then, when they couldn't handle Denis in school anymore, I gave him to Sean Murphy. Everyone thought I was crazy because Sean was a drunk and a crazy man. But I saw Denis sit quiet watching Sean play his fiddle and mandolin. And now he plays better than Sean did, rest his soul." She was heaving back and forth now, the covers barely over her.

"Denis will claim all your time and energy. If you invest in his ups and downs, you'll be worn out by morning. And I'll have him forever—he's sure to outlive me, given my luck thus far." Her eyes were glistening and she hid her face as quickly as she'd raised it. "He has no evil intent. He simply acknowledges no life but his own." She caught me staring. "Just like the rest of us, only moreso," she added and rolled away, taking the covers with her.

In another minute, his wails died down. In five, I heard him snoring.

≠

The rain was still dripping on the window; dim light still damping the clouds. She was awake, I could tell, though her back was to me still and she wasn't moving. Can a back be tense? Or maybe it was just the sound of her voice in my head, echoing *It doesn't mean as much to us as it does to you.* It was an awful sound, more awful for being so deadpan.

If this was ever to be a vacation romance, that was over now. I knew the ache that comes when you don't mean as much to her as she does to you. The ache was in my right side, just where you get pains from appendicitis. I didn't have appendicitis—I had Jillian.

I carried my clothes into the bathroom and dressed as quickly as I could. As I came out, Denis emerged from his room. I held a finger to my mouth to shush him and made for the door as fast as I could but he followed me right outside.

"You have to help me, mate" he said, hand on my shoulder to prevent me escaping. "Help a fella out, willya?" His tone would have been breezy but for that clamp of a hand on my shoulder. I knew little of Denis but 'breezy wasn't in him. He stood oblivious to the morning's drizzle, slippered feet smack in a puddle, t-shirt and jeans growing damper by the second.

"Help you with what?"

"With a girl, mate. Come on," and now he moved ten feet down the block before turning back to check on me. "Come *on*," he insisted and I went.

We spent ten minutes tracing streets along the border of town, where the backs of townhouses met lumpy long-grass farmer's fields. Denis turned left and right and left again, dead reckoning at each corner. But eventually he turned down a path alongside a burnt orange bungalow and straight into the kitchen door. I lingered outside the doorway, uncertain to follow until he stuck his arm out and dragged me inside.

It was all of 7am so I wasn't surprised there was no one up but he knocked at one of the bedroom doors, persistent in the way Denis could be persistent and finally the door cracked open.

"What do you want?" a just-awakened voice asked.

"Talk to him," Denis urged and she looked through the door crack at me. She'd done some mileage and had a few scrapes—the look in her eyes didn't expect much.

"What do you want?"

"I don't want anything," I said, sounding as innocent as I knew how. "Denis said I should help you. He wasn't clear what kind of help."

"*Talk* to him," Denis demanded and now he was getting worked up. The last time I'd seen him like this, he nearly punched the wall of a train compartment.

"He can talk if he wants," she said and pulled the door open.

Once she took the seat across from me, I recognized her as the occasional singer at the pub, the barmaid who wasn't Jillian. She tightened her bathrobe and waited for me as I waited for some idea of why I was there. Denis settled into a corner filled with musical instruments and started plinking away, which only pointed up the cavernous silence.

"I'm Sheila," she said finally. "Has he introduced me? I suppose not. Why does he think you can help?"

"I have no idea. What do you need?"

"Ha!" she stared harshly at me. But her face softened as she turned to Denis. "Denny you can't just bleedin' drag people over here. I'll go to England in a few —"

"No England!" Denis said abruptly. "Sheila, I want it."

"You don't know what you're sayin'" she scoffed. "I'm sorry he got you involved in this."

"No! *Talk* to him!" If you were waiting for Denis to really talk, you could hold your breath. But the stream of notes from his eight-stringed trebly thing kept up a running commentary; staccato when Sheila barked at him, lyrical and beseeching in between. And she was obviously vulnerable to this sort of cajoling; I watched her soften as the music worked her over.

"And what should I tell him?" She turned to me, stoic. "He's knocked me up and wants to have it. At my age."

"We can!" Denis said fervently. "People do!"

Sheila looked at me like *You see what I'm up against?* Clearly this was a continuing discussion. "Denis, it's getting late already. I'm going to England. Best put out of your mind."

"It's *not* best!" Denis cried and now the playing was cacaphanous, a mad flurry of notes and chords jangling and off-tempo.

"Does your sister know about this?" I asked quietly.

"Hmph! She's the trouble! Everybody worries about my damn sister!"

"Denis—she means to help you, in her way," Sheila pleaded. There was more sincerity in the *in her way* than seemed strictly necessary.

"I don't need her help—I play great." He put down the eight-string thing, picked a mandolin and played an amazing run of notes, then followed with the same display on guitar, banjo and zither. "People like me make records. They're on television. They do what they want." From him, this was a soliloquy. "I don't have to listen to her."

"You live in her house."

"I live here."

"You stay over. You come after closing and go home before morning. That's not living here." Sheila was worn down but she wasn't giving in. It was amazing to watch her persist—Denis could wear down a mongoose.

"You know someplace we can go," he said, turning his whole weight of absurd certainty on me. "You travel. You know someplace we can go. I can play. We could be together." He burned those big green absolutist family eyes into me. "You know someplace," he repeated.

I was stunned. I slumped in my chair. Even if the next step was just 'I can't help' and leaving, it wouldn't be easy. Finally, Sheila stood up. "You want some tea?"

"Why not?" I said, relieved for a moment to collect myself. Denis continued playing one instrument and then the next. He'd done his talking. But the melody changed when Sheila left the room, and changed again as soon as she returned.

By then, I had at least found a question. "Does Jill know *anything*? How can she *not* know?"

Sheila shook her head. "She doesn't think of him as a…she's protecting him, she thinks. Or she's afraid he'll hurt someone."

"I'm a pup if you listen to her," Denis growled, voice deep as a river.

"She has reason," Sheila reminded him. "He's good with me. He's never laid a hand to me in anger and that's more than I can say for some. She treats him as though he doesn't know he's a man." She rolled her eyes. "He knows."

"But she wouldn't keep him away if you wanted to be together, would she?"

"I don't think she's even considered him that way. As for me, Jillian...she went to Dublin, to London. I stayed here. I'm not her sort. She'd be furious. I'm amazed no one's told her already. He's afraid of her—"

"I'm no such thing!"

"—he cares what she thinks, despite all his blustering. And I won't breach her either. I've known her my whole life."

"That's why we have to go," Denis said softly. "It's *her* fault." He continued playing and listening, pretending he wasn't.

I leaned over the couch, close to her. "If you could, you would have him? With—with his problems?"

She smiled. "He's aware of them, you needn't whisper. He's *real*. He doesn't know how to lie, which makes him a rare man indeed. When he tells me I'm pretty I know he means it, crazy or not. When he tells me he loves me I know he does. And when he doesn't say it I know he does also." Denis reddened at this but a smile was on his lips, the hidden smile Jill showed sometimes when she wasn't thinking. "A girl could do worse." She looked at him warmly and the music changed once more. We all basked in the sound of it.

"He could make a living playing," she went on, "but not with that local shite he's stuck with!" Her voice rose in his direction—he hunched lower over his instrument. "But in Dublin or Galway—certainly."

"I could lead a band," Denis said, with conviction. "I lead this one. I would do everything for her. I want a *family*."

All of a sudden, taken entirely by surprise, I misted up. Sheila wasn't one of the beautiful people. She wasn't Jill and she wasn't Em. Men weren't throwing themselves at her. Denis was a bullying, slow, egocentric manchild, but Sheila saw the value in him and, like most of us, he'd responded to being found. We frogs don't become princes but we grow in the sunlight of a woman's attention and I could see that happening here.

And Sheila was formidable, a piece of that red earth I'd seen through the river flying in. If she was with Denis and with child, he'd make a living—she'd make damn sure he did. He'd have his family life and learn to regret it, most likely, like the rest of us.

All this warmed the cockles of my heart for a few seconds—until I realized they expected me to somehow infect *Jill* with this sentimentality.

"But what's this go to do with *me*? Why would she even listen?"

"She *fights* with you," Denis said.

"Doesn't she fight with *everybody*?"

"Usually she's just right and no more to be said about it," Sheila put in. "When you argue, she listens."

"She never *agrees* with me," I argued and Sheila looked at me like I was simple. And maybe I was. I sure didn't see things the way anyone else did.

"I'll talk to her," I said, throwing up my hands. "I don't know what good it'll do but I'll talk to her."

The light was on in Em's studio as I pulled her car into the driveway. I made no effort to keep quiet—what was the point? We would have it out now, not that the result was in doubt. I had wounded and abandoned her—without even being her lover first. I was entirely outside the bounds of moral behavior.

She was stalking back and forth in front of an easel when I came in, staring at the shack painting as though it might attack her. She mixed colors on her palette but ridiculous colors, bright pink and lavender, totally out of place in her earth-tone macro lens universe. Not that I cared.

Not that *she* cared either, I bet. The whole thing was just a sideshow to put off our confrontation. Sooner or later she had to bark at me, tell me off, put me in my place. Sentence me for the afterlife.

"I emailed Maeve that they were done," she said vacantly, as though there was nothing else on her mind. "So now I *have* to finish them."

She wanted to talk about her *paintings*? The paintings that hadn't changed in thirty years? The paintings she kept adding drops of color to without coming close to completing? She stalked the easel, eyes gone to slits.

"I almost slept with Malcolm last night. I basically threw myself at him. That's where you left me."

"Whoa! Give me a break—I'm a crappy friend, but how am I on the hook for *that* one?"

"You kept him at a distance. He couldn't miss we'd had a row. You left me no cover."

"You could tell him you were too upset to think about anything else," I offered. Women have pulled that on *me* enough times.

"Well, maybe I did, without putting it in words," she replied, circling the canvas, brush dangling droopy. "He said he couldn't take advantage of me in a moment of weakness."

"Oh terrific. What the hell kind of man is he?"

"Don't posture. You didn't take advantage of me when *you* had the chance."

"Yeah, well what kind of man am *I*?" If she would just go ahead and get pissed, I could feel properly guilty and start getting over it. Maybe I could even resent her a little for kicking me when I was down. Instead she was complaining I'd left her at his mercy while clearly frustrated he hadn't taken advantage of it.

"So what happened?"

"He brought me home. And kissed me, in the driveway." There was an unmistakable thrill in her voice—she was loving the situation and blaming me for it all at once. I was finally getting the hang of women's logic. It really was a great gig—wasn't there some way for me to get on the *winning* side?

A moment later she leapt to the contact point, spreading thick lines in garish pastel across her super-realistic windy field. I almost jumped to intervene—my first reaction was that she was defacing her own work. But something had changed in the *way* she attacked the canvas and it stopped me.

Emily had always painted with tunnelvision focus, building out from narrow detail. Now her whole body was grinding, shoulders and arms, wrists and legs and fingers. This was a physical act of creation.

The first attack took a minute and a half, maybe two. When she was done, I was so caught up in the experience of watching her paint that I couldn't see the picture for itself. And then, as she moved on, I did.

In the foreground of her insanely detailed field now stood the figure of a woman—a lithe young shape, beginner's curves. But not really a woman—a *design* for a woman, a filled-in line drawing, broad form without detail. A cipher with a peach face and a lavender Edwardian dress, skirt billowing, wide-brimmed hat at a coquettish angle and an abstract quizzical expression on an outlined face. Elegant and distant, she crossed that twenty-five-year-old field of windblown grass, stooped as if searching for something hiding in the weeds.

I'd told Em at Sarah Lawrence to add something that jarred, to make the viewer pay attention. And now she had. This painting, finally, grabbed you by the throat, powerful and enigmatic.

She placed the canvas on the floor near five others lined in a corner, narrow stands barely separating them. She picked up the second and placed it on the easel. She took a rag and began cleaning brushes and palette in turpentine (the smell hit me in the *eyes*), regarding the new canvas like a surgeon looking for the cut line.

A set of photos hung on the wall, pictures she must have taken of herself or parts of herself. Acting as her own model. I hadn't seen them before. When had she taken them?

"So—do you have anything to say?" she asked.

"I have to look at it a while," I answered, staring at the canvas. "It's a big change."

"I mean about last night," she said and I struggled to get back to square one. The whole thing was a whole lot more complicated since *it doesn't mean as much to us as it does to you.*

"Uh—I don't know…what to say. Yesterday I was prepared to apologize a thousand times over but you seem to have weathered the storm pretty well, as usual."

Em attacked the second painting—a roiling stream in closeup, mottled stones and a crushed beer can beneath the water, grass and weeds on the banks—adding a woman's calf and pointed ballet toeshoe flitting across the surface of the brook, almost levitating. She filled in the outline—the leg was wearing stockings. But what she'd added was as spontaneous and unfinished as the background was exhaustive and obsessive. The finished image, a minute later, was simultaneously innocent and fallen and ominous.

"You should know better than to judge by appearances," she remarked.

"Oh? What else *is* there? What else do you offer?"

"That's mean," Em retorted. "I've seen your temper before but that's low." Well, here it was—she was finally, actually angry. Bad timing, sweetie, because I was rolling again, back in bed with Jill, throwing blasting caps at the nitro.

"Okay, let me try to lay it out. You bring me here to be your beard without a word of preparation, you dangle the retreat job— only the greatest job in history and you know it—in front of me without any indication you'll ever actually *do* anything about it. You tell me to fuck other women and get pissed the first time I do. You're pissed at Malcolm for not attacking you and me for not protecting you from him. Meanwhile, you're repainting your old canvases to snag Maeve's approval, though you can't be in a room with her without going to pieces. You want everyone to be in love with you but you don't seem able or willing to decide who *you* want. Am I leaving out anything?"

The upset actually traveled to Em's always-placid face. She shook her head and bit her lip. Her forehead knitted right where American women by the droves were injecting Botox.

"You don't understand—anything!" she barked. It was the first time I'd ever seen her fighting for control. "It's not about love. *Nothing's* about love!"

I was louder of course. Em had no experience raising her voice and I'm an expert. "Well, if it's not about love, then what the hell *is* it about?"

"It's about—*desire*."

The word issuing from her mouth was triumph and relief, something she'd held in forever and, at the same time—to her—the most obvious thing in the world.

"Since puberty, I've had men continuously running after me. And women too, I guess.

"I was twelve, we were driving to Gram's on the Garden State Parkway. Some man—he must have been close to thirty, he seemed incredibly old to me at the time—in a red Mustang convertible followed us for twenty miles, staying alongside our car, winking and smiling at me. I didn't have a clue what to do about it. But I felt right then the *power*, that I would always have a secret life my mother and father and brother would never know anything about. He *wanted* me. I knew right then just how strong desire is."

She wiped her brushes clean, carried the finished painting to the corner and placed another on the easel. A big city chrome and glass skyline, street signs in foreground dictating 'No Parking 8am-12 pm Mon-Fri,' 'Diplomat Parking Only 12-6 pm Mon-Fri,' 'No Standing Anytime'.

"Chemo and radiation take everything but your life. When I got sick, I shriveled up for three years of medicine bottles and doctor's offices, of thinking about dying and clinging to life without any idea what life meant." She drew in the outline of an arm below the parking signs, the hand holding something I couldn't make out yet.

"And then I was in remission and they told me I was clear. I gained forty pounds all at once because suddenly I could hold my food down but my thyroid wasn't working. And these pounds didn't go away like they always had before. My hair grew back but just baby chick fuzz. I tried a hundred wigs but nothing looked right. I found one I almost bought—if I was looking now I would, it was a hoot, bright red and straight as a Japanese woman's hair. I probably could have been someone interesting in that hair in the right mood but it wasn't me and all I wanted then was to be me again." The arm in the painting was now clad in shiny cartoon leather; the hand holding a spray can of paint. She filled in the brand name in blocky, rough letters.

"And you became you again," I said.

"Yes and no. Something very basic changed in me then." She paused, considering the painting—or her story, who knew which?

"There's two kinds of loneliness and when you're an attractive woman you only know the first, which is not meeting the one you *want*—the one who satisfies you or meets your expectations or whatever phrase you like." She waved her hand in the air to dismiss the ghosts.

"When your whole life is people coming after you, that seems like real loneliness. Whenever I was blue, I could always go to a bar and think 'this is somebody's lucky night.' Loosen a button, bend over more than usual, smile and *know* I wasn't leaving alone."

She laid this painting beside the others and placed the last on the easel. She was moving fast by anyone's standards and quantum-physics fast by hers. This whole day was some kind of watershed, the dam breaking.

"But now, with my extra pounds and fuzzy-chick hair, I went to the bar and smiled and watched every man in the place look right through me. I was invisible and stayed that way for a year. When you go that long empty, that's *real* loneliness and I found out what it was like, until I'd whipped myself back into shape. And then I went out and proved I was desirable again, proved it a few times. It wasn't unpleasant, to tell the truth, but it wasn't me.

"I just don't want the sex, which is the only thing anyone thinks of. But I *wanted to be wanted*. Doesn't everyone? I've put so much of myself into... this," she ran her hands across her shoulders and breasts, her belly and hips and thighs.

"*Desire*. It's the most powerful constant, more than money or power or love. Anticipation's better than reality, over and over. And I'm going to have to give it up—soon. Women's bodies wear out faster than men's. I might be a better person when it's gone—but I don't really believe that. And I surely won't be the same. It's my power. No one gives up power in this world voluntarily. Not countries. Not people. No one."

The canvas on the easel now was one I'd never seen. It was unlike the whole rest of her work—an expansive landscape from above, from the point of view of some wandering hawk or circling airplane: mountains and setting sun through layers of cloudbanks.

Again, she jumped to the canvas, adding an old woman, stooped over and withered, to the crest of a mountain. The figure was tiny, almost invisible if you weren't paying close attention. But, if you were, it cast a sadness across the scene. It became a story of loss instead of a postcard.

I was about to tell her she'd done it—not that I was sure yet quite what she'd done—when we heard gravel crunching under tires and a silver Jag appeared in the driveway.

"Jesus! She's here!" Em hissed. "I was going to bring the paintings to her."

She dropped the brushes on the floor, sending them skittering across the planking and rushed into the doorway. Then she stopped dead. "I'll stall her," she ordered. "You clean up." And then she was gone, sprinting down the hall.

A second later, I heard her intercepting Maeve outside: *You haven't seen the property, have you?* But what I heard even louder was her surreal command: *You clean up.*

I stepped over to the kitchen door and took in the carnage. *You clean up.* I was to hide six years of pillage and destruction in the time it took the two of them to circulate the yard. I She could fuck herself. This was impossible. But the muscles went to work while the head was still chewing.

I grabbed the foyer rug and dragged it—along with peat logs, rubber boots, umbrellas, old coats, banana-colored rain slickers and two extra toilet seat covers—into the kitchen. I shoved the whole collection as far into the living room as it would go. Then it was the kitchen tablecloth, lifting by the four ends and depositing the newspapers and pill bottles, computer discs and glue pens, highlighters and trade paperbacks in it onto an existing living room pile, which quivered like Jell-O on Jell-O.

I threw open the kitchen cabinets and discovered Em only used one—everything on the counters went into the other one, in whatever order I picked them up. I slammed the doors shut and said a silent prayer they would hold until Maeve left. The floor was roughly swept in ten seconds and the broom thrown somewhere on the living room pile. Then I shoved hard at the mound nearest the door to get it to close.

The only thing left was the hallway. A middle door stood between mine and the studio—it had remained shut the whole time I'd been here. When I threw it open, I was astonished to find this one room tidy as a chapel, with a desk, bed, a few photos and books.

Not for long.

I picked up all the debris of the hallway—magazines, an oak coatrack, several liters of motor oil, the inevitable horse blankets, clothes (some with tags still on them), canvas stretchers, ancient palettes and spatulas, wood spoons, a model airplane kit, a pair of roller skates, two brand-new computer keyboards, a pearl necklace and what looked like a year's worth of the Irish *Times*—and tossed them through the door.

Outside the studio window, Em and Maeve were heading for the door, Maeve lecturing and Em asking questions, gaining me a few precious seconds.

Sweeping the hall floor was hopeless. I grabbed a flat shovel from the kitchen (what was it doing *in the kitchen?*) and pushed dirt, sticks, broken eyeglasses and leftovers to the far end, threw the window open and shoveled the whole collection onto the field outside.

They were coming—all that was left was the shovel. I tossed it after the rest and shoved the window closed as it hit the ground with a resounding *Clang!*

I wandered back to my room as the two of them made the turn through the kitchen. Relief and gratitude was on Em's face but it wouldn't last—now that I'd pulled *this* off, she'd surely expect lunch for five thousand from five loaves and two fishes.

Em laid the paintings out for Maeve to judge and the dynamic between the two women flipped completely in five seconds. Maeve of the previously-sharp tongue stared with wide eyes; Emily of the previously-quaking knees stood relaxed and confident. She had the goods and knew it. For no reason I could understand, this annoyed me to death.

Maeve, after multiple reps eyebrow-flexing, suddenly turned to *me*. "What do you make of her?" she demanded, indicating the abstract young woman who suddenly, finally, joined these paintings together.

"Visually she's powerful," I said. "But she's a cartoon."

"Is she?" Maeve prodded. "Maybe it's a cartoon universe. Maybe the universe makes her *feel* like a cartoon."

I'd done my time in liberal arts hell. I'd gotten laid a few times from art appreciation but this clearly wasn't going to be my party so I didn't give a shit. "This is someone who doesn't fit in the world, who think she's neater, brighter and more pure than everyone else. She prefers her illusions to the messy complications of coping with reality."

Em, standing behind Maeve, clearly didn't like this analysis, which suited me fine. I was warming to the subject pretty good now.

"She flits across field and stream in fancy dress and toe shoes, without any chance of grass stain or shit sticking to her. If other people exist in her world, the only evidence is parking signs or beer cans in a clear stream. They're either invading her world or she's alien in theirs but they're always at a distance, never at her level. The only connection she makes is defacing a sign with spray paint. She's either disturbed or totally narcissistic."

If I'd been hot when I started, now I was boiling. Em was stone-faced. So much for making up. I didn't even really know why I was angry but there was no doubt *that* I was.

Maeve watched me curiously. Then she turned to Emily. "They're powerful," she pronounced. "They have their own life."

"What about the contrasting styles—?" Em asked.

"That's what makes them," I said, ignoring my sincere desire to be hurtful.

Maeve nodded. "Power trumps style," she continued. "Power is the *point* of style. You will affect people with these pictures. That is the artistic point, which is your concern. The financial concern, of course, is mine." She clapped her hands and rubbed them together like a silent movie villain. "I envision a considerable success here—not simply *succes d'estime*, mind you, but a real financial killing. Not necessarily a villa on Lake Como but almost certainly a summer place in Nice or Tuscany, if handled properly. We simply have to make certain they're noticed. Do you know Celia Markham at the Irish *Times*?"

"I've read her reviews," Emily said. "She's a pompous ass."

"If she likes these, she'll make your reputation. Her opinion is the only Irish one read in London and Paris. Or New York for that matter."

"I think she's brilliant," said Emily.

"She's an insipid toad," Maeve sneered. "She looks like a toad. She *smells* like a toad."

"I still think she's brilliant," Emily repeated and Maeve nodded.

"That's a good spirit," she soothed. Then she turned to me. "So will you sleep with this critic? Wild impersonal sex with no repercussions? She won't remember your name the next day? To sweeten things? For your dear one here?"

It was just disturbed enough to suit my mood. But Emily grimaced before I had a chance to answer. "Paul's gotten ethics at the wrong moment," she said, which was news to me.

"It's always the wrong moment," Maeve answered. "So what about *you*?" she asked Em. There was an undertone in the question, an instant tension in the room that couldn't go unnoticed. Here was Emily's chance but she froze, as always.

"Alright," Maeve sighed, not looking a bit surprised, "where's the fabled promiscuous artist when you need one? I shall simply have to handle things myself."

Emily nearly lifted off the ground. I thought the air might evaporate just from the energy shift. It was hard to believe Maeve didn't notice but she was lost in the paintings, in dreams of money and prestige and maybe in the knowledge that she, Maeve, had pushed this big leap out of Emily. The two stood side by side, entirely at cross-purposes while the connection between them slipped away.

"Why don't you two tagteam her?"

What made me say it? Like I had any idea? Was I helping my friend? Or punishing her by forcing her toward something real, towards the step, whatever it was, that came *after* desire?

"Excuse me?' Maeve started.

"Maybe...we could approach her together," Em jumped in, with a smoothness that took me totally by surprise—and probably surprised her as well. "If you wanted to."

"Well, it wouldn't take long," Maeve replied tartly but all her usual sharpness dissolved. "You would —?"

The way they were staring, it took a moment for me to realize their attention was on *me*. I headed for the front door; no one made any effort to stop me.

$$\neq$$

I stalked down the rutted path at a clip, pumping over stones and tree branches, pushing myself to panting. I wanted space between me and that house, between me and all the connections piling up inside. Of course, no space could ever be enough. We carry our connections with us.

As long as we desired women, they won.

Men needed to actually possess a woman, to have her choose us, for the night or an hour or two or *something*. For women, a hungry glance was a victory, if it came from a man worth wanting. If not, of course, he was a pig for paying unwanted attention.

Our needs were ridiculously childish but theirs were just as shallow. Everybody was counting the cards and angling for control. There was that word again, that stinking filthy word. At least control was filthy if you didn't have it.

Jumping an Irish ditch, I flashed back to a couple hours with Jane, the Network Vice President of Marketing. It was the winter of 2000, before everything fell apart; we'd been working non-stop for two days on Asian market presentations and clip reels, selling my show to advertisers who'd barely heard of the network, much less me.

Somewhere in the second afternoon, we'd become aware of the buzz, the electricity between us. I'd suggested dinner. She already had a date, with the head buyer for some conglomerate. "But I'll be done early," she winked naughtily. "He's getting *dinner.*" She agreed to a second date with me around 1030.

Instead of dinner, we had bubbles—champagne bubbles and bubbly lines tossed back and forth on the giddy exhilaration of two bodies wanting each other.

After a few drinks, we stepped into the street. The snow was making little whirlpools in the air and every moment was weighted with the knowledge that she was flying to Tokyo the next morning. I cornered her in a doorway up the block and we began to kiss and paw. She gave as good as she got.

And then just as things seemed to be peaking, she led me to the corner, hailed a cab and leaned out the window to kiss me, saying with exasperating feeling, "You made a good case for yourself tonight—real good." Like it was a compliment. I couldn't help but hear John Lennon's mocking voice in my head as the cab pulled away: 'Thanks to you ladies and gentlemen—I hope we passed the audition.'

The moment had driven me crazy ever after. I wasn't madly in love—compared to Emily and Jillian, Jane was a pale player indeed. But surely at least the *lust* had been real.

What kept nagging at me, looking back, was her face in the cab window pulling away. She was triumphant, while, by my standards, nothing had even happened. After playing that picture over and over in my head, I'd come to the conclusion she didn't think I'd last. The conclusion didn't really fit the facts but it was all I could come up with.

But now I understood.

Jane was another of the world's entrepreneurs, an opportunistic player in the flesh market, forever seeking acquirable, perishable assets. *So many men, so little time.* Surely that t-shirt hung in her closet; I simply didn't get far enough to see her in it.

For a desirable woman, the game was to prove and reprove her desirability, to prove that someone—better, a platoon of someones wanted her. Even if she didn't want them back. Hell, she probably got bonus points if she didn't.

I'd spent my professional life trumpeting the values of the free market and here it was in all its wretched glory. Love couldn't be quantified, but desire—desire could be made evident, obvious.

On our night leading up to the taxicab, Jane's stock rose 62.3% because she'd been out with two men and both tried to go home with her. She'd enhanced her value further by refusing but retaining an option on our services at a later date. Maybe she'd had another guy waiting for her at home, who knows? Either way, she was advancing in a bull market.

Emily in her ditzy confusion was racking up points on two continents. Jill had a diversified portfolio on a more localized basis. *Think globally, act locally.*

The new liberated woman didn't just want to get laid like the old Hefner man but she counted the notches on her belt just the same. We'd given the sexes a chance to become equal and they'd chosen to become equally shallow, equally parasitic, equally oblivious to real feeling.

Who would protest this turn of events? Most guys certainly wouldn't complain about getting laid more often, assuming they really did. The rest of us were just losers anyhow.

I reached Balynkill, pumping past the market and the church on the hilltop and tilting toward Jill's pub on autopilot. I wouldn't find answers at Jill's. All the place offered was the bottom of a glass and maybe the bottom of my anger and that felt like enough at the moment.

The front room was quiet, two unsuspecting tourists in a booth, not realizing they were missing all the action. Sheila was wiping the bar. I felt a pang, passing her—I'd promised to talk to

Jill about her and Denis. But I'd forget that promise with several drinks and several were in the offing.

The same crowd as...Saturday (the days were getting hazy) occupied their usual places in back. I was greeted by name all round, now a regular. I took a stool at the far end. These were nice people. It would have been wrong to singe them and that was all I had in me. Happily, John the burlyman followed right behind me with Rudy the Hound of the Baskervilles and the room's attention shifted.

"What're you up to, John?"

"Tendin' the new horse."

"For the American?"

"That's Emily—Paul's friend." Glances in my direction for the benefit of newcomers, not that there were any.

"Yeah, she's a slavedriver, that one," John complained. "Back and forth, back and forth. Walk him up, walk him down. And then brush and feed and the usual."

"Such nerve. Asking you to *earn* your money?"

"It's not enough I have Rudy to take care of," John protested to widespread laughter.

A couple of times I caught expectant glances from the crew, that it was my turn to offer a joke or comment, to contribute. I was certainly closedmouthed this day. I was aggrieved. Too many muscles I'd forgotten now hurt too much. I was waiting for Jill to appear so as to know exactly *how* much.

A moment later she stepped around the bend of the bar and her eyes lit up and something sick happened: I got warm all over. Something in me melted despite my determination to piss all over the place. I was miserably happy to see her.

"Another orphan redeemed," she lilted, stepping to the tap.

"Umph," I said. It was as close to rational communication as I could come but she didn't seem to notice. She threw me endearing smiles, only ten hours after *we don't care about you as much as you care about us,* only an hour after Em explaining to me what women want (*Where's Freud's agent? I've got the answer!!*).

I knew this was only more proof of the insincerity of women. Yet somehow everything inside me gave way to her smile and the tenderness in her eyes. Longing trumps anger and I was flooded with longing. We believe what we want to believe and her power over me was to make me want to believe. We were a Vietnam of feelings, the two of us on the road together, the sky full of light, the mud up to our ankles and snipers waiting with their dark eyes behind the trees.

"How's the boy?" she asked quietly.

"He's seen better days."

"Sorry." Hands wiping glasses, sticking them back behind the counter. "Nothing's simple."

"I am. I'm just a simple guy."

"Says you." When had we become languid? It was bizarre; I'd never felt so crossed-up. Maybe she'd relaxed and I'd collapsed.

"But I *am*," I insisted. "I really think I should be able to get what I want. You too, as long as what you want is me."

She sniffed a laugh but her eyes were huge on me. There was feeling there. I checked twice to reassure myself but she kept giving it right back.

"Why *can't* we have what we want? Just like that? When it's right in front of us anyhow."

"We fight ourselves," she said. "We know how unreliable we are. We remember how often we thought we knew what we wanted and…" and raised her hands in surrender.

"I remember when getting laid *stood* for something," I whispered across the bar and we laughed. It was a shock to laugh together again. It felt temporary though. "For men, sex used to be the proof. A girl wanted to date you, she wanted your ring, that might still mean nothing. When she had sex with you, you were special. I kind of miss that certainty." I heard Em's voice as I echoed it. "We all want to be wanted."

"Is this some roundabout way of calling me a tart? Not that you'd be the first."

"Quite the opposite. In New York, you're a normal girl. But you never have to declare yourselves like men, do you? You merely pick among the boys who've declared themselves for you."

"So I never really get to choose at all then, do I?" she answered, with a wistful smile. We both felt the fall from the high place we'd found at first. The mud was around her ankles too and I repented if I'd put it there. Part of me still blamed her for the swamp though.

"We'll talk about it tonight," I offered.

She stared at the ceiling a long moment before replying, "I...can't. I...have plans." And I faded out. Everything faded in me all at once.

Too much, in twenty directions. Too much pain to feel, too much anger to process, too much disappointment, too personal, too absurd, too *much*.

So many big picture items—liberation, entrepreneurship, free love, democracy, marijuana—seemed to offer real potential for improving human life and ended up merely a 3% return on investment for 4% of the people involved and everyone else reduced to drudgery, terror or addiction. Why did hope always end up pounded down to the smallest seed?

I stepped off my stool and staggered a bit putting foot to floor. The group at the bar offered a sympathetic round of chuckles but it wasn't the drinking. It was too much history, too many disappointments, too much heartache to let me stand without swooning.

Who wants a fever? No one. But once you had one, all your judgments went off-scale. None of the fucking useless pharmaceutical companies made inoculations against women. And if they did, the fucking useless insurance companies would rule they weren't a necessity and charge $750 a dose. Which would still be a bargain.

I would go for men if I could. But I'm a straight man, the only choice that guarantees sexual insecurity. Gay men see men as attractive. Women these days—*all* women—know exactly how attractive women are. If you're a straight man, you're a mess, because you never understand why anyone would want to have sex with you.

I'd spent a lifetime chasing women, trying to find someone who thought I was as special as I always seemed to think they were. I'd found one who made my knees quiver and whose smiled warm me even when I was mad at her, who happily obliterated any degree of common sense I had left.

What I seemed to arouse in women, on the other hand, out of self-protection or self-preservation or rank self-interest (and how many articles had I written extolling the virtues of self-interest?), was not love, not feeling, but the need for buffers, all-organic insulation, gel insoles, high-tensile fiber gaskets—or at least more options.

Em's place wasn't my place but I had nowhere else to go. Her driveway was visible at a distance so I saw Malcolm arriving as I stomped up the last stretch of dirt road. Maeve's car was still nestled behind Em's, next to the ancient lorry—Malcolm stood staring at it, indecisive for a long moment, but surely doing the math. An offkilter canvas blocked the studio window. By the time I arrived, he'd just gotten around to knocking at the door.

"The car's here but she's not answering the bell," he said a little too absently. "I'll just come back."

"She might be in," I said, stepping to the lorry to pull the extra key from under the floor mat. "Sometimes when she's painting, she doesn't hear anything." I wasn't thinking about what I was doing. Or maybe I was. Maybe I was tired of women doing whatever they wanted and counting on men to play by their rules. Or maybe I was just tired of trying to figure anything out any more.

"Oh, no bother, it doesn't matter," Malcolm stammered and began edging back toward his car, speaking louder than necessary. "I—I just wanted to drop off some things for her. Some tack and her good boots—she always leaves them at the barn." I knew Em had six brand-new pair of boots in the house—I'd upended almost that many just clearing the hall. "Actually, we should talk, don't you think? About McCarthy? Why don't we get a pint at the pub?"

"I don't like that pub," I said quickly. But what came to me, listening to this stammering run-on, was that Malcolm *didn't want me to go inside.*

"There are five others," he replied. "We should square away the details of our deal before McCarthy signs the contract, don't you think?" He kept motioning toward his car and speaking louder than necessary.

"Plenty of time for that," I answered. He was protecting *Emily.* His loyalty only made me angrier, though I was having trouble narrowing down who I was angry at. "Ron said he'd send the contract tomorrow. Knowing him, it could just as easily arrive Friday."

The surprise showed instantly on Malcolm's face. "McCarthy's already got it," he said.

"He *has* the contract?"

"He got it this morning. He'll sign by the end of the day." I played this back three times to make sure I hadn't misheard. "We really should go over the details, don't you think?" He gestured towards his car. I pulled my cell out. It was getting good signal. No messages from Ron.

"Our deal stands," I told Malcolm. "If you want to, have your lawyer—solicitor, whatever you call it—draw something up and I'll sign it." I took another step towards the door, saw the look of alarm on his face and something inside me shifted. The guy was decent to the point of comedy. I couldn't torture him. I pointed to Maeve's car and nodded. "It's okay," I said quietly. "I know about her."

"Of course, of course," he stammered, the words spit out at a fervent pace. "They're discussing art." And here something in me changed course. I'd been feeding off on my own need, my own pain, my own anger. I knew all about Maeve and Em, but I'd missed the fact that Malcolm the Eagle Scout actually had feelings that were being torn to shreds.

"That's right," I answered, a bit late to sound convincing. "Em has some new paintings."

All at once, I was overwhelmed with sympathy for Malcolm. I was brimming with sympathy for anybody who cared about anybody else in the world. I was the one who thought everybody should get what they want, right?

Malcolm's face took on a stoic repression, the soldier in him moving to the forefront. "Well, if there's nothing to discuss…" his voice drifted off. He got into the Mercedes and backed onto the street.

I unlocked the door and stuck my head through. "Decent?" I called. "Just," Em replied. As I reached the studio hall, Maeve barged out, pulling her silk dress around her as she went. Her face was a reddened mask. Her car was out of the driveway in seconds.

When I peeked into the studio, Em was wavering back and forth on a little divan shoved against the wall. She was attempting to tuck her blouse back into her jeans but this seemed too complex a task for her at the moment. She attempted to stand twice and slumped back down both times. And I was the one who'd been drinking—at least I'd gone out with the intention of getting drunk though I couldn't remember taking a sip now.

"Are you okay?"

"He has *never* shown up here before," she said. She was speaking like a drunken Emily too, enunciating extremely clearly as though her mouth might start detouring if not kept under strict watch. "The one time I have someone else here? *That's* when he shows up?"

"He said he had tack and boots of yours—"

"Damn! Shite! We're hunting tomorrow!" she hissed, pushing herself forward to stand and then leaning back, defeated. "Oh hell...oh hell." Her hair was tangled, her eyes smudged, her expression glazed. She was a mess. She looked glorious. Sensuous, languid, reduced to jello by another woman's touch, for the first time in all the years I'd known her, Emily was truly sexy.

I waited. I didn't need to ask. We'd always told each other everything.

"It was...overwhelming," she whispered "but I can't enjoy ... anything." She swayed back and forth like on shipboard. "I don't know what's wrong with me. She's got an amazing body and—she was so sweet. Who knew she could be sweet? And it felt amazing. So...deep..." Her face screwed into a tribal mask, lines coming from very old places, big dark expressions. "I got...tense instead of happy. I...resisted. I don't know why. I wanted it so bad." She could barely get the words out. "I think she thought it was *her* fault."

And here was the answer to the question I couldn't answer, about me and Em, the red stop light I'd seen every time I thought of touching her. Only now was it clear that the red light came from her, not me.

"It wasn't her fault," Em continued. She was still glassy-eyed. Sure didn't look like bad sex to me. How high were her expectations? That might make one more reason never to have sex with her.

I went to the kitchen to get her a glass of water. On the way back and forth, I passed two sets of brand-new hunting boots, which made me think of Malcolm, which made me think of...

"Will you be okay for a minute if I make a phone call?" I asked and Emily nodded, though she continued swaying and humming disconnectedly.

I retreated to the kitchen to phone McCarthy.

"No, I'm still reviewing," he said. "You can't rush such things. But it should be less than an hour now, if you're in a hurry."

"I'm not in a hurry. Can you review one section with me now?"

"Of course."

I hadn't had the slightest belief I'd actually find a distributor on this trip. Nonetheless, I'd covered enough lawsuits to know that deals were what appeared on paper, period. I pulled my copy of the contract from my laptop case.

"Let's look at section 29F, okay?"

I could hear pages fluttering near the phone.

"29F, you say?" he asked. "29E, that's all there is." I bit my lip for a long moment. "You mean 29E?"

"Seamus, would you be willing to fax me a copy of your contract? And not sign anything until I call you back?"

"Of course," he said immediately. "I made a deal with *you*." He added this as a reassurance, though I needed more reassurance now than he could offer.

I took a second look at my contract. The clause detailing my rights and standing appeared right where it was supposed to be, but now I saw Ron had never initialed it. The devil's in the details, as they say. Business aphorism #36. Maybe #1.

Emily wavered slowly down the hall. "Do you have a fax?" I called out.

"Uh sure—I have one here someplace—still in the box!" She wobbled toward the living room door.

"Oh, that's not a good—" I started but too late. She pulled the door open and the whole place let loose, boxes collapsing and saddles cascading down the piles I'd created that afternoon, clanging, scraping, crashing noises echoing through the house. Em just remained by the door, wide-eyed and dizzy. "Ooooh," she hissed like a deflating tire. I covered the phone receiver. "Seamus, I'll call you back with the fax number, okay?"

"I'll be up till ten," he said. I doubted I'd last that long.

Half a block from the mini-market, the sign read 'Internet Access-Fax-Cellphone Service.' I had seen it the night we arrived and thought of checking my email a few times but it's not as though anyone was missing me. Now I drove down and called McCarthy with their number. In five minutes, I had the contract in my shaking hands. "I'm going to bed," he said. "I'm not dead yet but I finding pleasure in the comfort of my dreams. Speak with you in the morning."

I knew what the contract would be, and it was. Nary a mention of me anywhere. Now that there was a deal, Ron was cutting me out. I'd covered several cases like this over the years, companies sued by the poor shnook who was owed a fee or percentage. The game was old and the outcome predictable. Ron's lawyers would file motions—motions to postpone, motions of discovery. They would offer to negotiate a settlement, which most courts would welcome, if only in hopes of clearing the docket. They would offer nothing and take forever to do so. My counter-offers would provoke a thousand questions. And all the while, my lawyers would be charging by the hour and his would be on retainer. No one ever beat a company at this game. It was business at its most grinding and pitiless.

A producer I worked with once told me, "When I pitch an idea to a network, the crucial moment is when they say, 'Okay—we have your idea—what do we need *you* for?' If I don't have a compelling answer, I'm done."

I was now officially done.

I wandered out into the dregs of the evening. The sun was setting, the streets packed with people heading home to families and dinners, lovers and children, gardens and ballgames on the tube. Or to the pub to down a few with friends before bed. Everybody had someplace to go. I needed someplace to go. I needed a reason to go somewhere.

I wandered half a block before walking smack into Sheila. She stopped just quickly enough coming out of the minimart to avoid a collision.

"Sorry."

"Not a worry," she said. "Lettuce, cabbage, tomatoes and eggs. They shorted our delivery this morning so I'm filling in." She said this indignantly, as though I'd accused her of stealing.

"That was the closest market?" It was as innocuous a question as I could think of.

"It's the *furthest*," she answered. "She could ask someone to deliver—they wouldn't mind—but they'd charge a few pence, so instead she sends me. If she's sendin' me, I'm not going to be quick." She was talking about Jill of course.

"I'm sorry I haven't had a chance to talk to her yet," I offered. Not that I was likely to either, but I wasn't digging a bigger pit for myself, the Grand Canyon already being available.

"No worries, I told you," she sniffed. "Some people waste their life hoping. I'm not of that crowd."

"Well, I'll talk to her. I just don't know if she's going to listen." I really didn't know if I could face Jill at all. Not yet. I was a mess. I needed time. I needed a *vacation*. I kept hemming and hawing in hopes Sheila would let me off the hook. And she kept doing it, but not in a way that offered any peace.

"I'll go to England. Time's running out where he won't be able to argue with me anyway." And she patted her stomach, where the billows of the dress camouflaged her shape and I understood something that had been in front of me for a while.

"You're going for an abortion?"

"You go to England for abortions," she nodded, deadpan, withdrawn, tight as a drum.

I drove a friend to get an abortion in college. She went into the facility a shallow irresponsible sweet girl and came out sober and grown up and not in a happy way. So Sheila's declaration rumbled in my stomach. She was a lot older than my friend had been—everyone in my world was older than we used to be—and a much tougher cookie but that only made her evasions scarier.

Denis would be ravaged if Sheila went—and they'd be torn to shreds by his response when she came back. I'd seen lives go off the tracks before and an abortion was not a little glitch in the works.

Everywhere, you saw people who'd lost their balance—just a little at first, maybe, but from the first slip, momentum started running against them at an ever-increasing rate. They drank too much; they stuck needles in their veins. Some became barricaded in habit, a teacup in the same spot on the table until it became part of the table, pushing off company because they'd miss their soap opera or Ira Glass on the radio, people who thought of the UPS guy as a personal friend.

Stunted, blocked, lost, passive-aggressive, plainly aggressive and vengeful, people whose energy inexorably, inevitably turned bad, until their only satisfaction was to fall asleep across a subway bench or block in an ambulance with a double-parked car, to hack a website or walk into a restaurant with an automatic weapon or a bomb strapped across their chest. The international brotherhood of neighborhood terrorists, people who couldn't fashion any better payoff than kicking back before you kicked them first. People who little by little had reached the end, the point where futile resistance was the only dignity they could muster.

The gap—between them and Denis and Sheila and me—didn't seem very wide at the moment. I could feel the first stirrings of vertigo, the fluttering swoon before a succession of 360's down a sandy grade.

She said "Uh-oh" when I walked in, like there was trouble just in the sight of me. The place was quiet—four or five stragglers at the end of the bar, whispering and throwing darts. Denis and the boys must have been on break, which was a blessing.

"I have to talk to you."

"Here it comes." She bit her lip and stared at the ceiling. "I'm sorry. Go ahead."

"No no, you lead. You've already decided why I'm here so let me in on it."

"I told you I had plans tonight. And here you are. Two days and I'm not allowed plans that don't include you." She smiled her superior woman's smile. "You just can't help yourselves. Men are bred for conquest."

I held my tongue. To be precise, I went blank. Eventually I heard words coming out of my mouth like I was someone across the room.

"If I'm here another three days," this wasted voice that sounded like mine said, "I want to be with you from now until then. I hoped you'd feel the same way about me. That's all."

"Maybe I'm not as sure of myself as you are," she said, voice softening. "Maybe I don't trust my own feelings the way you do."

"Maybe you do—maybe you don't. Why don't you know? Or do you know but you're just not willing to say?"

"Why would I do that?"

"Because maybe you're still counting the cards. Because maybe you like gamesplay better than anything you can actually have with someone else." I gulped saying it. I wasn't trying to hurt her anymore; I was just talking to myself. "That's the thought that truly terrifies me."

She seemed truly thrown by this. Hurt by the words but somehow not angry. Or maybe hurt by them but considering the thought anyway.

I fell back, dutifully, to my objective. "Anyway, I'm not here about that." She raised an eyebrow. "It's about Denis."

" You're going to lecture me on *Denis*?"

"Not lecture. Just talk…"

"About what? I put numbers on the labels of his clothes so he knows which match."

"He's got a woman in love with him," I cut in. "And he's in love with her. They aren't pretty but they *work*. And if you ignore the situation—I can't believe you're not a little aware of it already—if this blows up, it'll be on your conscience forever. And they asked me to so I'm talking to you. Okay?"

She stared at me as if waiting for a password. Fifty emotions slipped across her face before it tightened into sullen anger, at which point the family resemblance was really pretty striking.

"This is a sham," she said. "What do you care about Denis?"

"He's your brother. That's what I care."

"He has a handicap. He has no judgment, whatever his blather. He'll harm himself—and her."

"Oh, and we un-handicapped always have clear judgment? She's chosen him, Jill. He's chosen her."

"Who'd have him?" she growled. "What's he offer a girl?"

"He *feels*—he may be an open sore but he's open," I answered and felt the words catch in my throat. "She sees what's big in him, so around her, he's big. His flaws don't scare her so they shrink. They've found the way, Jill, the way we can't seem to find. They grow each other."

Her eyes were fierce. "This is just a way to tweak me, to get at me."

I put my hands to her cheeks and drew her close. "Leave me out of this. I'm really trying to do something right for a change. Go see them. Give them a chance. Will you do that?" I let go and she nodded.

"And *soon*," I warned. "The train's leaving the station."

I kissed her–the kiss was all on my side but I'd remember how she tasted— and then I was hoofing out the door. I passed Sheila on the way. Her face held a lot more hope than I had for the outcome.

I wandered the riverbank for a while. *Done is done*, I told myself. Life would move on eventually the way it always did. I'd remember her in front of that dark window, drawing slippery connections between raindrops. Maybe she'd be my last woman.

I wallowed in sweet misery for a few obligatory moments. Then I heard her laughter in my head. *Rubbish*, she mocked. *Sentimental rubbish. Love is a fraud and misery a sop. Real feeling passes as soon as the moment is over.* And maybe she was right—who could say?—but there was her voice, ringing in my head, already a part of me. I hated every word it said but I kept listening over and over until the words lost their meaning and I could just lose myself in the sound of her voice and the way it made me feel.

Longing, I decided, was like chemotherapy. It ate away everything in you that wasn't longing, until all you saw everywhere was longing, until everything tasted of longing, until anything unrelated to longing seemed unreal, drained of substance or reality. It was a dead end that felt like truth.

When finally I wandered back to the middle of town, the first thing I saw was Jill flashing by in a black Alfa Romeo driven by—who else?—Liam. Serves me right, I thought.

There was bile in my throat and I reacted in the only way I could: I made the circuit of the pubs of Lisheen. I drank my way up the hillside. Pints of Guinness, jiggers of cognac and some idiot bought me a whiskey to finish me off.

Several kind civilians made attempts to save me over the course of the evening, but you don't go into a pub to be saved. All I wanted was to leave a big fireball when I went down.

Well after midnight, I stumbled toward the outskirts of town. Boulders blocked the road at odd intervals—actually, they seemed to be leaping *into* the road as I approached. *Caution: Life may appear larger in the mirrors.* My goal was still to shut my brain down completely, though that hope dwindled when all that booze failed to get the job done.

A whitewashed stone wall cut across an expanse of field, broken by several narrow roads slinking serpentine uphill toward Em's. In the general direction of Em's, at least. They all looked the same at the wall, and, three feet beyond, everything—I mean *everything*—faded into darkness. Not faux-dark like it gets in the US, where there's always headlights or highway lights or some chemical plant spewing God-knows-what into the atmosphere after dark when they think no one's watching. Pitch-black dark this was, like the world came to an end right over *there*.

After a while, a certain woozy clarity set in. It really didn't matter which road I chose—they were all roads to nowhere so they all went the same place, didn't they? It was a rhetorical question, not that that stopped me from asking and answering several times. Wavering at the wall, I discovered one of the advantages of futility: once you slipped over the edge, you had all the time in the world.

There was no sound anymore. No cars, no voices in a backyard or TV static from a second-story window; not even voices in my head. Not my father's, Jill's, Emily's, not even my own. Real silence—real peace, for a moment. I took the closest road because it was the closest road and, if you're not thinking too hard, that seems like the best offer. Three feet up the hill, I couldn't see my feet, couldn't see the ditches along the edge. I'm tall but that was spooky. I wandered into bushes, hedges, trees. The damn road kept moving around. The second time I walked headlong into a treetrunk I gave up. The ground at the foot of the tree felt like grass or moss or at least something comforting instead of mud or cowpies. It was just a stop on the road to nowhere anyway, so I leaned against the trunk, sank to the ground and surrendered to sleep.

TUESDAY

I woke out of a vivid dream. I was wrestling with Naomi Watts. She was naked. She kept trying to slash me with a big knife. She wasn't angry—she was smiling and laughing and giving me those really seductive eyes while waiting for a chance to cut me. She was really strong too, so I had to keep hold of her wrists and keep her at a distance but at the same time she was naked and she was Naomi Watts so who wanted her at a distance? I wanted her to have whatever she wanted because she was naked and Naomi Watts even though she had the knife and...well, that's all I remember. Of course, I knew all along that she was Jill even though she was Naomi Watts...and even though she had my ex's voice. That *really* threw me.

I was hovering in that morning place before thought and with my ex's voice still echoing in my head. And all at once I vividly remembered what it felt like when we had just met and were madly in love. All those feelings rushed back like a long-wrecked ship washing up on a beach. If you think *that* isn't disturbing, you've never been married.

Confused and a bit dizzy, I sat up and began to take stock of the dawning world.

It was chilly and very damp. Ireland, in case I'd forgotten, the locus of dampness in the world. I was about six feet off the road, lying at the foot of a very small tree in the front yard of a tidy little house that hadn't had one single solitary light on last night. Not even a night light in the kitchen if you needed water. What kind of people turned *everything* off at night? The sky was dim, just the promise of sun beginning to creep through the clouds. Purple clouds. Everything was shades of purple, now that things were starting to register. It was probably 5:30 or so—that would explain the light and the fact that no one had appeared with a shotgun to roust me off the lawn yet. I pushed myself to my feet and creaked onto the road to beat them to it. I wondered where my watch had gone. My mouth felt like leather but my head was only pounding a little.

It took an hour to reach Emily's house. When I arrived, she was rushing around like a greyhound on a track. She'd somehow pushed all the furniture and boxes in the living room against the walls, opening a tunnel between the kitchen and her wing. There was no longer any place to sit in the room but apparently that could wait.

"Your timing is perfect. I've left clothes for you in your closet."

"Clothes?"

"You don't have anything proper to ride in."

"I told you I wasn't riding."

"Of course, you're riding. You don't come to Ireland and not get on a horse. It'll be fun."

"I'm a Democrat. The PETA contingent will skin me alive."

"Oh don't be such a snob. You don't know any animal lovers but me. You're lucky if you know someone who owns a dog."

"I slept with a woman who had two Dobermans. I slept with them too."

"Not more than once, I'll bet."

"You win." At least we were bantering like ourselves again.

But when I followed her into the kitchen, there was the telephone pitched sideways into the center of the table, atop a pile of paper crammed with doodles and Maeve's name written over and over in Em's fastidious handwriting. She caught me looking and her eyes got watery. "What happened?" I asked.

"I don't know. Maybe nothing," Em said, and the tears began to roll down her cheeks. "My calls just ring and ring and then go to the machine. Although I don't know what I'd say if she picked up either." I came over and put my arms around her. She jumped back all at once. "What happened to *you*? You're sopping!"

"I slept in a meadow. It was softer than your guestbed, by the way."

She chuckled and leaned again against my shoulder. "At least I don't have to worry about ruining your clothes," she said and cried for a minute. Emily crying, nice and polite, not loud. Not whimpering. Dignified crying. Emily always had loads of dignity—maybe that was the thing in her I couldn't relate to. But now I rubbed her hair and got some satisfaction from being a decent friend again.

Finally, she straightened up. "Do you think she'll still sell my paintings?" she asked and sputtered a laugh. "I want her to love me, dammit—but even if she doesn't, I want her to sell my paintings. I want the summer house in Nice if I can't have her."

"Hey—*French* lesbians," I offered. "Just think."

"I'm terrible, aren't I? Thinking of money at a time like this?"

"She might be hard at work selling your paintings right now, sweetie," I reassured her. "You don't know why she's away from the phone. And, in the end, we all do what we have to do."

"Do we?" she asked. "You too?"

"No, not me. There's always some nice cliff nearby to throw myself off." We were both laughing now.

"Things still not going well?"

"Things are stopped," I said. "Everything's come to a halt, all round."

"Me too," she said. "We're both stopped."

"Well, we'll just have to start again," I said.

"That's right. So ride the horse, will you? Just to make me happy? I picked a nice safe one for you. You hold the reins and he'll follow the pack. Okay?" After all I'd done, she was still here, still looking at me like I was truly her friend.

"Okay. But not immediately, right? I have to take a quick shower and make a few phone calls."

"Use the middle bedroom" she said. As I started down the hall, she added, "And grab the neck strap when the horse jumps."

"*Jumps?*"

The getup was hanging on my closet door. I grabbed it and carried it into the middle room, to try on while working through phone numbers.

It was as spectacular a suit of clothing as I'd ever seen, much less put on. Black riding jacket, tan breeches and helmet, boots to the knee gleaming like the ocean at midnight. They were rented—the arms and legs were a little short and there was a patch on the seat but I still looked like Errol Flynn on steroids but not as good. I admired myself in the mirror while dialing but then the various overseas connections clicked through and I had to focus.

"Shmuel, it's Paul Roget from New York, I was with Ron Levine at...yes, that's right." Shmuel was one of the Israeli inventors of the Getaway Bed. We had met two months earlier when he came to New York for a technology conference (Ron was convinced the visit was an excuse to spy on us). He had given me his business card and it stayed in my wallet because I'd written the names of several women I'd met in bars on the back of it. None of them ever worked out but I kept the card to remind myself to stop going to bars.

"Shmuel, I have a question: Your deal with Ron—does it only cover the US territory?"

I had awakened in the field with a fragile sense of survival. Nothing in my life was working but I was still here. The sun came up again in the morning, even if it remained behind the clouds. I had options. I could *make* options.

The whole conversation took ten minutes. It turned out Ron hadn't expected me to find an Irish distributor any more than I had—he'd never secured the rights. He'd left Shmuel a message the day before but only after they'd closed for the evening— apparently he was still shaky on timezones. And they weren't rushing to respond, as he was still haggling over the wholesale price of the display beds they'd sent him. Shmuel was only too pleased when I offered myself as an alternative. He promised to stall Ron and gave me 48 hours exclusive to secure an Irish distributor and first option on the EU as well. By the time I hung up the phone, I was the second Jew in history to be resurrected from the dead and the first in a really spiffy riding outfit. *It is double pleasure to deceive the deceiver:* Niccolo Machiavelli. A business quote I hadn't learned from Ron—one I hoped he would learn to regret.

Something was happening. I was breathing deep—the morning air mingled with the manure of the field outside, that putrid gagging airtaste I will always associate with Emily's house. Thank God I don't have much of a nose. But my life was in my own hands for the first time in a long while.

A few more phone calls and Web research nailed down details—shipping companies, points of Irish and EU law. I took in the photos on Em's desk waiting for people to return my calls. One photo I remembered from way back, Em and Dyson and me at some school festival (Mayday? Halloween? No, the clothes were wrong) and another I'd taken of the two of them together, in proximity but not close, tense and awkward in each other's company as always. The oddest of couples.

"Seamus McCarthy."

"Seamus, it's Paul. Would you rather work with Ron or me?"

This conversation took five minutes flat. McCarthy had made clear the other day (yesterday!) that he didn't require a pitch. Nonetheless, I made one, and realized as I was spinning it out that it was my pitch for myself, the open credit account I kept in my head over the years to reassure myself that I was indeed a decent human soul—capable, possibly a bit flakey but hopefully in an endearing way, someone fundamentally trustworthy with a plan for the future. I put it over pretty good, working through my doubts as I went, tamping down the fear that I had only my last few chances to prove it more than a pitch.

"I can't say I'm surprised to see you break with him, m'boy" he said when I finished. "The man's a viper."

"In America he's just a run-of-the-mill boss."

"It's a better world where his type are vipers," he chuckled. "Paul, I don't doubt myself at this age. I trust you. I don't trust him. You have my support. What do you want me to do?"

"Just sit tight for now. Keep reviewing the contract. Let me get the details straightened out. I need a good Irish lawyer."

"Political or non-political?" was his instant response.

"At the moment, all he has to do is vet a contract. But connections won't hurt down the line, will they?"

"I'll give you my own man. He's got a tab goin' at all the major parties and across the northern border as well. They even like him in London, except for the Thatcherites but they're all dying off." He took a thoughtful space, a pause. "Are you sure this is what you want?"

"What do you mean?"

"I don't know exactly. I always wanted my own business. Made me a bit of a king, even when all I had was a farm, three old houses in disrepair and a lorry in rust color. It's like having a child though. They get bad-tempered and willful. They need what they need and they don't care much what *you* want. You sure you want to take this on?"

"I'm still getting used to wanting *anything*."

"Alright, well you think on that," he advised me. "If there's something I can do, I'll do it, within reason."

And that was that. A kind of uneasy peace settled over me. The coup was underway. The troops were massed on the border, tanks moving into position at the front of the columns. I collected my pile of notes and enjoyed the breeze taking the curtains and the dust motes floating in the sunlight. And then I glanced at the other pictures on the desk—and one in back jumped out at me.

It was certainly Dyson and it must have been Emily—it was her photo, after all. After picking it up and angling it into the sunlight, I could see it *was* her, just very young—maybe 14 or 15. The body language in the picture was a particularly ungainly example of their familiar tension. On second view, Dyson looked pretty loose by his standards; it was Emily who was all torque. What gave me a start was *where* they were—a hillside in front of a shack. *The* hillside, *the* shack, the one from Emily's painting, the scene Emily had been obsessively painting for twenty-five years, the picture Dyson hated. Dyson and Emily had actually been together at the shack that spawned her art, however much of it there was.

All of a sudden, that painting morphed inside me: cartoon girl in a photorealistic world, a woman totally out of place in her surroundings, uneasy in her own body. And barreling right behind came the cuts on her arms and the dentist's chair look in bed. And then I stared at the photo again, at the body language — the man so uncharacteristically drowsy and the woman so tight and contorted — and I got a chill and knew there was no curing it.

I carried the photo into Emily's wing of the house. She was sitting on her bed, pulling on her boots, when I held it in front of her.

"It's the cabin — the one in your painting. What happened there? What makes it so important?" She just stared at me. Like it was perfectly obvious. But not as though it was none of my business. We were old friends — everything was our business. "You and Dyson. The two of you."

"What's the question?" she answered. "What do you need to know? It was another of those things that…didn't work out the way I expected. Or hoped. Things that *hurt*." Her voice was flat, affectless. As deadtoned as Sheila had been on the street, talking about cabbage and eggs and not expecting anything from the world. "I attached more significance to pain then than I do now."

"That's it?" I stammered. "That's all you have to say?"

"What more do you want to know? I wanted it — not quite the way it turned out maybe but…" She shrugged.

"Well how old were you? Thirteen?"

"Fourteen."

"He was eighteen or nineteen. He knew better."

"I led him on. I teased him. I never said 'No.'"

"Mmm—that makes it okay."

"Well, I don't think he knew much more than me. He wasn't experienced, I can guarantee you that. He was guilty forever after."

"He had a strange way of showing it."

"Dyson had a strange way of everything. He couldn't handle people, you know that. Quarks and neutrinos were charming but not when they turned into anything bigger."

"I can't believe you're just shrugging this off."

"You want me to perform for you?"

"Don't perform. But *nothing*?"

"I won't be a *victim* for you!" Emily burst. She rose up yelling and the world around went silent. I couldn't think. I was totally blanked, while she was as defiant as I'd ever seen her.

"I've had cancer. I've been raped, if you insist. That just makes me another woman. Men get judged by their work, looks, social standing, character under fire. Women get judged by sex, by the effect we have on men. Period. If you wonder why women burn out on sex, that's why."

She walked to the closet and pulled on her coat like a shell. "I raise my horses. I paint my paintings. My life is a mess but it's mine. What's inside me, no one can take away. Who has good sex? For how long? If we make our happiness on that, we'll be happy three days a year."

She stood facing me, defending the part that was all her, that wasn't about men, wasn't about sex, wasn't defined by sex in the slightest little degree. And something came to me like it was drifting on the air.

"*It just doesn't mean as much to you,*" I murmured, "*as it does to us.*" Jillian's voice and my own joined and intertwined in my head, the words sounding very different now than they had.

"Sure," Em shrugged, as though it was obvious. "It doesn't take that many times to know it isn't love, it isn't friendship. It isn't even a good time all that often, because of all the baggage we attach to it." She smiled her indulgent friend smile. "We can't figure out why you guys haven't noticed."

As we putted up the hill into Malcolm's courtyard, several men were loading his black beast onto the lorry in the corner. I'd come to think of that thing as a piece of architecture—it was a shock when Malcolm actually got behind the wheel and fired it up. While it was warming, Emily led the grey up the ramp.

"Roy Rogers, I presume?" Malcolm's smile made me feel like new money. This was still better than feeling like no money, which is what I *really* was.

He was modeling his understated green Defence Force uniform with a slightly smaller spread of decorations across the chest. "McCarthy tells me there are to be changes in our arrangement?"

"No change in ours, "I told him. "I'm just not rewarding people for sneaking around behind my back." His eyes went a bit squinty and I realized that was just how he felt about *me*.

My life was about as racy at the moment as it ever got but the truth was nothing to the carnival in Malcolm's head. And yet here he was, smiling politely and helping Emily bind our horses inside his trailer. Waiting us all out.

What a stubborn race the Irish were! There was a determination and devotion to the guy that I had to admire. I hate being wrong about people but I've had to get used to it.

The three of us squeezed together across the front of the lorry. Things were a bit stiff after the previous night's follies, Em unable to be her usual breezy self with Malcolm and him pretending not to notice. My inevitable bad jokes met terse smiles. There's nothing more deadening than sincere people being polite—it sucks all the air out of the room.

We wound up in a caravan of trailers and riders clip-clopping down the middle of the road. No sign marked the hunting grounds but they would have been hard to miss—just take the gap in the stone wall surrounded by the wall of screaming protestors, waving placards and specific fingers at you as you passed.

I spied Jillian, of course, front and center with a profane placard of her own original design. I looked for Liam but not very hard. Reworking old banners to replace innocent Iraqis with innocent foxes wouldn't have taken the whole evening. I straightened in my seat to look a little defiant but I didn't feel it.

Malcolm found an open parking spot under a huge tree. Four or five men appeared out of nowhere to pull down the ramp and help with the horses. I'd expected everyone to be as formally dressed as we were—I was surprised (and not happily) to find we were the fashion plates of the crowd. The man skipping up the ramp wore what were surely—twenty years ago—expensive riding breeches now overrun with patches, a dusky moth-eaten undershirt and suspenders falling loosely off his shoulders. His cap carried earflaps pinned up along the sides like unfurled wings.

The crowd at the wall increased the volume of their taunts. "Wherever we go, we raise a crowd," I remarked.

"Cruelty to animals, of course," Emily sniffed. "They're talking about banning hunts in England next year. Like it's disrespectful to hunt a fox."

"Well, isn't it disrespectful? To the fox?" I asked.

Malcolm looked pained. Em simply said "No" and continued only after seeing the look on my face. "It's the highest respect. Foxes can run rings around the hounds. But you have to challenge them to be at their best."

This sounded an awful lot like *'they're motivated — by fear'* " in my head. What if the fox didn't *want* to be challenged? What if he was just some wage-slave hanging around the forest stealing nuts and berries or eating rats or whatever foxes do and collecting his paycheck on Friday afternoon?

"But isn't the point to *catch* the fox?" is how it came out of my mouth. I thought I'd boiled the subject down to its most innocuous face but the other riders melted away from me like I had a disease.

Em led a big chestnut horse off the lorry and handed me the reins, like I would know what to do with them. "Just show him you're the bigger horse," she said and started up the ramp again.

The thing threw me a look — without moving, just the eyeball screwing over for a peek — and then began to crowd me, clopping sideways right into my chest. I stumbled back a foot or two before gathering myself and putting both shoulders into it. I shoved back hard, the way I'd seen Em in the field the first day. The eyeball swiveled over at me again and the horse stood still.

Em led the grey down the ramp, cradling its huge head in her arms. Malcolm followed with his horse and the group of helpers pushed the ramp back into the lorry.

"The fox is unpredictable," Malcolm answered and clearly, he'd made this explanation before. "He has no rules or course to follow. He knows the hounds follow his scent so he'll run along a streambed to deaden it, jump a fence and double-back on his own tracks to confuse them. Which means we're not just riding a course but doing something *real*, something with a little chaos in it."

He popped up onto his mount. Em followed. I had the reins in hand. I looked hard into the eyes of my horse and sent him a telepathic message that I'd punch him to death if he so much as twitched in the next minute. Then I hoisted myself up and into the saddle. Apparently he was a mindreader.

"You look pretty natural," Em said to bolster me. I tried to smile. "How do you feel?"

"I don't know," I said. "I was flashing back to Doctor Levitz' Jewish history class. Historically, my people have always been the fox."

"Not hugely different from the Irish," Malcolm answered. "If the choice is hunter or hunted, enjoy the upside."

They flicked their reins lightly and made cluck-cluck noises at their horses. As they moved forward, mine followed.

The riders assembled by a gate in the inevitable plain Irish stone wall. Looking over and beyond, I could see Malcolm wasn't kidding: there was no course. A wide collection of broken fields stood ahead of us, mud and grass and tangled bushes, streams cutting through behind stone walls at all sorts of heights and odd angles.

Em looked first at me and then at Malcolm and burst out laughing. "We get a nice ride in the open country," she said. "Don't take it so seriously—the fox is symbolic. The hounds go first and we take off after them. Hang back if you like. Roddy'll follow the pack all by himself."

"Roddy?"

"That's your horse."

"*Roddy*? Hi Ho *Roddy*? You've given me an effeminate horse!"

She laughed and began sidling into a better position up front of the pack.

Malcolm clicked his horse up beside mine. "I'm a peacekeeper," he said, so soft I had to lean to hear him. "I spend half the year between neighbors who desperately want to kill each other. There's always an insane reason, some awful snub from 1500 years ago, retold and retold and retold. And I place forty or fifty men across the road or along the river to hold them off for a year or two, so we can pretend it's not bleeding on us."

Some of the horses got skittish but the riders quieted them and happily, my Roddy held his ground.

"Out there, *civilization* feels artificial, like a foreign film in subtitles. What's real is chaos. So today, we're simply getting in touch with our real nature."

"That's real—chaos? Nothing else?"

"I think feeling is real, as long as it lasts," he said. "Even the most bestial humans will do anything for their families. Sometimes that's what turns them into beasts. But the feeling is genuine." He looked around. "In the middle of this hunt will be moments that are truly real—and I'll feel wonderful once we've had our ride and no one's been hurt and we get back to the Pub for a pint or two."

He scanned the field of hunters and shrugged.

"Death is real," he added. "Life is a dream and then we wake up."

And then I heard the yapping of hounds and suddenly we were all galloping.

If I clicked the reins, it was news to me, but suddenly we were moving fast. The crowd in front sucked through the gate like water through a drain and we were in the open field. The pack spread out instantly and the horses started hitting their stride. It was all I could do to stay in the saddle. The wind kept getting knocked out of me just from the bouncing up and down. The sound was overwhelming, the pounding converging from all directions. Two kids who couldn't have been more than thirteen went flying by me on horses as big as mine. I collected myself just enough to watch what they were doing and tried to imitate. I leaned forward a bit and let my ass bounce up and down with the horse. This didn't require much work—all I did was relax and lean and it happened.

The field was a complex mess. One hoof would hit rock while the other sank into moss that gave as though there was an air pocket beneath. The horses ahead of us were tearing up the ground wherever they ran, sod and dirt flying everywhere. It was barely controlled chaos like Malcolm had said and pretty damn thrilling, once I stopped worrying.

The riders at the front of the pack rippled upward and then dropped out of sight. A four-foot-high stone wall appeared just ahead, ancient and unyielding and coming on at an alarming speed. The riders just in front of us tensed and jumped and then it was our turn.

It wasn't as though I couldn't think—it was as though I didn't know *how*. That might seem like a petty distinction to you but I spent several crucial moments pondering it instead of the fact that I was about to become a pile of meat against a stone wall.

And then Roddy (a ridiculous name for something the size of my kitchen) heaved mightily and launched into the air. All the ferocious churning and pounding and the barrage of sound turned to eerie silence and stillness—and a moment later, we were on the other side, pounding up the hill and I was still on the son-of-a-bitch. It was a miracle but I gave myself credit like I had something to do with it.

After that, I let the scene run away with me: the air rushing past my ears, the thrumming hooves, the cries of riders and yelping of hounds, the pounding and bouncing and careening from side to side as the pack turned first one direction and then the other. I leaned over Roddy's neck and flicked the reins, making clucking noises like I'd heard from Em and Malcolm but faster, more insistent and urgent.

Suddenly, I wanted to *go*. Everything was about *going*, going faster, more speed, more wind in the face and more power over the ground. Roddy quickened his pace, hunkered down, strides lengthening. We came to another broken wall and actually gained in the jump, making up space between us and the pack ahead. I could see Em towards the front. I had no idea where Malcolm was but I didn't care at the moment. Everything was about *going*.

The group turned wildly to the right, scrambling up and down a gulley between thick bushes. I could see the hounds suddenly off in the next field—like Malcolm had said, the fox didn't know from property lines. It was strange to even think of the fox now. The fox was just an excuse.

As we came upon the next wall, higher and more formidable than the others, I saw frantic movement on the other side. Apparently, some of the protestors had gotten onto the field with mischief in mind and were now caught in the wrong place at the wrong time. They were scrambling behind the tangle of vines and stone, trying to get to safety. They looked puny and stupid, out of place and foolish for putting themselves at risk.

And then I heard Jill's voice inside my head—she was inside my head all the time now. *This is what it is to be a bomber pilot*, she warned. *You don't have to hate the fox. You just have to forget him.*

Suddenly I was trying to ride Roddy, to get him to do what I wanted and he wasn't interested. Or maybe he just didn't understand, me not being fluent in horse. I lost the rhythm.

Suddenly I was banging against the saddle again, out of synch, my hands gone clammy, sweating like a pig, no time to think and no way to stop. I was a non-functioning extension of an instinctively-reacting horse chasing brainless hounds after a symbolic fox. That was too many damn layers removed from reality.

When that thought hit me, the whole thing got real and all I could think of was getting out of that field alive and in one piece. The front pack went over the wall just ahead and disappeared down the bank on the other side. I clutched the reins and banged against the saddle and held my breath.

Roddy's jump was awkward, off-stride. I felt us wobble in the air and heard stones flying behind—he must have clipped the wall with his rear legs going over. He stumbled a bit on one leg as we landed and I was leaning for an endless moment over the wrong side of him but then he regained the downhill bank and we burst across the stream bed upright and at a gallop, flashing past another horse trying to scramble, frantically, to its feet in the riverbed. A riderless horse. A charcoal horse, stirrups flailing.

We were halfway up the hill in half a second before I realized it was the grey. I pulled the reins over hard, harder than I probably should have but we burst out of the pack and I was able to look back down the hill. Where was Emily?

She was already in Malcolm's arms. He was bent over her in the water, cradling her head and carrying her away, out of the path of the next pack of riders. The grey stood idly a few feet away, drinking stupidly from the stream like nothing had happened. Em's eyes weren't open. I don't remember riding back down the hill or getting off my horse.

"Hopefully it's just a concussion," Malcolm said. A couple of riders were standing by, apparently out of the next group. Malcolm told them to fetch the doctor and a stretcher and within minutes Emily was being carried through the field to a hospital van. Malcolm was a whirlwind of instruction, first with the doctors and then me. "Go in the ambulance," he said. "I'll meet you at hospital."

Em came to in the ambulance and muttered a few words. I swear she wanted ice cream but she was very quiet so no one was sure. The EMT's kept arranging a plastic-bag cushion around her pelvis, which had apparently been cracked or broken when the grey rolled over it.

I was terrified but everyone else seemed very matter-of-fact, one step following the next. I kept thinking they should call a proper doctor for instructions but they all pretended to know exactly what was needed. They kept talking at Em and encouraged me to do the same, to make sure she stayed awake until the hospital.

I read her every warning label in the van and there were plenty, the usual assortment of stretchers clamped to the floor, racks of bottles and vials and specialized equipment, all with complex decals. I read every single one and they kept her awake, which only showed how off she was. Who ever expected anyone to actually *read* that shit in an ambulance? Whose ass was being covered *there*?

And then we arrived at the hospital and the hours just blurred together. There were several consultations about her pelvis and a CAT-scan after two doctors had examined her for concussion. I knew her mother was dead and she hadn't spoken to her sister in years, so I told them I was her nearest and dearest. After that, they reported to me — and to Colonel Lowell, of course. No one seemed to question why he was there — he was Colonel Lowell. The Pakistani doctor didn't know him but all the others did so he went along.

Malcolm ensured she had a private room — no small accomplishment in an Irish hospital — and had her personal physician tracked down when the hospital couldn't find him at a conference in Cork. He finally arrived late that evening. When he came to report, Malcolm made sure to include me, though the doctor made a beeline straight for him. Not that any of this mattered in any practical way—I just appreciated it personally.

The doctor went on and on and Malcolm kept nodding but I can't imagine he really understood much more of it than I did. The pelvis was broken favorably and should heal on its own—though Em would be on crutches for several weeks—and no *indication* of permanent damage from the concussion. The rest of it was Sanskrit and who cared anyway?

They kept her isolated much of the evening. When we did get to see her for a few minutes at a time, the experience was disturbing. She was sedated, irritable and spacey, mumbling about things and then forgetting her train of thought in the middle of a sentence. "It's normal," Malcolm said as we returned to the waiting room.

"You seem awfully relaxed about this," I accused.

"Riders get injured. I've been peacekeeping—getting shot at—for twenty years; I've had six operations," he said, "all but one from riding. She was on a new horse. That's why I hung back, in case either of you needed help."

We slept in the waiting room. Somewhere along the line one day turned to the next.

WEDNESDAY

We kept waking during the night, Malcolm and I, first one, then the other, padding around in our socks, having long since abandoned our boots to the green-carpeted floor. The coats stayed on—the hospital was as cold and damp as every other place in Ireland in March. I wished now I'd gone riding in a full-length coat, not the cutesy short-waisted number. We stared out the windows and drank tea until we ran the dispenser dry.

Maybe there was something in the tea because we were both bouncing tipsy in the wee hours. Or maybe it was just the empty hallways and the busy silence—the beeping of the bedside monitors, the hum of the fluorescent lights and not one human sound.

"Actually, it's a shock to see her this way," Malcolm said at one point. "I've seen her fall before but I've never seen her injured. It just seems out of character. She's always at the front with her head up."

"That's what she projects," I said, staring at a pulsing fluorescent lamp overhead.

"It's not just projection. Most people carry their failures in their riding. You can tell where they fell by the way they approach the spot. Emily rides as though she's never fallen."

"She's fearless—on horseback," I replied and he took immediate offense.

"Most people don't know what fearlessness is. For Emily, it's what she means to be."

I guess he saw the confusion in my face—I was too tired to be polite.

"Who we're trying to become—it's a crucial part of us, isn't it?" he continued. "It's the part that still has hope."

"You told me hope was an illusion," I said.

"So choose your illusions *carefully*," Malcolm mocked, wagging his finger like a school superintendent. "You may become them." He sat back in his chair, a bit overwhelmed by this sudden eloquence.

I remembered the man at the airport, giving up his terminal to Emily and stunned by his own generosity. This was Em's effect on people. She aroused them to break through their boundaries.

Malcolm seemed to be thinking along with me.

"She makes me hopeful," he offered. "It isn't my natural state. I find myself wanting to protect her, even when she hurts me." The confession alone was exotic territory for him, even at three in the morning. And then I must have fallen asleep.

I woke later and saw his eyes drowsy-lidded on the opposite bench. He mumbled, "When you're an athlete, you're always a bit injured" and I said "Who isn't?" and we both drifted away again.

And then there was light coming through the trees outside and Jill in the chair next to me. I smiled and she smiled back and I felt the warmth pour through me, just as I recalled the last time I'd seen her, driving off with Liam Mr. AlfaRomeoMultipleBodyPiercings.

"I wasn't sure we were talking," I said.

"I assumed we were being dramatic."

"That sounds like us," I admitted.

I sat up, dazed and confused. I was really sure she'd dumped me or I'd dumped her or we'd agreed I wasn't as important to her as she was to me the other night. Last night? Two nights ago. Whenever. It sure didn't show on her face. It hurt to see her but that still felt better than seeing anybody else.

"Did you talk to Denis?" I asked as sternly as I could. If she was going to drive me fucking crazy, she at least owed me *that*.

"I'll go this morning—I promise," she said, like I hadn't seen it coming. "It's funny. I organized the protest at the hunt and then—I had other things to do last night. But all the way through, I kept hearing your voice in my head: *Talk to Denis. Talk to Denis.*"

You're always in my head too. "I don't seem to have had much effect."

"Well—I'm aware I *should*," she said. Her head dipped in the mildest of apologetic shrugs and I melted all over. It was all I cared about—what I wanted *mattered*. Not enough to do anything about, maybe but enough to feel guilty over, at least a little. If my ex could only have offered that same gesture three times a year, I'd still be married. I felt terribly, childishly grateful.

"I had to come here first," she said. "I saw Emily go down. And… you're here." She struggled with that part but she said it. And then Malcolm appeared in the doorway and called me to Em's room.

Jill didn't want to come along. "She doesn't want to see me," she protested until I dragged her bodily. I think I actually lifted her off the ground the last few feet. Malcolm threw me a hard look the whole way, which didn't help.

Em was in an electric hospital bed with metal rails all around, IV dripping, monitors beeping, head raised, pelvis on some sort of cushion. It was the demented version of the Getaway Bed. Or maybe Ron's was the demented version. She looked tiny in context, pale and flattened, the world's only blonde Modigliani.

"They changed the sheets," she pronounced dazedly, recognizing she had company but not necessarily sure who.

"It was morning," Malcolm shrugged. "They hadn't changed them so I insisted." I couldn't imagine what would happen the first time he set foot in Em's *house*.

"I was riding—?"

"The grey. He's fine. He took a tumble on you."

She looked *relieved*. The *horse* was fine.

It was really hard watching Em struggle like this and I thanked God selfishly I wasn't around when she got the cancer diagnosis. I knew now I couldn't have handled it.

She threw a steady gaze at Jill, who fluttered under the scrutiny. But she sucked it up and waited Em out and finally came the smile, the recognition. Em held her hand up, just off the bed and Jill leaned over and took it.

Malcolm seemed totally thrown and I couldn't blame him really. Jill's didn't have the whole story about Em and me but Malcolm had *nothing* straight. Every idea he could possibly have had about us was off by about half a mile.

Meanwhile, I was kvelling, swollen with a kind of abstracted pride. Both these women, whom I loved, had longed for a friendship, a relationship, that included men but wasn't about us. And now, here it was, at least the beginning stages and it felt kind of thrilling seeing it happen.

And then Em jerked suddenly against the sheets, squirming her shoulders for just a moment. This was more than enough for Malcolm, who was out in the corridor demanding pillows in a flash. We could hear him being referred to the desk down the hall. Em turned to us with a woozy smile.

"He came," she murmured.

"He's been here the whole time. He's been running this wing of the hospital. I don't know if you've got the best care but it's surely the fastest—they just want to be rid of him."

"At our age," Em said, indicating herself and me, "you know you'll be in the hospital at some point and the most important thing is that someone's outside waiting for you. So you have to get better. Because they're waiting, you see?" She smiled at me. "Paul was with Dyson—he was my husband—when he died. He wasn't around when I had the cancer or you would have been with me, right?" I saw Jill's face quake—Emily's cancer was always a shock to anyone the first time they heard about it.

"Sure I would," I said, hoping it was true.

"And Malcolm's here now," Em repeated in a soft voice, almost like a lullaby. We could hear him bustling back up the hallway with what sounded like a posse. "And you too," she said peering at Jill. "Thank you."

"It's okay," Jill said, fidgety all over again.

Malcolm returned with two attendants in close formation carrying fresh sheets and blankets, flowers in a vase and a portable radio that played "I Say A Little Prayer for You" as soon as it was plugged in. The room was packed all of a sudden and Jill popped up and out the door.

I caught her at the end of the hall. She grabbed me by both arms and dragged me out onto the ramp by the emergency entrance.

"Don't ask me to stay."

"Fine—just say goodbye and—"

"I can't," she gasped. quivering and sweating. "I hate hospital. Mam and I spent two years, almost every day in hospital with Denis. I can recite every prayer for the redemption of the sick and wounded from memory, in Latin and Irish and English. And I don't believe a whit."

I reached for her cheek, to touch her, to try to drain off some of whatever it was that kept her feet from ever touching the ground. She retreated from me, the way she had from Liam on the train. And something turned in me again.

"This isn't about the hospital," I said. "You can't handle Em being nice to you. You were entirely comfortable fucking me behind her back, not that I needed convincing. But when we hurt her, you were thrown. And you *really* can't stand when she turns out okay with us, when she thanks you for showing up, for being decent. You insist you want to be bad but that nasty conscience of yours just won't let you enjoy it. So why do you keep trying?"

She shivered like someone had dumped her in a storage locker. She looked all around but whatever she was looking for wasn't in sight.

"I said it the other night:" she muttered, as though talking to herself, "'*If we can't know, how can we trust?*' It wasn't my line, it was Mam's. After Da died, she found out all kinds of things about him—debts, women, things she didn't tell me for years. He ate her up but she stayed...*stupidly* loyal to the man till the day she died! Every time I yield to a man, I give up a piece of myself — and end up small and mean and resentful. I don't know that me, I don't like her. Better to keep to myself, to my causes, to stay independent. " Her eyes were full on me now. "I get close with you, I really do. But you're right; I hold back. Something stops me every time."

I wanted to reach for her but it would have killed me to see her pull away so I didn't.

"Jill, I want you to know my couple of stupid secrets. I want to know the name of your dog, your first boyfriend, your favorite Beatle. That's *real*. Fox hunts aren't real. Iraq isn't real. Neither is the Zionist Entity, the Dow Jones Average, the Holy Ghost or poetry you never let anybody read. If we make the world better, it's by coincidence. But you can give me little things that'll make me feel loved. And I can do that for you. That's *real*. All you have to do is decide you *want* it."

She tried to locate a nice smile for me, something better than wistful or bitterweet. But she wasn't getting there.

"You always have answers, don't you?" she accused.

"Sure. I'll have five more tomorrow if you don't like these."

"You could pause momentarily before hitting the nail on the head," she said and marched away fast across the carpark.

I stood on the verge, watching the ambulances shuttle in with the dead and dying and those that would die later, the rest of us. I could watch that. I couldn't watch her go.

So many people had disappeared from my life. Each left a space that didn't fill in. Dyson dropped dead before I knew what he was. My old man tormented me but left a deep hole once he was gone. My mother disappeared or died, I'll never know which and I'll never stop wondering. My life was full of spaces where there should have been people.

The room was all primped by the time I got back. Em had drifted off again. She was propped onto mountains of pillows and surrounded by bouquets of flowers. The cards were from Malcolm and me—we were a couple now.

I found myself squirming at this goody-two-shoes generosity and realized I was doing what I'd just accused Jill of—recoiling from real feeling. And it wasn't like I had anywhere else to go. All I had left was Em and Malcolm was steadily advancing on the territory between us.

I found him in the waiting room, nursing his 75th cup of tea. "The doctors will check her when she wakes. They'll probably let her go home in the morning."

"How come you're not a general?"

"I'm sorry?"

"You should be. You're a natural leader," I burbled. There— I'd done it. I'd paid him a sincere compliment and it hadn't hurt, not really, though the side where my appendix was felt a little sore.

"Well, thank you," he said graciously. It really was frustrating, all this good fellowship. There had to be a dark side to him but it didn't show.

"Look, I don't know how to put this but—why didn't you give up a long time ago?"

"I'm sorry," he said, not looking a bit sorry. "Am I crowding you?"

"No, actually I'm welcoming you in my own weird way. I just need to understand a bit better. She means a lot to me too."

"I know. I know you care about her, despite everything." Thanks, pal.

His eyes were piercing now. They fit the uniform, the military side of him. "I didn't expect things to go easily," he continued. "She takes some keeping up with, Emily does. Honestly? My appraisal is that eventually you'll all go away and I'll still be here. And she will appreciate at some point that I am."

He stared at his cup for a moment. "I don't enjoy life as I should," he continued. "But I do when I'm with her. I feel *alive* when I'm with her." He shrugged. "You asked the other day what's real. Maybe that's it—maybe that's all there is."

It took about thirty seconds for the statement to hit me, for the truth of it to ripen inside. And then I was hurtling out the door, looking for a cab to catch up with Jill.

Her house was quiet though her car was parked outside. When I got to the pub, the cook told me she'd taken the day off. He sounded Moroccan or something, now just another New Wave Irishman. Neither Denis nor Sheila were anywhere to be found and a woman I'd never seen before was stationed behind the bar as though she belonged. This was disturbing, like the Hitchcock movie where the whole train says "What woman? You weren't with any woman." I stepped outside along the river and my cell rang.

"I have a contract from my man which I think will suit you," McCarthy said. "Shall I fax it to that same number?"

"Give me five minutes. I'll call you from there," I answered, force of habit, the body twitching response while the brain remained comatose. I was feverish over Jill, but what was the point? I knew I had to find her but I had no idea what I would do if I did.

Two-and-a-half hours went by, filled with redrafts and clarifications signifying nothing. I exasperated McCarthy and confused the shit out of myself. I thought about jumping out the window, but it was a one-story building and wouldn't even hurt.

And then I heard McCarthy's voice over the phone: "I asked you before: Are you sure this is what you really want?"

And the sound of his voice was like a fresh gust of air. I heard myself answer, "It's not everything I've ever wanted—but it's enough." And suddenly everything was fine and five minutes later I had a signed piece of paper containing everything I needed.

Then it was Ron's turn.

"I must have sent the wrong contract," he said when I confronted him with the missing clause—the missing me. "Anyone can make a mistake."

"Ron, the slightest change to your documents and they have to be saved under a new name. You have the only three-room office in the world with a computer keycard system so you know exactly who went where when. If the chairman of the Nuclear Regulatory Commission told me he made a mistake, I'd believe him. Not you."

"Now don't get upset."

"Too late."

"You still work for me."

"Not anymore."

"What does that mean?"

"It means you didn't nail down Irish distribution rights before you sent me over here. I hold them now and I've made my own deal with McCarthy."

Silence. Two beats.

"You're just threatening. You know it's too late for me to check with the Israelis."

"I'll fax you a copy of the contract if you want."

Silence. Three beats.

"But the process is all mine!" he squawked, voice up an octave. "The flow-chart, the sales process, the End of the World — that's proprietary information that was done as my employee!"

"If McCarthy liked any of that, he'd have signed with you. He thinks you're gumming up the works."

"He doesn't understand modern business."

"Happily they're primitive here."

I could hear him fuming across the Atlantic, the steam whistling out the pores.

"There's a no-compete clause in your contract — three years," he burst finally. "If you think I won't use it, you're out of your mind."

"I never signed it."

"What do you mean?"

"Go check your files. I never signed the contract." I knew from day one I had no intention to stay, that I would take the first out that presented itself. I had stalled and raised niggling questions and objections. The process had gone on far longer than I expected — there really wasn't any work for me out there — but eventually Ron had just taken me for granted and stopped asking.

"You accepted my wages." He was sputtering now. "There's an implied contract."

"I was work for hire. I accomplished every task you gave me. This is my vacation. I made my own contacts and negotiated my own terms." Long tedious expensive stalemate in court, if it ever got to court, and we both knew it never would.

I could hear scraping sounds—the desklamp going west, the phone north by northeast, the shiny black memo pad rotating to windward. When Ron got upset, he cleaned his desk. It would gleam before he went home tonight.

"I will sue," he said finally and inevitably.

"And bleed your profits away to lawyers. McCarthy has fleets of them—and politicians—on retainer over here. Lawyers of long standing in the EU, where you would have to litigate." There was a long pause. I could hear Ron taking a big swig of his environmentally superior bottled water.

"Okay. What do you want?" he said, deadpan and wary.

"From *you*? Nothing. I have what I want."

"I have the States locked up. You're burning your bridges in a much bigger corporation."

"I don't *want* the bigger corporation, Ron. I like the one-on-one, person-to-person thing over here."

"But that doesn't *work*," he whined. "Individuality leads to dependence on the employee. Dependence destroys management control. Lack of control increases risk. That's the sum lesson of thirty years of American business."

I had a thought here and it made me smile. I wished I had suspenders like McCarthy so I could snap them.

"So what you're saying is that America has finally *transcended* individualism."

"*Exactly!*" Ron thundered. "That's a great insight. It's the Next Step."

"Well, good luck. It's my gift to you," I told him and hung up.

$$\neq$$

Victory never feels as good as defeat feels bad. And this was just a regional skirmish in a minor campaign.

Would I like exile to Ireland if I *wasn't* with her? The thought chilled me to the core. And then, thinking of her, Sheila popped into my head. Of course (!), Jill had finally gone to Sheila's to talk. *That* was why the bunch of them were missing. I had to go to Sheila's.

God knows how I'd find the place. Denis had taken me through five counties on the way. I headed for Jill's, hoping to remember the first few turns and there was Denis in the front seat of her car, cranking the engine like a video game.

"Whoa there," I called through the window. "You'll never start it like that."

"Sheila's gone!" he answered, frantic.

"Where?"

"The airport. England. We've got to stop her!"

The car started before I could disappear. I tried to step away but he jumped out of the seat and round the other side. "You drive," he said. "I'm not good." Having seen his sister drive, it seemed like a smart move. But I wasn't getting in the car yet.

"Where's Jill?"

"She's the reason! She came to Sheila's house and Sheila showed her belly and Jillian *pushed* her! She got real upset. So I threw her out."

"You threw her out?"

"I yelled at her. I shouldn't have done that."

"That's all you did?"

"Yeah, yeah," he waved his hand dismissively. "I broke a vase. I threw it. But in the other direction. Sheila says I have to control my temper. But when I came back to the house, Sheila was gone! And Jill's gone!"

"What do you mean 'gone'? How long ago was this?"

"Maybe an hour. Well, maybe two. I had to cool down so I went to the pub and had a pint. And played a little. Almost three, actually." The time I'd spent faxing and revising. My heart thumped.

"Where'd Jill go?" I said again and stalked up the block to her house. Denis trailed half-heartedly but he knew what I would find. Which is to say, nothing. No answer at the door. Silent and empty through the windows.

"She left with Liam," he added. He seemed entirely unaware how those words twisted into me. "The hell with her. What about *Sheila*? We have to go after her!" His voice was the wailing cry from two in the morning at Jill's. It pierced me. I knew what it was to need someone who wasn't there—I'd known it since I was three or four.

The car was still running when we got back. You probably could have left that car unlocked and running in Brooklyn for days and no one would steal it either. A minute later, he was directing me out of town.

I hung my head out the window—I couldn't drive my best if I was knocking myself senseless at every turn. We followed the ribbon of local road to the N18 without difficulty. Not much traffic on a Wednesday evening but Denis hung out the other window shaking his fist at every driver who dawdled in our path. He told me the entire history of Planxty, some group that combined Irish and Bulgarian music, I think. Who knew he could talk? But now he was nervous and upset and wouldn't shut up.

I spent the whole trip trying *not* to think about Jillian, which is to say I couldn't think of anything else. It would have been totally out of character for her to be placid about Sheila but I'd expected her to keep control. Sheila's belly had been too much reality. We'd all had too much reality lately—it wasn't good eating.

Denis was already out on the tarmac and striding toward the terminal before I'd finished pulling into a parking space. I caught up with him at the whooshing electric doors and my heart sank. The place was packed to the gills with soldiers as well as the usual tourists and business travelers. The crowds were so thick we'd never make a dent.

"How do you expect to find her?" I asked. "She's got what? Two hours lead on us?"

"The bus would take hours," he said. "And then she'll have to wait for the plane." That was actually pretty good deductive reasoning, but hopelessly logical now that we'd arrived. "We have to find her," he said, grabbing my sleeve. "I want this baby. I need this family. I don't care if Jill never talks to me again." I did, of course. I cared for Jill's sake and Denis's. I knew enough already to know this was a family that made mistakes in haste and regretted in leisure. Was that a quote?

No way were we going to find Sheila in these crowds. No way were we going to see *anything* that could help. Which is, of course, when I saw something that helped: a couple of teenagers, blowing bubble gum into the camera of a cellphone. Giggling and poking and snapping pictures while waiting for their flight to board.

"Denis, do you have a cellphone?"

"Yuh."

"Is there a picture of Sheila in it?"

"Should be."

"Get it out. Have a wallet?"

"Yeah."

"Give it to me."

I stuffed the wallet in my laptop case. "Let me do the talking," I warned.

It took three minutes to find the airport Garda station, past the lost and found down a long hallway in the back of the building, across from the bathrooms and just forward of a door marked "No Exit—Official Use Only." The whine of jet engines leaked in around the edges.

I pulled Denis to the counter and held the camera up to the sergeant behind the desk. "She flirted with him and lifted his wallet," I said. "Maybe five, ten minutes ago."

That sort of complaint, lodged in a New York City police station, would have resulted in two hours filling out paperwork, all the while being politely discouraged and reminded how unlikely it was that our property would ever be recovered, though certainly the police would make every effort, etc.

"Connolly! Download this image and get it on the floor!" the sergeant bellowed immediately.

"She said she was getting on a flight," I added.

"They often do, though they're rarely going anywhere," the sergeant answered. "Nonetheless, we'll check the gates." Connolly took the cellphone and disappeared into the back. There were ten desks scattered about but only the two cops. "You aren't cramped for space," I remarked.

"We're all over the floor tonight," the sergeant answered.

Denis pulled me into the hallway. The jet noise was really loud there but he checked up and down before speaking.

"Are they going to arrest Sheila?"

"Once they find her, we'll explain what's up. They won't be happy, but I'll bet it's not the first time. They probably won't file charges...in the end. "

"You're not sure?"

"You want to stop her?"

"Yes," he yelped, all doubt erased.

"Okay. So now you've got a crew that can go all over the terminal. Let them get as mad as they want *after* they stop her. Right?"

"Right!" This was Denis, Mr. Emotion, firing on all cylinders. The man who always *knew* what he wanted. I bristled with envy.

"But remember: in the meantime, you're just a guy whose wallet's been stolen. You don't know her and you can't get frantic about her. Okay?"

He nodded. And then Connolly emerged lugging a ream of paper and we were off. Up the hall, onto the floor, rounding corners, through locked staircases. Every section of the terminal contained a checkpoint with several officers; Connolly handed out the pages and instructions at every stop.

We circulated for more than fifteen minutes, my heart sinking every time I heard the roar of a takeoff. I kept Denis close and away from Connolly in case he overcooked.

We hadn't finished the second level when the officer's cell rang: Sheila had boarded a plane. It had not yet left the gate. She would be removed and returned to the boarding desk for questioning. We hustled off to the spot.

When we arrived, she was surrounded by Gardai and arguing with her usual brusqueness. "Take *another* time through," she snapped as they went through her bag. "I've never stolen anything in my life." Then she saw us coming and her whole face changed.

I said I know longing and it's not bragging to say it. It's not the kind of thing you want to be real familiar with, because basically it almost always means you didn't get what you wanted and who wants to be familiar with that? But now Sheila took a look at Denis coming down the aisle and her face clouded over with the most awful terrible longing I've ever seen. It was as though she'd been stricken with happiness. She fought it hard, fought to maintain control, to keep that determination she'd worked so hard to build for days or weeks or since the first fear she'd had of being pregnant.

And then Denis got close and burst into tears and she pulled him into her arms, all her resolve washed away, reduced by him to feeling, dragged against her will to sincerity.

"There there," she cooed like a mother bird, stroking his hair.

"Don't go," he begged, naked as always. "I'll do anything you want. I'll do anything."

She held him, helpless, rubbing the back of his neck and whispering in his ear until he calmed down. Then she glared at me like it was all *my* fault.

"Don't go," I urged.

"And what do we do about *her*?" she said and I knew who she meant of course.

"Defy her," I said. "She'll come around. She likes defiance. She respects it."

"You're a grand sort of optimist," she said drily.

Connolly was clearing his throat repeatedly. When I turned to face him, he threw me the same face Ms. Stouffer did when she caught me doodling in seventh grade math class. "In the States," I told him, "they'd call this a domestic situation, I think. Sorry we weren't more upfront about it."

"Hmmph! The copies cost three Euro," he answered. I handed him a fiver. He made change and insisted on writing me a receipt.

We threaded down through the main terminal, Sheila and Denis knit together. How many couples like them had I stared at over the years? I was tired of staring, tired of envy. I wanted something better, something with that real-world chaos in it. I wanted some poor schnook to envy *me*.

We were almost to the electric doors when I spied Sweaterman and two of the other back room revolutionaries in a corner, grouped around an Internet terminal, whispering and pointing at the screen like a middle school clique.

What made me stop? Nothing that won't get me locked in a rubber room. I snagged Sheila's arm to get her to wait and headed over for a look. The group was packed so tight around the screen they didn't even see me coming.

Grainy video filled a small window on a makeshift webpage, a green nightvision image of a woman in a ghostly burka wading close-up through hip-deep grass. Behind, a huge American transport plane bathed in spotlights. Her eyes were just a slit between headdress and veil, the camera hand-held and shaky, the video low-res, digital cipher. My stomach, however, was already churning.

The headline on the page read: **PEACE VIGIL AT SHANNON**. The text under the video window read: 'Tonight, until she is arrested, an Irish woman activist will retake the grounds of Shannon Airport to read aloud the neutrality section of the Irish Constitution and a letter to President Bush, Prime Minister Blair and Taoiseach Ahern, requesting that they turn away from their reckless...'

It's not like there was any doubt who was out there. Who else could it possibly be in a nation of only 4 million? Part of me, I'll admit, started counting the nights of no sleep and bad sleep I'd already had on this trip: the hospital bench, the damp meadow, Jill and I pulling a monthly gym membership in a crypt, Ron calling on Borneo time. That part of me longed to get in the back seat, let Sheila drive home, crawl into bed and pull the covers over my head.

But then the burka-wearer started reading—and of course it was my sweet coloratura, all sharps and flats ringing majestic. My Jill, forever the first volunteer kamikaze pilot reporting for duty. I started laughing—I couldn't help it. When I looked down, Sweaterman and the others were staring at me, expectant. I pointed toward the runways and they nodded.

Then things started to happen quickly. I returned to Denis and Sheila.

"Did Connolly give you back your cellphone?" I asked Denis. He began searching his pockets.

"Jesus you'd lose your head if it wasn't—"Sheila groused.

"Don't worry about it. I'll fetch it and get a ride back with our friends here. You guys go on ahead," I said and tossed her the keys.

I retracked through the checkpoint to the Garda station. The sergeant stepped into the back room with a growl and returned with Denis' cellphone. "Just going to use the bathroom if you don't mind, " I said and ducked into the hallway outside, the hallway ending in the noise-leaking door marked 'No Exit—Official Use Only'.

I waited a moment for Connolly to step back to his desk behind the counter. Then I marched straight to the door and grabbed the handle. One long deep breath, soaking up the whine of the jets on the other side, and I pushed hard.

Sheets of sound tore through me. An Airbus was rolling out across the tarmac, backwash scattering ponderous plastic containers like pizza boxes. The door alarm began shrieking the instant it opened, of course. I took off at a sprint along the outer wall, ducking around baggage carts and gasoline trucks, scanning the outskirts for the transport. And there it was, making no attempt at subterfuge, bright and isolated at the farthest end of the field, close by a thirty-foot wall of earth where the runways ended.

I ran out of building pretty quickly and then out of the lights. The end of the runway was maybe a hundred-yard run. I mounted the earthen bank and for a moment all the noise fell away. The ground was spongy, the grass wagged in the wind, a typical Irish field if you neglected to look around.

As I hit a soggy patch of turf, I saw lights and turned to see a jetliner turning for takeoff at the far end of the runway. It wobbled and shimmied, the engines ramped up and it gathered speed so quickly it seemed like an optical illusion. Ten seconds later, with a whoosh like Godzilla's vacuum cleaner, it leapt into the air. For a second, the headlights were right in my eyes—my heart jumped before I had a single sensible thought—and then of course it was already thundering by, 200 feet up and climbing like San Francisco.

As I started down the far side of the bank, the transport loomed like an ocean liner with wings, freakish, bloated and comical, dwarfing the other planes, the trucks servicing it and even the hangars behind. Carefully set in its own space, wide cover all round, ringed in spotlights and soldiers on light trucks keeping guard. They didn't look particularly threatening but they probably didn't feel particularly threatened—this was Ireland, after all, leprechauns and four-leaf clovers. A continual stream of palettes hauled by low-slung tractors shuttled between the hangars and the open belly of the plane.

As I reached the bottom of the hill, I spied them in silhouette, moving through the high grass, Liam crouched and panning his camera, Jill declaiming in a loud voice over the continuous whine of the transport's engines.

Of course—they'd been *planning this all week*. She had...*other plans*. She couldn't have confided in me, of course. Security as tight as the Pentagon. Maybe *that's* why Liam had been so freaked out when I broke into the meeting—was that possible?

I stopped for a moment and watched the two of them together. Jill was gesturing, telling Liam where she wanted the camera. He was nodding, making his own suggestions, but generally doing as asked. Solid, loyal, reliable. A good friend. Maybe reluctantly so, but a friend.

Not my competition.

All at once, it was clear to me. What was wrong with Emily? Jill had asked. Nothing, of course. *Nothing* was wrong with Emily—which was what was wrong with Emily.

Em was my friend because she accepted me for what I was, supported me right or wrong. Didn't ask me—wouldn't think to ask me—to be anything else. She was good and true. Reliable and safe. My good faithful friend.

Jill was a pain-in-the-ass. She lectured and prodded, demanded I raise my game. She saw a bigger me than I did and demanded I reach for it. And made me want to. She was mine as long as I earned her. There was nothing safe or secure between us. Not my friend—my lover.

I bounded the last several yards into the field. "You picked a fine night for it," I called, dropping down behind them.

"Jesus!" Liam jumped.

"Did you bring Gardai?" Jill asked. *That* stopped me.

"Huh?"

"We've been running around this field since half eight," she complained, as though picking up a conversation from five minutes earlier. "I've read the damn Constitution three times. We've been webcasting the while—you'd think someone would notice."

"Why don't you just head into the spotlights? They can't miss you there."

"It's a seduction," she sighed. "These things have rules. We hide; they seek. They're not holding up their end."

"Maybe they're tired of seduction. Maybe they want you to declare yourself."

"Not very thrilling."

"Better than being ignored—or forgotten," I replied. Liam raised an eyebrow but didn't argue. "They don't want to arrest you—they want to *ignore* you. They want to keep you symbolic, like the fox."

Even through the narrow slit, I saw the look she shot me. Tough. I was in television—I know how to be a *major-league* pain-in-the-ass. Finally, she grudgingly asked, "So what are you doing here?"

"He wants you to stop," Liam sneered. "Home in the kitchen, not out in the world causing trouble." He was sneaking looks over the viewfinder, cueing her to agree but she waited on me. She removed her veil now so I could see her waiting.

"Denis," I answered. "I came for Denis." Her eyes bugged out like a grouper—it wasn't pretty. "He *begged*. Sheila was getting on a plane for England."

"England?" She knew why alright but I explained just to make sure.

"For an abortion."

"Shite!" Jill exclaimed. She stalked around in a tight circle, her arms thrust out stiff, fists clenched. She was thrown by this way more than I'd expected. "Dammit! I'm totally against abortion!"

"You're not pro-choice?"

"This isn't politics," she snapped. "It's a *baby*." There was a wound in her voice that I would remember to ask about someday.

"Well, relax—she's not going. They're on their way home."

"No thanks to me," she muttered. She was really thrown. "Why—How did you...get him here?" Even her *syntax* was faltering! The girl who could cut you to ribbons at sixty words a minute!

"We took your car. He had the key. He was all upset...after you left." I was trying to let her off the hook—it was all over. But she couldn't.

She misted up. Hopefully none of the surveillance cameras caught Liam and me with our mouths open, staring at her.

"I showed up at Sheila's," she gasped, "like I was granting them ten minutes of my valuable time. I was doing *important* things, planning my *demonstration*! Denis wouldn't even speak to me and Sheila—" she trailed off.

"Denis said you pushed her away."

"Did I?" Jill murmured, as much as you could murmur over jetshriek. "I hoped I'd imagined that."

Liam switched the camera off and was looking around for the exit. I shrugged—I wasn't at Sheila's; I was no witness.

"The idea of Denis with a kid *is* kind of scary," I admitted.

It wasn't much but enough for her to smile, a tiny apologetic smile. And then Liam laughed, a full-throated laugh and the air pressure seemed to equalize. It was like we all took a deep breath.

Jill threw me her sharp appraising look, the one that had so intimidated me two days earlier. "None of this explains, after solving Denis and Sheila and the world's trials, what you're doing *here*?"

In the past, I'd have triangulated a response. Now, I shrugged. "You're here," I said.

This seemed to please her. "I am," she replied.

"Well, I'm on your side, right?"

"That's it?" she asked, eyes widening. "That's everything? No lengthy explanations? No historical quotes or footnotes?"

"Who needs footnotes? *I* know what I want."

And now I got the full-blown smile, the one that lit me up head to toe. We stood like idiots in the swaying weeds for a minute or so—or maybe it was ten seconds, who the hell cares—basking in each other.

"John," she said finally, softly.

It took me a moment to realize what she was talking about. "Well, of course," I exclaimed and she cackled. "Who else would it be?"

She kept staring at me, expectant, until I answered, "George."

"That is acceptable."

"I don't care—I like him anyway," I said and we shared another precious little laugh.

And then there was a sharp crack, a loud bad noise, close by in the dark. And we realized together that Liam was gone.

A little scuttling about and we found him, outside the nearest hangar, on a palette of wood crates, waving for us to join him.

Twenty or thirty palettes stood at the side gate, carrying crates in stacks four or five high. Squeezing between the stacks, we moved to the front of the palette and a protected view of the hangar.

A low deep-rumbling tractor scuttled out the side gate and grabbed the empty palette just ahead of us. It pulled the thing into the hangar. As soon as it was dropped, four soldiers converged on it immediately. They didn't any of them look more than nineteen, all gymrat muscles, camouflage and buzzcuts.

Two pulled a crate off the stack and opened it while a third pulled a squarish muslin packet from a shiny metal box. From the packet, he pulled a bright, spotless American flag. He and the last soldier unwrapped the flag and pulled it taut across the top of the crate, clipping it securely under the lid. The instant they finished, the first two laid it back on the palette and offered another to take its place.

Looking beyond, we saw teams like this all over the vast space, stacking crates, unwrapping and fastening flags, methodically and efficiently refilling the palettes. Tractors hauled completed palettes out the far door toward the transport.

I can't pretend there was anything confusing about what we were seeing; sometimes the mind rebels at simple information. And then, all at once, I was standing amidst a pile of undressed empty coffins and I jumped down from my perch as though stung.

Jill and Liam slowly followed me toward the gate. Liam pumped the camera onto his shoulder, swiveling slowly from one end of the hangar to the other. That was more presence of mind than Jill or I could muster. She was sleepwalking, taking in the weight of what was before us, what we all knew had to come.

All of us, that is, but the soldiers. They kept to their script, their repetitive tasks, controlled and detached, focusing on relentless, robotic execution. The world accepted the dignity of a job well done and these boys were exhibiting the only dignity now available to them. Tears came to my eyes and kept coming. Jill came over and put her arms around me and we watched for a long moment.

She traced a finger across my hairline. "*Not in our name*," she instructed me tenderly, like it was a lullabye. "That's our statement."

"The hell with that," I told her. "Let's go get arrested."

$$\neq$$

I would simply have marched around to the front of the hangar to be taken by the guards. We'd have resisted, made our point, for what it was worth. But Liam now grabbed the wheel. The dismal nature of the place, which sucked the spirit out of Jill and me, seemed to fire him up.

"This way," he said, stepping briskly into the mouth of the beast. He was tracking backwards, getting the shot of us behind him. I've seen cameramen do this my whole career and never figured out how they don't kill themselves.

As we stepped in through the wide hangar door, the night breeze came from the other gate and Jill's burka billowed out behind her like the angel of death.

I froze at the sight and so did she. Her spooky reflection shone fifty times in a pile of shiny flag boxes littering the floor and she stood transfixed for a moment staring at it. Then she bent, almost involuntarily, gathering herself into the goddess pose she'd struck for me by the lake and re-fastening her veil to complete the image. Liam—no fool—stepped over to a better angle and I moved out of his way.

Jill began to glide slowly across the stacks of flag-dressed coffins, moving as though she was barely touching the ground. Liam dropped the camera to waist height to accentuate the billowing cape.

After twenty years in the business, I know a money shot when I see one and here was an image people would remember long after this night had passed. Everything came together—Jill's sensuality and fierce pride, her grace and vulnerability, the woman she was and the woman she was willing herself to be. And, caught up in the moment, I thought: *Maybe this'll really do it. Maybe this is just enough to stop them—at least to make them think.*

Liam motioned Jill forward. We were just reacting but Liam had a plan. We followed him onto the back of a palette the soldiers had just completed and wedged between the rows as a tractor hooked onto the far end and started towing us out to the transport.

As we burst into the open air, I went lightheaded, tipsy from the bouncing platform, the misty night air between the coffins and the sight of that blimp-like plane looming ahead. *Something was happening.* Boy was it ever.

The palette jerked to a halt and we saw the tractor pull away. All around, we heard shouted orders and reaction, the barks and groans of military protocol. There was something surreal in the deadpan noises echoing between the crates.

This odd interval lasted maybe half a minute, the three of us waiting, listening to all the bustling activity we weren't part of. Then Jill gathered herself, straightened her shroud and stepped off the front of the palette into the blinding floodlights.

She was only two steps ahead of me but the shouting and pounding footsteps were all around us before I regained my eyes. We were in a close-up ring of soldiers in camouflage, full combat packs and rifles, maybe six or seven of them. The leader—at least the most belligerent—was three feet from Jill, bellowing in her face.

"Stop moving! Face on the Ground! Face Down! Face on the Ground! NOW!!"

His rifle still pointed skyward but it was waggling and he was spitting and wide-eyed. He'd laid in bed, surely, for weeks, preparing for Iraqis in battle dress, tanks and mines and booby traps. He'd cleaned his gun, gone over procedures ten thousand times. When he'd landed in sleepy old Ireland, he had to have decided he was on vacation. And now, here was this wraithlike apparition that wasn't talking or listening or seemingly concerned in the least with his gun or his training or his shouting. Or his fears. He was struggling, very clearly, with real fear, a real sense of breakdown. That sight set me cold.

Jill remained unearthly calm. As he yelled, she simply raised both sleeves into the wind and the burka unfurled behind her like a dark angry cloud. The kid staggered backward as though she'd struck him. The rifle came down off his shoulder.

"I'm an American!" I heard myself yelling. All at once I was between the two of them, screaming in the soldier's face while his gun barrel hovered at my chest. "It's a protest! Passive non-violent resistance! Martin Luther King, Medgar Evers, Watergate! It's my right as an American citizen!"

"*Prove* it!" Here was another voice, all at once, another soldier, black and much taller, more like my height, coming from the other side of the group. The belligerent kid's gun lifted away, thank God. You could see him pass authority, gratefully, to the black man.

All eyes were on me now. I had to say the right thing. I was afraid to go for my passport. I wasn't sure what pocket it was in and I was damned if I was going to get shot dead for fumbling.

"Marc McGuire was taking steroids," I burst. "He's a fucking cheat. Roger Maris should still have the record." It was the most American thing that came to mind.

"He was just taking Andro," the tall soldier replied. "I take it myself. Helps you recover quicker from a workout."

"It's still a steroid," I argued. "There should be an asterisk in the record books."

"The hell with an asterisk," said a third voice. "They should just give it to Sosa."

"They'll never do that. Black man can't have the record." Fourth voice. And then they were looking at me again.

"I don't give a shit about McGuire or Sosa. Or even Maris. I'm a *Mets* fan. I just want all your guns pointed at somebody else." They laughed when I said I was a Mets fan. But it seemed to help convince them we were harmless.

A moment later, one of the soldiers discovered Liam, who'd remained on the palette, shooting the whole scene from the shadows and sending it out on the Internet. This seemed to explain things to everyone's satisfaction and an hour later, we were in a Garda station, not the one at the airport but a proper one with interrogation rooms, the stench of sweat and urine and real metal bars on the cells. We spent half an hour giving basic information. *Do you have any tattoos?* "Three!" Jill answered excitedly.

"Show him the butterfly," I suggested and they told us to hush up.

The local sergeant faltered visibly when he heard my address—actually, the instant he heard my voice.

"I'm staying with Emily Ormond at Killreath Lodge, Malveigh, Killmoyle, Lisheen." There are no zip codes in Ireland. Everyone lives in a place that's off the road to another place that's off the road to another place. Emily, of course, was off *that* road, the farthest level removed. But as I was reciting all this, I could see the sergeant's eye's widen. When he pulled my passport from my jacket pocket (I couldn't myself because of the handcuffs), his face fell and it was clear something was up.

After that, the officers kept leaving the room to take phone calls or make phone calls and they seemed to be doing an awful lot of conferring. They left us cooling our heels for two hours in the holding cells. Jill in one cell, Liam and I in the other but directly across from one another so we could talk. It was a concrete room of course so any sound just boomed.

"I think felons in coed cells would be much more entertaining," I suggested.

"We're behind the times," Jill answered. "Coed *schools* are new here."

"Wow! They expect teenagers to think about schoolwork?"

"They're not that daft," Liam muttered.

"I'm a *convent* girl myself," Jill crowed.

"Doesn't surprise me a bit."

Eventually the sergeant came back in. "D'ya need anything?" he asked. "Coffee, tea, a ciggy? Someone had ciggies in her bag."

"That would be brilliant," Jill said and the sergeant immediately unlocked her cell.

"I smoke too," I said instantly and Jill tried to stifle a laugh.

"You weren't carryin' anything in *your* pockets," the sergeant said.

"I'm trying to quit." When he squinted at me, I added, "I'm not going to quit in jail—you *want* it to be nerve-wracking, don't you?" And he let me out.

The three of us ended up leaning against a squad car in the courtyard behind the jail, me puffing shallow to keep from choking. Jill and I were entwined from the first moment. The sergeant, whose name really was Murphy—are Irish cops a cliché in *Ireland?*—shot us a look and I said, "You couldn't give us a few minutes, could you?"

"I could *not*," he responded and then they called him inside for a phone call. So there we were alone in the courtyard, the rear gate not five yards away. Jill laughed, took the cigarette from my hand and crushed it underfoot. She buried her head in my chest and I just started breathing different. As though the world was different. As though I could forget for a little while what it was really like.

Then all of a sudden, six or seven photographers appeared on the other side of the gate, demanding Jill's picture. She'd just begun posing when Murphy returned and shooed them away.

He was grinding, Murphy was, moving slow, flexing his shoulders and neck, taking dark snorts of breath. The poor guy was totally weighed down and I felt generous again, willing to help anybody who needed it. He came over and put his hand behind my shoulder—as high as he could reach—and actually steered me a short distance away from Jill, toward the gate at the far end of the yard.

"We've no charge for you," he said. "We'll return your things. Your friends'll be arraigned in the morning and then all will be right, you see?"

"Excuse me?"

"You're free to go." He tried to steer me back toward the station house now, while Jill remained leaning against the squad car. But I wasn't being steered anymore.

"Whoa whoa whoa," I said, stopping dead. "Not that I'm ungrateful, but you can't let me out and keep them."

"We've no charge for ya."

"I was with them. How'm I any different?"

"She resisted a direct order to lie on the ground. No one recalls telling you to lie down."

"They did."

"We've no evidence."

"I'm confessing."

"I'm off-duty."

"Well what about Liam? Nobody spoke to him either. Why is *he* arrested?" It was a bit strange, demanding to be arrested, but I didn't like the way things were playing out. And I was groping for leverage, a leverage I could sense I had though I couldn't for the life of me imagine why.

"He was hiding on a truck, according to testimony. Attempting to evade arrest. You stepped off willingly, presenting yourself." He flashed an entirely unconvincing smile. "They're not terribly serious charges, you see. Wouldn't be the least bit surprised to see them dropped when the judge comes in. So no bother. Thanks for coming 'round."

"Thanks for coming *round*?" I spit. "You brought me in a paddy wagon!"

Murphy shrugged. "These things happen."

He wagged his hand in the air, dismissing me. But the weight of the world was on his shoulders. He was that most miserable of creatures, a sincere policeman, a man with a conscience and a job to do that he didn't like one little bit. I was sympathetic as hell but I shook my head.

"If they're arrested, I'm arrested," I told him.

"I can't," he repeated. "We've no charge." But by now, all remnants of resolve had collapsed. He was out of arguments. He was simply pleading with me.

"I'll *make* you arrest me if necessary."

Jill had wandered over and was standing wide-eyed and suspicious, taking the scene in, both of us trying to figure the angles. Murphy looked exhausted.

"This comes from *way* above your pay grade, doesn't it?" I asked finally. When his eyes shut down, I knew I was on the right track.

I sat on the steps. Jill immediately took up her position next to me, arms locked together, years of hunger strikes and sidewalk demonstrations become force of habit. The whole thing was comical but it had an effect on Murphy, who was probably used to sleeping through half his shift. And then all at once I located my leverage.

"Wouldn't it be nice if we all just went away?"

"I couldn't allow that," he said, now glancing nervously at the gate.

"Not on your own authority, I understand. But what if you were *ordered* to let us go?"

He threw me a long skeptical look. "That would be extremely convenient," he admitted. "If it could be done."

"I'll take my phone call now." They'd offered me a phone call earlier when I couldn't think of anyone to call. Em was surely still in the hospital and I was not giving Malcolm the satisfaction. But now I had a better idea.

Murphy led us inside and showed me to a phone. "I have to dial for you," he said.

"I don't know the number," I told him. "It's Seamus McCarthy in Dublin."

"He knows you?"

"He *likes* me, for some reason."

"I told you I'd help you. Bailing you out wasn't what I had in mind," McCarthy said when we'd dragged him from bed.

"You're not bailing me out. They refuse to arrest me. For some reason, the fix is in."

"Is it?" he murmured and I could hear the TV click on in the background.

"This is a business opportunity, Seamus," I explained. I recited the web address for Jill's airport video and repeated it three times while his wife—I assumed it was his wife—typed it into the computer. "So I'm here now with a group of dangerous radicals."

"I see," he said and the twinkle was back in his voice. "You stand out in a crowd. So does she. She looks formidable."

"That's another subject. But if she was released, wouldn't the papers scream about these dangerous fanatics roaming the countryside? Making everyone nervous as cats? And you opening a spa and relaxation facility in two weeks? With Getaway Beds designed to make people forget the World's troubles?"

I could almost hear McCarthy straightening, standing taller, across the phone line. "That *is* a lovely coincidence," he admitted.

"I figure this is a proper democracy. You know all the right people. A few words in the right ears and they'll let us all go. Think of the headlines."

"On page thirteen," he said sadly.

"Not necessarily. It all depends what kind of a news day it is."

"There's the rub," he answered and I could hear the TV booming in the background. "The reason they're not arresting Americans at Shannon tonight."

"What reason?" I sputtered.

"It's started," he said. "You're bombing Baghdad."

Well, that sunk it. Just the way he said it—*You're* bombing... I wasn't bombing anybody.

I kept the news to myself. I just couldn't find a way to spring it. It was a long walk back to the cells and a long wait for the local solicitor to come spring us, while the other two celebrated our being released. They were bubbling—we'd pulled it off, put one over on The Man. Jill even owned that McCarthy might have a use in life.

We settled into the back seat of the solicitor's long gray car, Jill almost in my lap now, buoyant. As soon as he fired up the engine, the radio came on and I didn't have to say a word. There was no commentary for almost a minute, just the sounds of explosions, of bombs going off in the streets of another city. It could have been New York of course, but we all knew it wasn't.

The solicitor gunned the engine and we headed home, listening to the concussions, as clear and immediate as though they were going off around the corner.

I slumped, shriveled in my seat. Jill glanced at me finally— her expression was hard. Then she threaded her arm through mine. "Not in *our* name" was all she said.

The sun was coming up over the hills, those silly Irish hills with their sheep and planted groves of trees and the stone walls that kept jumping out at unwary motorists. It was not a practical country, not really. Everything needed work. Everything needed tending.

~~~~

AUTHOR'S NOTE

This book took nine years from first sketches to publication. A huge crew of people helped but a few must be named: Dianna Dennis, Maureen Gallagher, Elaine O'Sullivan, who actually protested in a burka at Shannon Airport, Jennie Fields, who told me repeatedly (when I had no interest in hearing) what the book needed, Sara Leiser at www.chronofhorse.com, who published the first bits to see light, Barry Nisman, Billy, Toni and Joe (always Joe) Papaleo, Christy, Andy, Donal and Liam for giving me the heartbeat and all the wonderful people I met in my trips to Ireland, particularly the Galway barmaid who lectured me mercilessly in 2005 ('How could you *re-elect* that eejit?!!!).

Read a Preview of
'Swindler & Son,'
The new novel by Ted Krever
On Sale December 2018

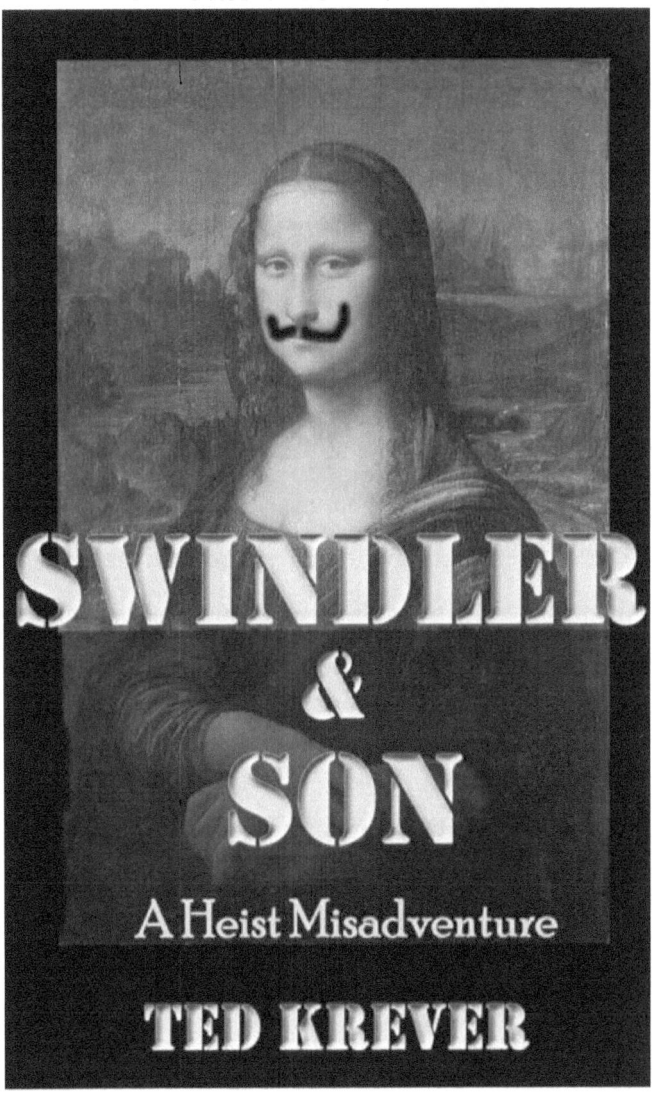

THE START

-So how does it start?

It starts with the sound of my own name spoken aloud.

Call me Nicholas, I'm fine. Nick or Nicky, even better.

But 'Nicholas Marsh' enunciated, first and last, all the way through—when I hear it *that* way, I know I've done something I'm about to pay for.

Hearing it in French, every syllable twisted and slurred and leaking from the earpiece of a Parisian counter-terrorism officer in a Kevlar vest, his back to me and his binoculars trained on my kitchen window—*that's* rock-bottom.

That's how it starts, in the snowy garden of the *Hopital Saint-Louis* in the Tenth Arrondissement, just past sundown on Christmas day, at what I fervently hoped was the end of one of the worst days of my life.

Well, actually, no…

Actually, it started about fifteen minutes earlier, on the other side of the canal, where I was mugged by some twenty-five year-old junkie in a purple-tinted mohawk and a leather jacket. And several nice tats on his neck that distracted my attention when I should have been focusing on his oncoming fist. He took my wallet and phone and left me aching and dizzy, which is why I wandered groggy several blocks out of my way and approached home through the garden.

I love that garden but none of the official exits land anywhere near my apartment. A few years ago, I found a back door, through the *Musee des Moulages* on the hospital grounds, that let me out near a construction gate right across the street from my building.

I'm just opening that back door when I hear my name and see GIGN, French Special Forces, two officers, huddled like Martians in flak suits, gas masks and sniper rifles, peeking through the construction gate at the wide corner, the entrance to my building and, eight floors above, at the dead coleus drooping from my night table.

Frozen in place, I scan the rooftops and find a squad of dark gray uniforms—and, in case I harbor any last doubts, hear my name one more time from the headset hanging from the blonde officer's right ear. I back instinctively into the doorway, sweating and making twenty-five different plans at the same time.

The bus! They won't be checking the bus on the Boulevard de la Villette, that's an answer. Having any sort of answer helps calms the quiver in my legs, brings them back into something like working order.

This is a mistake—it's got to be. If I'd done something to deserve counter-terrorism, I'd remember it, wouldn't I? More importantly, why in hell didn't somebody tip me off? Who do I know at GIGN?

Out through the door and the museum, retracing my steps, back out the far end of the compound, past the *Chapelle* to the *Rue de la Grange aux Belles*. Up toward the roundabout at a regular clip, walking briskly like a Parisian.

Am I thinking of escape? Hell no, I'm just getting pissed. Why hasn't somebody warned me? Why haven't they given me a chance to buy my way out of this?

Oh sure, GIGN makes it look serious but that just raises the price. I know somebody in every department of government and what they cost. Serious things have been undone before.

By the time the bus makes three stops, I know who to talk to—Beltoise, the second man at the *Surete*. He was at our Christmas party just last night.

I *own* him! At least, I should. If I had a middle-class clientele, if I dealt pot or owned a brothel, I could expect a phone call 24 hours in advance of a raid. It's common courtesy!

He'll be at *D'Azur*, of course, charging his dinner to us as usual.

When I arrive, he's tucked into a dim corner. He rises before I can reach him.

"Why is GIGN all around my apartment? You don't warn me?"

His eyes bulge like marbles. "Where's your phone?"

"Phone? Stolen. I got mugged."

He looks *relieved*. "That's why they're not here yet," he mutters and pulls me into the private room in back.

"Nicky, our past history—and the fact that I like you—is why I'll give you a minute's grace before I call you in." He's serious! His face goes cold—not like he doesn't know me, like he's never *seen* me before. "Normal corruption is one thing—but this?"

Normal corruption? Normal corruption is my *specialty*! He's reducing ten thousand years of civilized give-and-take to a catchphrase. Not to mention, it's fed him quite nicely, thank you, over the years.

I look at his face, at the disappointment and condescension there, and realize what a farce it all is. You treat them like princes but the first time you actually need them to put out...they might as well be in insurance.

Faced with this ingratitude, something inside me just gives up.

"Okay," I tell him. "I surrender."

"What?"

"I'll confess, right now. It's the jet ramps, isn't it?"

He looks confused.

"We have this client, a dictator...you know the old joke about, you're not really a country unless you have your own stamps, your own airline and your own beer? Well, he's got commemorative stamps, a brewery, a Mercedes stretch limo and a portrait of himself as Julius Caesar. But he gets embarrassed when his guests have to descend a staircase off the plane.

"There's a staircase on Air Force One' I tell him and he says, 'They could have a ramp if they wanted one.' So when Kumbatta collapsed, we flew a cargo plane in and liberated a couple of jetramps. The guy was so happy, he painted two Cessna's and proclaimed them the national airline. I don't think we *hurt* anybody."

Beltoise settles into the nearest chair, not saying a word.

"That's not it?"

Silence.

"Okay, Napoleon's penis—that was a good deed, I swear."

"*Excusez moi?*"

"It's your Minister of Defence's fault! Not the present Minister, the old one. He had this...thing about Napoleon's penis, that it should be back in France where it belongs."

"It is in France! Napoleon's body is at Les Invalides!"

"The body, sure, but his penis was removed during the autopsy and it's floated around ever since from collector to collector. It's now owned by a urologist, naturally, in Philadelphia."

"Don't be funny."

"It's true. The BBC measured it a few years ago and found it a bit small. Naturally, that outraged the Minister, who insisted the English don't know how to measure. The urologist's price was just *outrageous* so we found a...more generously-sized one around the same age, for a price the Minister could afford. It made him *happy*."

"You found him another penis?"

"Another *old* penis! You think that was easy? How many three-hundred-year-old penises you think are floating around?"

Beltoise stares at me with—I can't tell if it's respect or concern. The odd thing is, to me, this is actually beginning to feel pretty *righteous*. Confession really *is* good for the soul. "Okay, not the answer. Give me a chance. The eighteen identical one-of-a-kind Moroccan emeralds—"

"No."

"The Van Gogh with the wrong ear missing?"

Beltoise rolls his eyes. "We've never met," he warns, "except for a few state dinners with hundreds of other people I've never met either—but my advice is, you find a quick way out of France now. And don't bother replacing your phone—they'll find you as soon as you do. You understand?"

This is terrifying—Beltoise is a glorified flatfoot with a fancy office. I'm *begging* to be arrested and he's not biting. It's *unnatural*.

"Throw me a bone here," I say. "I don't understand what's happened."

He grimaces. "You know damn well it's the bomb."

"The *BOMB*?"

Of course, I know all about the bomb. I'd arrived back in Paris the day before, just in time for the funerals. Twelve dead, 37 injured, a miracle it wasn't more. A mountain of flowers in plastic sleeves heaped on the rubble, candles arrayed like soldiers in front of the dress shop left somehow intact on the corner.

And a march from the *Place De la Republique* to the *Place de la Nacion*, thousands, orderly and dogged, middle-class families and university students, *Le President* and his rivals, butchers, bakers, artists and computer technicians shuffling through neighborhood streets between broad public squares, solemn and chattering, sombre but fashionable—Paris, formal but somehow intimate. Great buildings and beautiful women dressed in black. Paris is a grand dame, maybe a bit past her prime, but she still knows how to put on a funeral.

'It's an escalation,' they say, the voices that multiply in crowds. Just a few years ago, 'they' were content to shoot up a restaurant or concert hall. Now, somehow, they bring in a bomb the size of a safe to bring down half a block of five-story apartment buildings.

The size of the explosion makes people nervous. Nobody builds a bomb that size to bring down the Rue Breguet. We all sense a grander plan that went awry and the fact that no one claimed responsibility only seems to heighten the tension. You don't even have the consolation of knowing who to be afraid of.

Beltoise, however, has made up his mind.

"It's your shipping certificate!" he yells, no longer caring who hears. "Your company's letterhead! Your *signature* on the bloody thing! You think I will cover for *that*, you're insane!"

I stand frozen for an endless moment, until words I never thought I'd hear myself say come tumbling out of my mouth.

"I didn't do *that*! I'm *innocent*!"

And then, I run.

RUNNING

-You ran?

It's an expression. I know better than to run. I walk at my usual quick pace but not fast enough to attract attention. Okay?

I lose myself in the tangle of back streets, staying off the boulevards, sticking to shorter blocks and parks where I can change direction at will. I stop short in front of angled store windows several times, switch direction several more, take a cab for a short distance and then another to double-back on myself. I'm overdoing it, in truth—if GIGN were really on my tail, they'd just throw on the sirens and take me. Once I'm sure I'm not being followed, I find a thrift shop that's just closing in a church, buy a pair of slacks and a short dark hoodie and wear them out of the store.

-This is tradecraft. Where did you acquire your technique?

Like you don't know. I had a very brief career in—what do you tell strangers at parties? About what you do for a living?

-I don't speak of such things.

Argentine tango couple are giving lessons one-on-one on the terrace and the star of the national football club is kicking balls around with enchanted kids and dazzled grownups on the south lawn.

In Paris, of course. That's our home base. It's one of God's jokes—Harry hated the French so, once we'd been thrown out of every other country in Europe, the only place left to go was Paris. Which, of course, he now loves because how can you not love Paris? It's *Paris*, for God's sake.

And the French love Harry. Big gnarly elegant gay Englishman, what's not to love? He ignores their culture, conducts himself like tenth-generation nobility fallen to trade or maybe a good Savile Row tailor, speaks only enough French to be fed and catered to but laughs and charms so naturally, they can't help themselves. Seduction is the French national pastime; they recognize a Master at work.

I was in Mumbai two years ago, picking up a load of Indian cotton. There was a rash of suicides among cotton farmers in Vidarbha and I was able to pick up several farms' entire crop just by paying off the bank loans. I told myself it was a good deed and a good deal. So I'm in the hotel bar at the end of the day chatting up some girl when a man behind me says, "Oh, you work with Harry Sandler? I was in a steeplechase syndicate with him in Ireland once. Took me for £65,000 quid. Most wonderful time I ever had." He bought us both a drink.

Everybody loves Harry; that's what nearly killed us all. As I watched the Iranian commandos lining up on the deck of the ship three hours ago, in their black stocking caps and their Kalashnikovs aimed at our temples, all I could think was, *Everybody loves Harry.*

Fucking goddamn Harry.

AUTHOR BIOGRAPHY

Ted Krever watched the Beatles on Ed Sullivan, went to Woodstock (the good one), and graduated Sarah Lawrence College with a useless degree in creative writing.

He spent several decades creating programs for ABC News, CBS, CNN, A&E, Court TV, MTV News, Discovery People and CBS/48 Hours, and as VP/Production of a short-lived dotcom.

He has driven a 16-wheeler across the Rockies, shot overnight news in NY City, managed a revival-house movie theater and married twice, in a triumph of optimism.

He was once accused of attempting to blow up Ethel Kennedy with a Super-8 projector.

Read more at www.tedkrever.com